A hand grabbed Jesse's arm and spun her around.

The fury in Char's eyes was unmistakable. "I never called you a whore, nor did I insinuate you were one. So don't put words in my mouth, woman."

"You never said it, but you were *thinking* it."

"The only thing I was thinking was how I'd like to beat that uncle of yours senseless for allowing you to live like that."

"Stop shouting at me."

"Then stop blaming me for something I haven't done."

Jesse jammed her hands onto her hips and glared at Char.

He glared right back.

Music and laughter drifted around them. The scent of sawdust and leather. The whinny of a horse tethered nearby. The thud of shoes against the barn floor. The sound of clapping hands.

Still, neither of them moved. Neither of them spoke.

Their eyes held in a battle of wills, then something happened. Jesse's senses came alive and fixed only on him. On the blue-gray of his eyes, the minute crook in his nose, the bronze of his smooth skin, the sensual shape of his mouth.

Her pulse picked up speed. This wasn't supposed to happen. She took a step back—and came up against the wall of the barn.

Char closed in, his eyes never leaving hers, their bodies almost touching. "Want to know what I'm thinking now?"

RAVES FOR SUE RICH'S
OTHER SIZZLING ROMANCES

RAWHIDE AND ROSES

"This exciting, fast-paced story is full of adventure and intrigue; lively, interesting characters; tender, sensuous love; and a great plot. This book is impossible to put down once started."

—*Rendezvous*

"A superb western romance that brilliantly mixes humor, action, and emotional tension into a rather tasty brew."

—*Affaire de Coeur*

MISTRESS OF SIN

"Ms. Rich has excelled herself in this gripping story . . . an intriguing, truly romantic story."

—*Rendezvous*

"A definite must-read for anyone who likes their romances with a twist."

—*The Talisman*

THE SILVER WITCH

"A masterpiece of historical romance, *The Silver Witch* will long be remembered in readers' hearts and kept on their keeper shelves"

—*Gothic Journal*

"Sue Rich enriches the romance genre with a fast-paced, action-packed, otherworldly romance filled with great characters. Readers will be enchanted from the beginning to the end of this novel."

—*Affaire de Coeur*

Books by Sue Rich

The Scarlet Temptress
Shadowed Vows
Rawhide and Roses
Mistress of Sin
The Silver Witch
Wayward Angel
Aim for the Heart

Published by POCKET BOOKS

Sue Rich

Aim For the Heart

POCKET BOOKS

New York London Toronto Sydney Tokyo Singapore

This book is a work of fiction. Names, characters, places and
incidents are products of the author's imagination or are used
fictitiously. Any resemblance to actual events or locales or persons,
living or dead, is entirely coincidental.

An *Original* Publication of POCKET BOOKS

POCKET BOOKS, a division of Simon & Schuster Inc.
1230 Avenue of the Americas, New York, NY 10020

ISBN: 0-671-89808-6

First Pocket Books printing February 1996

10 9 8 7 6 5 4 3 2 1

POCKET and colophon are registered trademarks of
Simon & Schuster Inc.

Front cover illustration by Vittorio Dangelico

Printed in the U.S.A.

Jessalea Jones, my sister, my
friend, and my inspiration for
this novel. I love you, sis.

Caroline Tolley, my editor, who
manages to turn my vague words
into a story. Thank you.

To the wonderful people who helped
me with research—even if I didn't
use it all: Marty Damon, Houston;
Julia H. Gahagan, Shreveport;
Margaret Rose, Corpus Christi;
Lucy Swanger, Victoria.

And, as always, to my remarkably
patient husband, Jim.

CHAPTER

❋ 1 ❋

San Antonio, Texas 1876

Char Daniels shed the last of his clothes as he watched the woman lying on the bed, waiting for him to join her. She was pretty, in a plain sort of way, with waxy blond hair and a slender, full-busted figure. It was clear that she wanted him, and he never denied a lady anything, if he could help it.

He slid under the covers beside Polly Whittaker. "Darlin', you've started a fire that's going to be hard to control."

"Oh, Char, you positively turn a woman's head." She drew him over her for a long, lingering kiss.

A door slammed downstairs. A man's thunderous voice ricocheted through the second story hall. "Pollee!"

"It's my husband!" the woman shrieked.

"What?" Char lurched upright. "You never said anything about a hus—*Ah, hell.*"

"Polly?" her husband rumbled again. Heavy footsteps pounded along the floor below them.

Char sprang to his feet and reached to pull on his britches.

"There's no time for that," Polly wailed. "Just take your clothes and get out of here!"

He glanced at his gun belts sitting on the bedside table, but discarded the idea of using them. He didn't want to kill anyone over something that never should have happened in the first place.

Shoving the clothes under his arm, he grabbed his weapons and boots with one hand and jammed his hat on with the other. "Stay outta trouble, darlin'." With a final, flirty wink, he raced for the open window.

Char heard Polly's soft sigh as he ducked under the frame and climbed out onto the slanted roof covering the front porch. Splintery shingles pricked his bare feet as he sidestepped from view of the tumbled bedroom.

An inside door banged open.

He flattened against the building, his naked rear pressed to wood siding. Holding the clothes to his chest, he placed one hand on an ivory-handled Colt, praying he wouldn't be forced to use it.

A summer gust fluttered a shirtsleeve against his bare leg. A sparrow flew over his head and landed on the eave. The scent of roses drifted up from a trellis at the side of the house. It was a warm, lazy day that should have been spent beside a pond with a pole and line.

"Where's my dinner?" the man's voice boomed again.

Startled, Char moved, and a sliver of wood impaled the cheek of his butt. He sucked in a sharp breath.

"I was getting ready to fix it," Polly said in a breathless rush. "I-I didn't realize it was so late, Moose."

Moose?

"I was taking a nap," she continued. "Guess I, um, overslept."

Char rolled his eyes.

"Well, I'm hungry enough to eat a longhorn on the hoof, woman. Get a move on."

Probably big enough, too, if the man's size matched the roar of his voice.

The bedsprings creaked, then the sound of rustling fabric floated through the open window. "Button my dress, will you?"

There was a long silence, then a soft "thank you" before the door closed.

Char released his breath and eased from the siding.

The plod of horses' hooves froze him in place. He swung his gaze toward the road that passed in front of the house. For the first time in two months, he hoped the rider was Buddy Hill, the youngster from Boston who'd been following him—and not someone who knew the Whittakers. The kid may have some pretty strange notions about how exciting it was to be a gunman, but at least he didn't know the Whittakers and wouldn't cause problems for Polly and her *moose* of a husband.

But it wasn't Buddy.

A young boy peeked up at Char from beneath an ugly, flop-billed hat. Near thirteen by the looks of him, he pulled his buckskin to a stop and stared. His eyes widened in shock, then crinkled with humor.

Embarrassed, Char scowled at the kid who was no bigger than a post.

The youngster smiled, then touched the brim of his hat in mock greeting and nudged his horse on toward town.

Cheeky brat, Char thought as he hopped on one foot to pull on his britches. The splinter poked farther into his rear, and he winced, rubbing the offended area. It felt as big as a nail—not to mention being imbedded in a spot where it would be very difficult to remove.

After strapping on his gun belt, he peered down at the ground. The distance made him groan.

Sighing, he dragged on his shirt and boots, then swung over the edge. He hit the dirt hard, and pain shot up his legs—and rear. "Ah, God. I'm getting too old for this," he moaned as he hobbled toward his mount, Black Duke, tethered in a stand of cotton-woods across the road.

Although the horse was well-trained, Char swore the animal was half human—an arrogant human at that. The critter carried his ebony head at a disdainful tilt, and pranced rather than walked, as if strutting his noble lineage. Even the black and silver saddle that came with him suited his regal manner.

Char hadn't had him very long, just since his other horse was killed in a shoot-out on the Nueces Strip, but then, it hadn't taken much time for the stallion to show *him* who really controlled the reins.

As he approached the animal, the Duke blinked an onyx eye, snorted, then resumed eating. He looked disgusted.

Not in the best temperament, himself, Char shoved his boot into the stirrup and mounted. With extreme care, he eased into the saddle. The splinter sank deeper into his flesh, and he drew in a hissing breath.

The stallion made a noise that sounded suspiciously like a snicker.

Char clenched his teeth and gave a swift yank on the reins, turning the animal toward San Antonio.

Alongside the lane lay the ruins of the sprawling plaza of the Alamo, and he inspected the crumbled chapel and twelve-foot-high stone walls. Grateful for what those courageous men did for Texas, he dipped his head in a silent thank you.

Entering San Antonio's town plaza from the east, he noted an array of colorful streamers draped from one side of the street to the other. They hadn't been there when he'd ridden in a few hours ago and saw Polly lugging a sack of flour down the boardwalk and offered to help.

More streamers were draped over several beams protruding from the top of one continuous adobe building with numerous windows and doors. Banners and flags adorned every available space from porch rails to the Governor's Palace to signboards.

Even the San Antonio River, which wound its way through the entire town, had flags posted along its banks for tomorrow's celebration of America's 100th Birthday.

He grinned. Maybe he'd get started on his own celebrating a little early—as soon as he got someone to remove the splinter. After all, the fourth wasn't only America's birthday. It was his, too. His thirtieth.

Jesus that sounded old. If he didn't watch it, he might start thinking about getting married like his friend Hayden Caldwell. And that was a fate worse than hanging.

Char had made it a rule to move on if a woman started getting serious, or if he felt himself slipping.

He'd never live the dull, boring, day by day existence he had as a child. He'd figured long ago that restlessness was in his blood. After all, his own pa hadn't even stuck around long enough for his birth.

Not wanting to think about the man he had never met, and the despicable couple who raised him, he clamped down on his thoughts. None of them were worth it. Guiding Duke around a corner, Char reined up in front of Thompson's Saloon.

Since it was dinnertime, only a few horses were hitched to the rail outside, which suited him fine. At the moment, he wasn't in the mood for noise . . . or trouble, which was bent on following him no matter where he went.

Just because *a couple of times* he'd been a little quick on the draw, he'd been labeled a gunman. Now every young upstart around wanted to test him once they learned his identity. No one realized if he'd been any slower, he'd be dead.

Ambling through the door, he strode to the rear of the room where he took a seat—very gingerly—with his back to the wall, maintaining his usual precaution. From there he could see the entire room and—he hoped—catch the eye of an accommodating saloon girl to help him remove the sliver.

No female was in sight.

Stale smoke, sawdust, and whiskey permeated the air. Brass spittoons were stationed by bar stools and tables, their dented surfaces stained by customers with poor aims.

Since there wasn't a saloon girl to take his order, Char rose and approached the counter where a long-faced bartender with a drooping mustache tapped his fingers in a nervous beat.

"What'll it be, mister?" the man asked in a clipped tone, his gaze flitting to the door and back, his manner skittish.

"Whiskey." Char tried to convince himself the man's edginess wasn't because he expected trouble.

The proprietor scooted a bottle and a glass across the bar. "That'll be four bits."

Fishing in his pocket, Char pulled out the appropriate coin. "You ever heard of a man named Otis Daniels? Or a name close to that?" he asked as he handed over the money. "He might have mentioned a woman named Emma from Charleston." After fifteen years, asking folks if they knew of his pa had become second nature to him.

"Never heard of either of them." The bartender shot another peek at the door and edged closer to the end of the counter.

Char didn't pay much attention. He thought again on Deke Webster's words, and for the hundredth time he wondered if the old man had heard Char's dying mother right. Deke claimed she had no man with her, nor was she wearing a ring when she showed up at his door ready to give birth. It was raining, and the Websters' was the only house on the road for miles. The name she had given was Emma, then after Char was born, with her dying breath, she had begged Deke Webster to take the babe to Texas, to his father, Otis Daniel—. She had died before she could finish the rest.

Deke assumed she had been going to say Daniels, so he gave Char that name. Since the birth took place in Charleston, Deke tagged that on him, too.

Resuming his seat, Char downed a gulp of whiskey and tried to rid himself of the aggravation he'd experienced so many times during his search for his real father. Too, he couldn't help wondering if his mother had started to say something else. Add more onto Daniel, like *son*—or whatever. Or even a third name . . . a *last* name.

It was damn hard to locate a man when you didn't know all the details. Brushing a layer of sawdust off the battered table, he focused on the occupants in the smoke-filled room.

A chesty saloon girl sauntered in from a side door.

Char gave a relieved sigh. Now at least he could take care of one problem. The splinter.

The gal's gaze drifted in his direction. Stopped. Widened in surprise . . . then softened with appreciation.

"Howdy, cowboy," the gal purred as she sidled up next to him and propped a high-buttoned shoe on the rung of his chair.

He appreciated the bright red color of her hair, the long sweep of her neck, and low cut of a tight green dress that didn't quite conceal her charms. "Howdy, yourself, darlin'." He inspected the net-covered thigh temptingly close to his right hand.

She trailed her long fingers down the length of that limb. "Like what you see?"

"Absolutely." He slid his hand up the inside of her leg, enjoying the feel of warm, female flesh. "In fact, I like everything about you." He arched a brow. "Where to?"

Licking her ruby lips, she nodded toward the stairs. "Room six."

She started to turn, but he caught her hand. "You got any tweezers?"

The girl whipped around, her eyes startled, uncertain. "W-what for?"

There was no way he'd mention the sliver of wood in his ass within hearing shot of the others, but he didn't want her to think he was *strange* either. He rubbed his thumb and forefinger together. "A splinter."

She relaxed. "I'll get them from the office, but give me a few minutes."

"Sure thing, darlin'." He watched the seductive sway of her hips as she crossed the room and smiled. After his problem was taken care of, they could spend a few enjoyable hours between the sheets.

He poured himself another drink and checked a clock on the far wall. He'd give her ten minutes. Swirling the amber liquid in the glass, he returned his attention to the room.

Three men, businessmen by the looks of their pressed suits and black string ties, sat at a round table playing cards. Across from them, two trail dirty, timeworn characters talked low between themselves, their eyes on the front entrance, their manner edgy— like the bartender had been earlier.

Char had seen anxious men before—too many times. He gave an inward curse and shoved away from the table, not wanting any part of whatever was brewing. Deciding to wait for the saloon girl in the upstairs hall, he rose, wincing when pain pricked the cheek of his butt.

Boots thudded on the plank walk outside.

The two characters stiffened.

Char swore and moved toward the stairs.

The front doors swung open, and the kid he'd seen

9

earlier swaggered into the room. Beneath the flop-billed hat, he surveyed the room and spotted Char. For a split second, a flicker of surprise widened his eyes, then his gaze shifted and settled on a heavy-jowled man playing poker.

The bigger man looked up, then threw down his cards and leaned back, the material of his vest tightening over a protruding belly. "Been expectin' you—Jesse, isn't it?"

"Yeah, *Boggs,* you got the name right," the youngster rasped in a half-whispered tone. "Now all you have to decide is whether you want to die here . . . or in the street."

"Ain't me who's going to die, boy."

Char gave a silent groan.

The other men at the table scrambled out of the way, scattering money and knocking over chairs in their haste.

Boggs continued to stare at the kid. "Way I figure it, ain't no need to stand out in the hot sun, neither. Things betwixt us can be settled here and now." As he spoke, he slid his hand down. A glint of silver flashed, then a derringer appeared in the fat palm under the table.

Char tightened his fists, but remained still. He *would not* get involved.

Then he saw the other two men behind the youngster ease to their feet and draw their revolvers.

His attention swung to Boggs in time to see the older man give them a secret nod.

Ah, hell. The boy didn't stand a chance. Char staggered forward, hoping to appear drunk. "Hey, kid," he slurred as he placed himself between the

10

youngster and the men behind him. "What say we have a lil' drink?" He looped an arm around the boy's thin shoulders and leaned into him.

The boy stiffened. "Get away from me, mister."

"Beat it," Boggs seconded.

"Ah, don' be like that," Char mumbled. "Listen up," he directed to the younger one. "I know this gal who likes lil' boys real good. Why, the other day a kid tol' me she even likes to . . ." He turned his mouth to the youngster's ear, pretending to relate some spicy tidbit.

Jesse tried to jerk away, but Char tightened his hold. "Boggs has a derringer on you under the table," he whispered. "There's two more guns at your back. Get the hell outta here."

A tremor ran through the boy, but he held his ground. "No."

Wanting to take a switch to that scrawny backside, Char mumbled a curse. But, deep down, he knew the young upstart wouldn't listen to reason. Bullheadedness wasn't hard to recognize.

Raising his voice for the rest of the men to hear, Char continued. "And that ain't all she done." He chuckled and again whispered in the kid's ear, praying the boy knew how to use his short-barreled .45. "We're both gonna regret this, but you take Boggs, and I'll get the others. When I give the word—draw."

Char gave a lewd laugh, then backed up, giving himself room to maneuver. He'd have to be fast since those back-shooters had already drawn their guns. "Come on, kid. I'll take you over to her place—*now!*"

Char went for his twin Colts. He spun—and fired both.

A roar of gunfire shook the room.

The two men crumpled, matching holes centering their chests.

Swallowing a sick feeling, he whirled around in time to see Boggs's chair topple over and crash to the floor.

Blood gushed from a crater where the fat man's heart should have been.

Char's stomach shriveled.

But the kid's features remained blank as he stared through the smoke still rising from the .45 in his hand. Yet his eyes reflected a mixture of hatred and horror.

Char holstered his irons.

The boy, Jesse, also reseated his gun, then nodded his thanks before he turned and walked out the door.

The kid's nerve was unbelievable. He'd strolled in here big as you please, shot a man, and was walking out without a word of explanation. *Like hell, he was.* Char started after him.

"Hold it, mister," the bartender ordered. "Now, drop the gun belt, easy like."

The man had to be kidding. Char turned to find the barrel of a shotgun pointed straight at his middle.

He sought patience from the ceiling. The proprietor didn't even realize that Char could draw and kill him before he pulled the trigger. God save him from fools. With a sigh, he undid his belt and lowered his weapons to the floor.

"Someone git the law," the bartender commanded. "And the coroner."

One of the men who'd been at the poker table bolted for the door.

Char was too frustrated to care. While they were so set on corralling *him,* the kid was getting away. "Shouldn't you be worried about the other one?"

"Nope. Sheriff'll git him. Knows this country like his wife's fanny. 'Sides, with nothin' but open plains between here and the border, and with them soldiers down to the other end of town, not many escape the law in these parts."

"What about the mountain range to the west? The kid could hide out there and never be found."

"Them hills ain't gonna help the boy."

Wondering at the man's confidence, Char lowered his gaze and fixed on a pool of blood, right where Jesse had been standing. Boggs must have gotten off a shot.

"Wow! That was some shootin'."

Char whipped around to see his hero-worshiping shadow, Buddy Hill, step through the door. This just wasn't his day.

"I ain't never seen shootin' like that," Hill gushed, his seventeen-year-old face alight beneath a mop of blond curls. He was dressed all in black, like Char, and he, too, wore twin, pearl-handled Colts on either hip. "And who was that other fella? He sure was fast." Buddy tossed Char that idolizing smile. "Course, not near's fast as you, though. Ain't nobody in the whole world fast as Char Daniels."

The bartender sucked in a sharp breath.

Char was going to strangle that kid. That's all he needed, for everyone in the country to know his identity. "Don't you have a home?"

Hill's dimpled smile sagged.

"Get those hands in the air, *Mr. Daniels,*" the

man holding a gun on him commanded in a strained voice.

Fed up, Char swung on the saloon keeper. "Now listen, you jackass, I didn't—"

A gun cocked, and another voice—a menacing one—grated from behind him. "Better do as he says, Daniels."

CHAPTER

❧ 2 ❧

Char stared through the bars, at the door separating the two jail cells from the sheriff's outer office, his insides churning with anger. He knew damned well he shouldn't have gotten involved with that youngster in the flop-billed hat, and one of these days he was going to listen to his better judgment and save himself a whole passel of trouble.

He could imagine what Captain McNelly would say if he knew about this. Or his friend Hayden. They'd never let him live it down. Char and Hayden had been Texas Rangers under McNelly for the last two years, and knowing Char's knack for finding trouble, the idea of him in the hoosegow for his involvement in the shooting of Davidson Boggs—*a mayor, for God's sake*—would send those jackasses into fits of laughter.

Stretching out on the bunk, he flinched at the pain in his butt and wondered about Boggs. Char had learned a lot about no-goods during his years as a county hunter and as a Ranger. He'd learned to read their eyes, and Boggs didn't strike Char as the sort to win votes honestly. Of course, he wouldn't be the first to *buy* them, either.

It was nothing to him, he decided. It was over and done with, but he wished all this could have waited until *after* his visit to the saloon girl.

He laced his fingers behind his head. Too bad the Rangers disbanded last month after that final confrontation on the Nueces Strip. He'd enjoyed the job, and if he ever got out of here, and if he ever found his pa, he might look for a similar position, like, maybe, marshal or deputy.

He lowered his Stetson over his eyes, recalling the bartender's reaction when he learned of Char's infamous identity. For sure that hadn't helped his situation any, especially now that the sheriff knew. Although he wasn't wanted by the law for any of the scrapes he'd gotten into in the past, folks still tended to think of him as an outlaw because of the way he dressed—and his reputation—which had made it easier for the sheriff to believe the lies Boggs's friend and the bartender told. Or maybe they hadn't been lies. Maybe those men did believe that he and the kid had planned the gunfight.

It didn't matter, though. Until the circuit judge came through next month—a man he hoped knew him—Char would stay behind bars. He hoped the sheriff didn't catch that scrawny kid and toss him in the same cell, though. Char was liable to castrate the troublemaking brat.

"Daniels?" a whisper drifted from the window. "Can you hear me?"

Recognizing Buddy Hill's voice, he tried not to

groan as he lifted the brim of his hat to see the barred window above his head. "What do you want?"

"I'm gonna get you outta there."

"The hell you are!" That's all he needed, to be hunted by the law. He shifted to the uninjured side of his rear and sat up. "Listen, kid—" The words clogged in his throat when he saw that Hill had disappeared, and there were ropes looped around the bars.

In stunned horror, he watched the ropes tighten, heard the wrenching sound of the bars giving under the pull of the kid's horse.

"No!" Char bolted to his feet. But it was too late, the whole wall collapsed in a rumbling roar. Dust rolled up like a bank of fog. Splintered wood and chunks of adobe bombarded him like tiny missiles. He shielded his eyes with his arm.

The office door banged open behind him. Gunshots exploded. A bullet zinged past his ear.

He dove through the opening and rolled to the side when he hit the dirt-packed street. The splinter stabbed deeper into his rear, and pain grabbed his breath.

Buddy was beside him in an instant, urging him toward Black Duke.

"I'm going to murder you!" Char roared. "Damn it, I didn't want—"

Another bullet slammed into the dirt.

"Shit!" Knowing he was going to live to regret this, Char leapt astride his horse. Gripping the horn to ease the pressure on his butt, he kicked the Duke into a gallop. They raced out of town and toward the mountains, their only hope for finding cover.

"I got your guns!" Buddy yelled over the pounding of the horses' hooves.

Nothing about the kid surprised him anymore. "How?" He darted a glance over his shoulder to see if the sheriff and his posse were behind them.

They weren't.

"After the sheriff locked you in," Hill shouted, "he went back to talk to those fellas in the saloon. I got 'em then." He grinned, his blond hair flapping beneath the rim of his hat. "A gunman needs his weapons, you know."

"A gunman needs privacy!"

The cheeky kid simply smiled and nudged his horse into a faster gait.

Dust, rocks, and dirt flew up from the dry ground, and Char was forced to draw his black bandanna up over his mouth and nose so he could breathe.

When they at last came to the shelter of trees clinging to a hillside, he turned Duke into the shaded coolness of thick cottonwoods and slowed him to a walk. Holding onto his rage by a thread, he lowered his bandanna and turned on the boy. "Do you have any idea what you've done?"

"Saved you?"

"Saved me! You jackass, you damned near got me killed, and you've turned me into an outlaw. Why didn't you leave me? In a few weeks, I'd have seen the circuit judge, explained the circumstances, *and walked out a free man."*

"That's not what Boggs's friend said. He claimed the townsfolk was goin' to string you up for killin' their mayor soon as word got around."

That shot a hole in his anger. He'd never figured on

a lynching. Still, apologies and thanks never came easy to him. "How'd you get my horse?"

"Sheriff wanted someone to take it to the livery. I volunteered."

Char had to give him credit. The kid was sharp. Drawing Duke to a halt on top of a rise, he searched the area behind them. No sign of the sheriff.

The youngster reined in, his gaze turning to the barren expanse between the mountain and town. "Why aren't they coming?"

Recalling the way the bartender had ignored the possibility of escape into the mountains, Char looked around for the answer. When he spotted the reason, he tried not to swear. "See that red flat over there?"

"Yeah."

"Know what it means?"

"No. Folks don't tie cloths to trees back east."

"It means we've entered hostile Comanche country and, more than likely, we'll be slaughtered before we can get out of here."

The kid paled. "What are we gonna do?"

"Try to survive. Hand me my revolvers." When Buddy complied, Char strapped on his gun belt, then reloaded the missing shells. He kept his gaze fixed on the trees as he tied his holsters on his thighs. "Come on. Let's get out of here."

A horse whinnied.

Char drew his guns and swung toward the sound. Deeper into the woods, he saw a restless buckskin, its sides heaving.

"The horse belongs to that kid, Jesse," Hill whispered. "I watched him ride this way after the shootin'."

Char recognized the animal, too, and wished he didn't. He refused to get involved again. But visions of the kid's blood on the saloon floor wouldn't leave him, and he guided Duke toward the buckskin.

"Where'd the boy go?" Buddy asked in a hushed voice.

Char stared at the riderless horse, at the blood on the saddle, on the ground. But there was no sign of the gun-toting kid.

"I bet the Comanche got him."

"If they had, they'd have taken the horse." Easing out of the saddle, he approached the skittish buckskin. He placed a soothing hand on its sleek golden neck. "Easy girl. No one's gonna hurt you."

Buddy's indrawn breath startled him, and he whipped around.

The towhead stood by a thicket, staring at something in the brush. "What is it?" Char asked, but he already knew.

"Jesse. He looks dead."

Char strode over to where the youngster's body lay sprawled beneath a cluster of scrub brush. Fury tightened his muscles. His intrusion in the gunfight had all been for nothing—the kid was dead anyway, and now Char was a hunted man. He knelt beside the kid and reached for a pocket on his bloody shirt. Maybe he could find a last name for the grave marker.

A low, whimpering moan rasped from Jesse's throat.

Char jerked his hand back as if he'd been bit by a snake. "What the—?"

"He ain't dead!" Buddy blurted inanely. He scrambled down beside Jesse and placed a finger on his throat. "He's got a pulse."

"Pulse? Where'd you learn something like that?"

"My pa's a physician in Boston."

"Then why aren't you there with him?"

"I told you. I want to be a gunman, like you."

Char's frustration knew no bounds. He rolled Jesse over and picked him up, not surprised by the youngster's light weight. He looked half-starved. "Get the buckskin. We've got to get out of here and find some shelter."

It took them several minutes to locate a deep, narrow canyon. It had a small spring-fed pond, and from the bottom, they could see any approaching riders without being seen themselves. Wild grass, scrub brush, drooping willows, and cottonwood lined the ravine. Considering how difficult the pond was to reach, he doubted if the Comanche would bother. At least, he hoped they wouldn't.

Nudging the protesting Duke down the steep hillside while holding onto Jesse and trying to ignore the pain in his butt wasn't easy. When they reached the bottom, he had Buddy hide the horses while he laid Jesse under a canopy of sagging willow branches.

"Get a bandanna out of my saddlebags and wet it," Char instructed as he pulled the hem of Jesse's overlarge shirt from his waistband. He lifted it to see how much damage had been done to the boy.

Two beautiful, coral-tipped breasts stared back at him.

His breath caught. *"Son of a bitch."* He jerked the shirt down and stared at Jesse's face.

He explored the smooth skin, the uptilted nose, the soft, full mouth. All the things he'd missed before. How had he ever thought she was a boy? Jesus. He really was getting old.

"What is it?" Buddy asked, coming down beside him with the wet neckerchief.

"Jesse's a"—he eyed the firm mounds of flesh outlined by the green and white checkered shirt—"woman."

"Jumpin' Jehoshaphats!"

With an unsteady hand, Char reached for Jesse's hat and pulled it off. Thick, dark hair spilled out, holding them both speechless. He had never seen hair that color. It reminded him of ripe blackberries.

Her small whimper snapped him back to his senses. She was bleeding from the gunshot wound in her side—and he damned well better do something about it. If she died now, he'd never know what was going on.

"What are we gonna do?" Hill asked, his voice filled with wonder.

"Try to save her life. Get a bottle of whiskey out of my saddlebags."

Buddy hurried to obey, while Char probed the gash on the girl's side. The injury wasn't deep or serious. It probably wouldn't even leave a scar. His gaze again drifted to her face, and he wondered why she was wearing men's clothes, why she'd killed Davidson Boggs—*why she was toting a gun and knew how to use it.*

He returned his attention to the wound. She'd bled quite a bit, but it didn't look like she'd lost enough blood to make her pass out. So why had she?

With Buddy's help, it didn't take long to clean the injury with whiskey and bandage her up with a piece of white shirt Hill had found in his saddlebags.

"Who is she, I wonder?" Buddy asked as he sat

cross-legged on the ground beside the young girl Char now guessed to be seventeen or so.

"A woman with a purpose, I imagine. She wanted Boggs dead, that's for sure."

"Wow. What do you think he did?"

"I don't know." Char eased down onto his side and rested on a bent elbow to study the girl. Pain speared through his rear end, and he flinched.

"What's wrong?" Hill asked in an anxious tone.

"You got any tweezers?"

"Yeah."

"Get them."

"What for?"

"I've got a splinter."

"Oh. Sure thing." Relieved, Buddy sprang to his feet and ducked under the drooping willow branches. A minute later, he came back, carrying the small metal instrument.

Char stared at it for several seconds. "You said your pa's a doctor. You ever help him?"

"Sometimes."

"Then I'm gonna trust you to remove the splinter."

"Where is it?"

Char sighed. "In my ass."

Buddy burst out laughing.

Char's scowl silenced him.

Clamping his mouth shut, the scamp's eyes still watered as he cleared his throat. "How-how'd it get there?"

"Never mind. Just pull the damned thing out." Hoping he had a steady hand, Char rose to his knees and undid his gun belt, then the buttons on his pants. He lowered the material down over his bare rear end and stretched out on his stomach.

The grass was cool to that part of him that rarely saw daylight, and he sucked in an unexpected breath.

"Something wrong?"

Char shook his head. "Nothing." He peeked at the woman lying beside him and shifted against a heavy feeling. Damn it. Why couldn't the gunfight have waited until after he'd visited the saloon girl?

"I'm not sure about this," Hill grumbled. "I never saw my pa take a splinter out of anyone's butt."

Char felt heat creep up his neck. "Just shut up and get to it."

CHAPTER

❧ 3 ❧

"Jess-ah-leee! Come in now. It's time to set the table for dinner."

Jessalea Richardson laid her kitten, Margaret, on a mound of straw near the barn door, then covered her with a square of material torn from one of Pa's old shirts. Mama had given her the blue checkered cloth yesterday when she'd given up trying to mend it—and it made a wonderful blanket for her kitty. "That'll keep you warm, Maggie," she cooed in a gentle voice, tucking the fabric into the straw. "I'll be back after dinner, when my chores are done, and read you a bedtime story."

Rising, she dusted off her calico dress and woolen coat, then ambled toward the distant house, kicking up puffs of snow as she walked. A cold February breeze blew across the open yard, fluttering the hem of her frock, and she quickened her step.

Her older sister, Susannah, was holding open the screen door, waiting for their little brother, James, as *he struggled to carry in a log for the fireplace. He was only five, but he tried so hard to be like Papa.*

Jessalea smiled with fondness, then slowed her pace to irritate Susannah. Jessalea still hadn't forgiven her sister for the switching she'd given her that afternoon. Nobody would have missed that stupid glob of ginger- bread dough, anyway.

"Will you hurry!" Susannah yelled, her smooth cheeks pink from the cold, her red hair fluttering against her neck in the icy breeze.

If it hadn't been for being cold herself, Jessalea would have slowed up even more. Just because Susannah was thirteen, she thought she was sooo big. Well, in five-and-a-half more years, Jessalea would be thirteen, too. Then her bossy sister wouldn't be so uppity.

A frigid blast lifted the hem of her skirt, sending a chill clear to her bones, and she started to trot.

The pounding of horses' hooves riding into the yard caused her to stumble when she turned to see.

Six men, hunched and cold, guided their horses toward the front steps. One, a big, hairy fellow, shoved his hat back with his thumb and stared at Susannah. "You got any warm vittles, gal? Me and my brothers are plumb froze to the teeth."

Susannah opened the door wider. "Come in out of the cold. I'm sure we'll find something." Her gaze darted over the yard. "Jessalea. Will you hurry up!"

All six men turned to stare, and for the first time in Jessalea's life, she felt afraid.

"Ow! Damn it, be careful."

Jessalea was startlled awake by a man's angry

growl. She opened her eyes and blinked several times, forcing remnants of the nightmare into its dark place.

Swaying branches of a willow came into view. Thin streams of sunlight danced with the warm breeze she felt moving across her cheek.

"Hold still," a voice warned.

In an attempt to locate the source of the sounds, she rolled her head to the side.

Two men came into focus, and she felt a tingle of fear.

One lay on his stomach, his dark head turned, resting on his folded arms. His black shirt molded the broad width of his shoulders and heavily muscled arms. Below that—*a totally naked male rear end.*

Good Lord! She moved to sit up. Her breath caught, and a spear of pain tore through her side. She clenched her teeth and felt the constriction of a binding around her middle. What on earth?

Like a bolt of lightning, she remembered everything. The saloon. The gunfight that left another Boggs dead. She swallowed to keep the threat of nausea under control.

She focused again on the men. The one in black, she remembered. He'd been on a porch roof outside of town and had later helped her in the saloon. But she didn't know the blond one.

She touched the bandage at her waist, remembering how Boggs had wounded her before he died. The men must have found her and tended her injury.

Knowing what they surely discovered beneath her shirt brought a flush to her cheeks.

"Jehoshaphats, Char. The thing looks like it's driven clear to the bone."

"Quit bellyaching and pull the damned splinter out."

Jessalea peeked at the blond man. He looked about her age and wore all black like the other one. How odd. He was leaning over the man called Char, and in one hand, he held a pair of tweezers, in the other, a bottle of whiskey.

He took a long swig, sputtered, then set the bottle aside. "Okay, here goes." He laid the metal against the man's flesh and wiggled it around, but he couldn't grasp the sliver.

"What are you doing? Digging to China?"

That brought a smile to her lips. Unless the younger one squeezed that firm flesh together with his fingers and forced the splinter upward, he wasn't going to get it out. Feeling beholden for the way they helped her, she offered a suggestion. "Why don't you pinch it?"

The man on the ground whipped his head around, and startling, blue-gray eyes met hers. For a heartbeat, they widened with surprise, then closed in resignation. "Lady. Your timing is lousy." He turned away. "Get on with it, Buddy."

The dimpled blond sent her a grin, then returned to his task, but when he went to place his hand on the other man's bare rear, he halted. "I can't do this." He drew back. "I'm not touchin' your butt for anything, Char."

"If you don't get that splinter outta my ass in the next thirty seconds, I'm gonna shoot your horse and leave you to the Indians."

"Ah, criminey. You wouldn't do that."

"One thousand, one . . . one thousand, two . . ."

Buddy grabbed a chunk of the man's flesh, forcing the end of the splinter upward.

"Ow! Damn it. That hurts."

The boy ignored the swearing as he set the tweezers to the sliver of wood and yanked. A splinter the size of a toothpick jutted from the instrument. "Got it," he crowed.

Char jerked his pants up, then came to his knees, his back to Jessalea as he buttoned them. When his clothes were righted and his gun belt in place, he rose and glared down at her from his imposing height. "Who the hell are you?"

His attitude irritated the stuffing out of her. Here she was, lying on the ground, injured by a gunshot wound, and he was snarling at her like she'd slapped him. Just because he was so big, he thought he could intimidate her. Ha! That would be the day. Disregarding the hard thighs and long legs towering over her, she narrowed her eyes. "You heard what Boggs called me in the saloon."

His abrupt nod caused a lock of midnight hair to tumble onto his brow. "Jesse. But, Jesse who?"

"Why were you standing on the roof of a porch—naked?"

"What? That's none of your damned business!"

"And my name isn't yours."

Buddy coughed. "Um, I think I'll see if I can't round us up some grub." He ducked under the branches, leaving her to the mercy of the scowling giant.

But she wasn't frightened. No man who put himself in danger to save another could be all that bad. "By the way, thanks for helping me out."

"Don't thank me. I've been kicking myself ever since for my stupidity."

"Why you arrogant—"

Footsteps pounded through the trees, and Char spun around, his gun leaping into his hand so fast, she didn't even see him draw.

Buddy dove under the willow. "Indians," he whispered. "On the ridge!"

"Ah, hell. Stay with her while I have a look." Char slapped his way out of the branches.

Jessalea was too stunned to move—and a whole lot scared. She remembered seeing the red flags when she was riding into the mountains, but in her pain and dizziness, they hadn't mattered much. She figured she'd die before the Comanche found her. If not from the bullet wound, from starvation. She hadn't eaten in two days.

Trying to control her nervous tremors, she eased into a sitting position and sucked in a breath at the ache in her side. But it wasn't as bad as the pangs in her stomach. The ground swam, and she touched her temple to slow the dizziness. When she could focus again, she drew her gun. "Help me up."

The kid's eyes grew wide. "You tryin' to kill yourself?"

"Quit caterwauling and help me to my feet. I'm not going to let your friend face those savages alone."

A flush tinted his cheeks as he gave her a hand. "You ain't in no shape to be fightin' Indians—and Char said stay here."

"No. He said stay with me. And, if you're going to do that, you'd better keep up." Giving her head a second to clear, and holding her side with her free hand, she parted the willow branches with the barrel of her gun and staggered through them.

Buddy followed, mumbling something she was glad she hadn't understood.

She found the scowling giant, hunched down behind a boulder. "How many are there?"

He whipped around so fast he nearly knocked her over.

"Be careful, you—"

A hard hand stopped the words. He dragged her against his chest, his hold so tight pain overshadowed his furious whisper. "Shut up before you get us killed."

He released her abruptly, then parted the bushes to watch the Indians.

Jessalea grabbed her side. The man's strength was incredible. He'd almost squeezed the breath out of her in that brief hold. And she'd never known anyone with skin so hot.

Buddy came down beside her. "How many—"

She pressed a finger to his mouth. "Shh." Not daring to move, she watched Char. The pearl-handled Colt in his hand was steady, his long fingers curled around it with lithe expertise, and she'd seen his speed with the weapon. He was a gunman. Just like—

"They're gone," Char rasped. "They were a scouting party." He reseated his gun and faced her. "Now, what the hell are you doing out here?"

She lowered her hand from Buddy's mouth and holstered her own weapon. "Covering your backside."

A muscle clenched in his strong jaw. "Lady, your help is the last thing I want or need. In the few hours I've known you, I've been in a gunfight, arrested, broken out of jail, and nearly attacked by Indians. If you help me anymore, I doubt if I'll live through it."

Arrested? Broken out? She wasn't sure what to make of that, but decided to let it pass. "I'm sorry you got involved, but I can't say I was sorry you were there. I'd probably be dead now, if you hadn't been."

"You better thank the stars it was him," Buddy pointed out as he stood and dusted off his britches. "There aren't many men as quick on the draw as Char Daniels."

Char Daniels. Heavens, had she been right when she pegged him as a gunman. Next to Cole Stevens, he was one of the fastest. And she knew all about that profession for sure.

Glaring at Buddy, Char rose and helped her to her feet. "Why'd you kill Boggs?"

"He deserved it."

"What did he do?" Buddy straightened to his full height, which would someday be impressive.

Pulling her hand free, she rubbed her side. "You ask too many questions." What Boggs did was something she couldn't even think about, much less discuss.

"Come on," Char urged her forward. "Let's eat, then get some rest. We have to get out of these hills and make a run for it as soon as it's dark."

Trying to control her body's jump at the mention of food, she steadied her voice. "From the Indians?"

"Yes, darlin', from them, first, then the law in San Antonio. Boggs was the mayor, and they didn't take kindly to you shooting him. Since they think I'm your accomplice, our only hope is to head south. I'll find a judge or sheriff I know and explain the situation, then put you on a stage for home."

"Like hell you will. I haven't finished what I started yet, mister."

"And you're not going to." He gave her a measured look. "What kind of man would I be if I allow a lady to traipse across the countryside on her own?"

"I don't know or care what kind of man you are. My affairs are none of your business."

"Jesus, woman. Didn't your brush with death teach you anything?"

"It taught me plenty." She put some distance between them. "I'll have to practice even harder on my draw and watch for back-shooters."

"She's good, Char," Buddy praised. "You was too busy, but I saw how quick she was. And I know she coulda got at least two of 'em."

Daniels narrowed his eyes on Buddy. "And the third one would have killed her."

"She was still good."

Char gave her a skeptical once-over. "You that fast?"

"Faster." She wasn't bragging. It was the truth. Still, she thanked goodness her injury was on the opposite side of her gun arm if the man wanted to test her vinegar—and the look in his eyes said he did.

His gaze drifted over her, then to a small clearing behind her. "That graze on your side hasn't slowed you down any. You up to showing me what you got?"

"Any time." The smugness he was trying to hide made her want to take him down a peg.

"Fine. But, no shots. I don't want to bring the Comanche down on us—and let's make it interesting. If you win, I'll help you track down the rest of those men. But if I win, you go home."

He was so sure of himself that her confidence slipped, but she propped it up. He wasn't as fast as the man who taught her. "I've got a better idea. *When* I win, you and your sidekick move on and let me take care of my own problems."

"And if you lose?"

She smiled. "I won't."

Amusement sparkled in those haunting eyes, making him look younger and more approachable. "You might be stubborn, but I like your spirit." He motioned to the clearing. "After you, darlin'."

It struck her that he hadn't agreed to her wager, but it didn't matter. She'd lose him—and his friend—when she was ready.

As she walked, she ignored the discomfort in her side and concentrated on her teachings. *Keep your feet spread, not far enough to threaten your balance, just enough for a solid stance. Let your hand hang loose at your side, no more than a couple inches from your holster. Keep your eyes on your opponent's and watch for a change that precedes the draw. Go for your gun the instant you see the sign. Keep your movement smooth and fluid. Never forget that a wounded man can kill you. Always, always aim for the heart.*

"Right here's good enough." Char stopped and eased into a lethal stance.

Buddy sidled off to one side to enjoy the mock battle.

Even though this wasn't a real showdown, she couldn't suppress a shiver when she saw Char's bottomless stare. The dangerous power emanating from his taut body was unsettling, and she was sure he used the effect often to unnerve his opponents. With those frozen features and menacing black clothes, he looked evil.

In that instant, she knew she had no chance of beating him. Char Daniels wouldn't give any sign when he intended to draw, which meant she'd have to outsmart him.

"You know, we could both stand here all day

waiting for the other to make the first move." She touched her side. "Truth to tell, I'm not up to it. How about if we draw on the count of three?"

He nodded, but his features remained unreadable.

She began to count. "One . . . two . . ." She whipped out her pistol—and aimed it straight at his wide chest.

Both of his weapons were pointed at her.

He gave her a slow smile. "Three."

"You cheated!"

"I went for my gun when you did."

"Jehoshaphats!" Buddy gushed. "I never saw anyone draw that fast." He was staring at Char, his expression filled with awe.

Char holstered his irons and advanced, pressing her hand down to reseat her own. "Since this isn't going to work, maybe we should try talking." He gestured to Buddy. "Build a fire—a very small one—and round us up something to eat."

"Yes, sir," the towhead bubbled, then headed for the horses.

Jessalea rolled her eyes and made for the willow.

Joining her on the grass, Char stretched his long legs in front of him and rested on his elbows. "Tell me why you're after the Boggses."

"I'd rather eat worms."

He didn't ask again.

She shifted. The man had no idea how unnerving it was when he stared at her like that. "Listen. What happened with that sidewinder isn't something I like to talk about. In fact, I never have."

"He must have done something pretty vicious."

"What he and his brothers did went far beyond vicious." She fixed on the overhanging branches framing his dark head. "They killed my f-family." Her fingers dug into the soil. "Listen, I don't want to talk about this anymore." She swept her gaze over him. "I'd rather find out how Char Daniels became such a fast draw."

He watched her for several seconds, then sighed. "There isn't much to tell. I learned when I was fifteen, and I was taught by a hired hand on the farm where I was raised."

"A hired hand?"

"He was a bounty hunter between jobs who worked there during harvest for a couple months."

Bounty hunters and gunmen were synonymous. How well she knew. "Did you become a bounty hunter, too?"

"Yes, darlin'. Then later, a Texas Ranger."

"There isn't much difference. They both risk their lives needlessly—and put their women through hell."

He studied her several seconds, then said in a quiet voice. "I don't have a woman."

Her pulse did a funny leap, and she could have kicked herself for the surge of pleasure that went through her. What was the matter with her? She had no girlish notions about Char Daniels. He stood for everything she feared. Everything she would avoid at all cost.

CHAPTER

❧ 4 ❧

Trying to ignore Buddy's ongoing praise as they ate hardtack and beans, Char let his thoughts drift to the young woman seated across the fire from him. Even in those God-awful clothes, she was a real beauty. But she had a stubborn streak that would make a mule take notice, and she was damned fast with a gun. Too fast.

He shoved in a spoonful of tasteless beans and chewed, wondering who'd taught her to handle a weapon.

"What time we leaving?"

Char glanced at Buddy where he squatted next to the fire, his empty plate in his hand. "Another hour or so. When it's good and dark." Setting his own meal aside, he spoke to the girl. "Where are the rest of the Boggses?"

She sopped up bean juice with her biscuit and popped it into her mouth. She hadn't paused in eating since she sat down. "One of them's in Laredo."

"Do you know which one?"

Blackberry curls rippled when she nodded. "Cecil."

"How'd you find out?"

"When I passed you outside San Antonio," she said, avoiding his eyes, "I was coming from Davidson Boggs's place down the road. I found a letter from Cecil in his desk."

As she spoke, Char noticed a slight tremor in her hands. Did talking about Boggs cause that? Or did it have something to do with her being in his house? "You think there's a chance Cecil Boggs is still in Laredo?"

"If not, someone's bound to know where he went."

"Then it looks like we're heading for Laredo. Come on, Hill. Help me pack up the gear."

"Look, I don't want you and your friend involved in this."

He stared at her upturned face. It was a perfect oval. "We *are* involved, darlin', and I don't take to murderers. That's why I've spent the last few years of my life chasing outlaws. Besides, the man I've been looking for myself might be in Laredo."

"Another criminal?"

He didn't want to explain his whole life history. "No. Just a man I'm anxious to meet up with."

"And, where Char goes, I go," Buddy piped in.

Char clenched his teeth.

Jesse rose. "Go wherever you like. But don't get in my way."

Her pluck made him smile. "I'll try, darlin'."

"Stop calling me that."

"Anything you say, sweetheart."

She whirled around and headed for her saddle, her lips pressed into a tight line, her limbs stiff with anger.

Char grinned and nodded to Hill. "Better go help her with the saddle."

A silver glow from the half-moon lighted the barren landscape ahead of them, yet not one of them was relaxed enough to enjoy the beauty. If the sheriff or his men or the soldiers spotted them, they'd go to jail . . . or worse. And she didn't even want to think about the Indians.

Jessalea tightened her fingers around the reins and squinted into the darkness. The plod of their horses' hooves and the creak of saddle leather was so loud she figured all of San Antonio could hear. She sent a peek at her companions.

Char's black figure blended with the night, but those pale eyes were clearly visible and in constant motion.

Buddy looked scared.

She couldn't blame him. Moisture dampened her own palms. She hated this. Fear did funny things to her—made her cold and clammy, then hot and sweaty, then shivery. But the knot in her belly stayed the same. Tight. Nauseating.

A bush rustled off to the side, and before she knew it, she'd drawn her pistol.

Char was beside her in an instant, covering her hand with his, lowering the gun, his voice gentle and reassuring. "It's just a rabbit."

She'd never been this jumpy, and it made her angry that she was now. Daniels would probably think she was some simpering female who was afraid of her own shadow. Ignoring the urge to defend her actions, she pulled her hand from beneath his and rammed her gun into the holster. "I know what it was." She nudged her horse into a faster trot.

"How far we gonna go before we make camp?" Buddy whispered.

"As far as it takes to find a place where we won't be seen from the main path."

That place turned out to be a cluster of mesquites they located five hours later.

Jessalea was so tired, she thought she'd topple from the saddle before her feet were able to touch the ground. She'd been riding at a killing pace for the last six days, anxious to reach San Antonio . . . and Davidson Boggs.

She'd miscalculated the expense of her journey, too. She'd used all the money she'd saved in the last year getting to Waco—to Patrick Boggs, so she'd tried hunting for food. She'd shot three rabbits and a squirrel the first few days, then her luck changed. Until tonight, she hadn't seen another critter for the pot. Nor had she eaten. Char and Buddy didn't realize they'd saved her life twice.

As she reached for the cinch on her saddle, a heavy ache rippled through her leaden arms. She felt like anvils were tied to her wrists.

"Jesse, why don't you put on some coffee while Buddy and I unsaddle the horses?"

Her relief was so great she sagged, then turned to see Char standing next to her, the taut lines of his face shadowed in the waning moonlight. The musky scent of leather and male drifted to her, and it was all she could do not to throw her arms around him in thanks. She stepped back. "Coffee. Of course."

She set about gathering small twigs and branches for a fire, and by the time the aroma of coffee filled the air, the men had tethered the horses and spread the bedrolls.

Jessalea filled a tin cup and sat cross-legged in the middle of hers. To her tired bones it felt as good as a feather mattress.

"How far do you think we've come?" Buddy asked, blowing on the hot liquid in his cup.

"Twenty miles. Maybe." Char watched her as he sipped his coffee.

She was entranced by the glow of firelight dancing over the sharp angles of his sinfully handsome face.

The corner of his mouth quirked as if he'd read her thoughts, then he set his cup aside. "I figure we'll reach Laredo in four or five days."

Interest brightened Buddy's eyes. "I'll bet we'll find a lot of gunmen there."

"I'm not looking for gunmen, kid, and I'd appreciate it if you didn't go blabbing my name around town when we get there."

"But—"

"Listen, Hill. I know you're trying your damnedest to get me killed, but I'm not ready to die yet."

"I am not."

"Fine, then don't mention my name. I have enough to worry about without looking over my shoulder for some hothead out to make a name for himself."

"Oh, all right," he huffed. Tossing his coffee into the fire, he flounced over on his pallet and pulled a blanket up to his ear. "I won't say a word."

Char smiled, then gave her a wink. "Better get some rest, darlin'. Tomorrow's gonna be a long day."

She clenched her teeth at the endearment, but she couldn't help thinking tomorrow wasn't going to be half as long as tonight. Especially when she saw him remove his gun belt and shirt.

Her breath became trapped in her throat at the

sight of his sleek, broad chest covered with a sprinkling of silky black hair. His skin was smooth and golden, and the hard muscles beneath that flesh bunched when he moved.

She didn't breathe again until he'd slipped into his bedroll. Still, she was very, very aware that not more than a half-dozen feet separated his bed from hers. The thought was unsettling at best. It would be much too easy to slide in with him. Learn the feel of that firm body. She shifted her head against the hard saddle.

Where in blazes were these thoughts coming from? It was a silly question, because she knew very well where. From Fanny Dupree, her uncle's mistress, the woman who raised her after the murders, the woman who had given Jessalea a home . . . in a whorehouse in Natchez, Mississippi.

She didn't want to think about Fanny—about how worried she must be by now over Jessalea's disappearance, even though she had left a vague note.

Closing her eyes, Jessalea sank into her bedroll, reminding herself to send Fanny a wire when they reached town. . . .

It seemed as if she'd scarcely gone to sleep when Char woke her with a cup of coffee.

They mounted up before the sun peeked over the horizon, but as the day progressed, travel was slow beneath the scorching Texas sun, and they had to stop often to water the horses from the canteens.

Char stuffed his bandanna inside his Stetson to insulate his head from the brutal heat.

Buddy draped his kerchief over his mop of curls and held it in place with his hat.

Jessalea's own discomfort wasn't limited to the

moisture trickling down between her breasts. In her entire seventeen years, she'd never seen anyplace so desolate, and for an instant, she felt a long-buried pang of homesickness. It seemed like forever since she'd lived in Missouri—on that peaceful little farm where nothing exciting ever happened.

"What are you thinking about so strong?" Char asked, guiding his horse alongside hers.

"How I used to complain about our farm being boring. I guess I never realized how well off I was, and, someday, I'm going to have that peace again. I'm going to return to that farm, raise a passel of kids, and live out my days in content and boring tranquility."

He gave a mock shudder. "I don't envy you. I spent the first half of my life living that monotonous day-to-day existence. I'll never do it again. There's a whole country that needs exploring, challenges around ever corner, excitement and adventure. Those are the things I crave."

"What about a wife and family?"

"With all the beautiful women in the country, why should I restrict myself to one? As for kids—I don't want any. Children mean commitment, and that's not for me." He turned away, his jaw hard. "I've had enough commitments to last a lifetime, and I know I'd make a lousy father."

She studied his determined profile, wondering what had caused him such bitterness.

"Riders comin'," Buddy warned, drawing his mount close to theirs.

Three horsemen rode toward them from the south. They appeared travel-weary and dangerous.

Char pulled his stallion in front of Jessalea and Buddy, shielding them. He motioned for them to stop, then drew up and waited for the others to approach.

He touched the brim of his hat in greeting. "Afternoon." No hint of wariness could be detected in his smooth voice.

She didn't know how he did that. She was as nervous as a calf cornered by a mountain lion. These men gave her the same scary feeling the Boggses had that day on the farm.

One with several missing teeth pulled off his hat and mopped his sweaty brow on his sleeve. "Right hot day, ain't it?" He eyed each of them, dismissing her and Buddy. His gaze returned to Char, to his sidearms, then up again. "Been travelin' long?"

"A spell."

"Me and my partners, here"—he swept a bony hand to indicate the men behind him, one with a heavy beard, and one with a scarred face—"been on the road nigh on a week now. Headin' for San Antonio for a few days . . . then on to Indian territory." He paused, waiting for the significance of that detail to set in.

Char didn't blink an eye.

Buddy swallowed.

It was all Jessalea could do not to groan. By the Schofield's on their hips, and the mention of their destination, it wasn't hard to peg them as no-goods. Indian territory was a haven for outlaws. Jessalea's hand inched closer to her gun.

Char smiled. "We were there, ourselves, a few days ago. Too quiet for us. Me and the *Youngers,* here, decided to see if there wasn't some excitement down Laredo way."

The man paled. "Youngers?"

One of the others drew in a startled breath. The scar over his right eye twitched.

"Er, Charlie," the hairy faced one interrupted. "It's gettin' late. We better head out or we ain't gonna make that poker game in San Antonio tomorra."

The leader cleared his throat. "Yeah, guess you're right, Pete." He nodded to Char, then with respect to her and Buddy. "Be seein' ya'll."

They watched as the men maneuvered their horses around them and rode on like they were being chased by the law.

Jessalea glanced at Char. "The Youngers?"

He grinned, his straight teeth white against his tanned face. "Didn't figure I could pass you off as Frank and Jesse James."

"That was pretty sneaky."

"But it worked."

Buddy continued to watch the others. "I think we should have shot it out with them."

"You would." Char nudged his horse into a trot. "One of these days, kid, you're gonna learn to avoid trouble whenever possible."

When the sun dipped below the horizon, and the coolness of evening descended, they came to a river Char called the Frio. It was a welcome sight with its slow-moving water, cottonwood trees, and boulder-lined banks—a perfect place to make camp.

After a meal of jerky, hard biscuits, and canned peaches, Char rolled a smoke, then he and Buddy settled around a flat rock to play a hand of cards.

Jessalea slung her saddlebags over her shoulder and headed for the river—and a much-needed bath. It was still light enough to see as she picked her way over the dry grass.

Rummaging through the leather pouches, she found a change of clothes, a towel, and a bar of soap, scented with honeysuckle. Although Fanny hadn't known about her leaving Natchez—especially dressed as a boy—Jessalea had taken the woman's advice that had been instilled in her over the years. *Always be prepared for anything, honey.* That's why Jessalea's supplies not only included the fancy soap, but bath salts, a nightgown, and a satin dress as well.

She caressed the hem of the cream-colored gown. Dear Fanny. She was such a kind person, always so warm and generous. Jessalea wished her uncle would see those qualities and marry the woman. Even though Fanny owned one of the most prosperous whorehouses in Mississippi, Jessalea's uncle was the only man who ever shared her bed. With Fanny's dark, sultry good looks, she must have given up a fortune because of him. Not a night went by in the brothel that some newcomer didn't offer for her.

Jessalea picked up her clean pants and shirt and walked toward the water. She felt sorry for Fanny, because she knew how much Fanny loved her uncle—and she knew he'd never settle down with one woman. Besides, considering his lifestyle, he probably wouldn't live to see his next birthday, anyway.

Keeping an eye on the line of trees between her and camp, she stripped down, then picked up the soap and waded into the river. The water felt wonderful after the killing heat of the day, and she sank low, watching the golden rays of dusk dance over the surface.

When she finished washing her hair, she wedged her

shoulders into the curve of a boulder, folded her hands across her middle, and rested her head on the rough rock. She listened to the evening.

Water lapped at her floating legs. A soft breeze rustled cottonwood leaves overhead, and crickets united in a peaceful serenade.

Then she heard another sound.

She jerked upright, and her gaze darted to the bank. She fixed on her pile of clothes.

The ominous rattle was coming from them.

Snatching her towel off a rock near the river's edge, she wrapped it around her and waded up onto the bank, keeping a healthy distance between her bare feet and the snake coiled on top of her clothes.

With slow, quiet movements, she inched toward the gun belt draped over her saddlebags and eased her .45 out of its holster.

In the growing darkness, it was hard to see, but the white under the rattler's neck stood out like a beacon. Taking careful aim, she fired.

The headless snake whipped up into the air, then hit the ground, twisting and flopping.

Char burst through the trees, guns drawn.

Buddy was right behind him.

Char spotted the snake at once, but it took Buddy a second to identify the threat.

"Wow," he whispered. "Great shot."

"Are you all right?" Char asked. He started toward her but stopped, taking in her near-naked appearance. "Jesus."

Buddy gawked.

"Hill, get back to camp," Char ordered.

"But—"

"Go."

With a mutinous scowl, Buddy whirled around and trudged into the trees.

Char returned his attention to her.

Her heart began to pound an uneven beat. The way he was looking at her did strange things to her innards. "The snake was on my clothes," she explained stupidly.

He hadn't moved, hadn't quit looking at her. Those heart-stopping eyes glowed bright silver in the moonlight.

The crickets' song grew distant.

She felt the breeze slide across her exposed chest like a soft hand. Her stomach tightened. She became self-conscious of the scar on her left breast.

"Put some clothes on, Jesse. Before I do something we'll both regret."

She couldn't move.

He took a threatening step toward her.

She panicked and thrust out her hand. "No! Don't."

He stopped, then explored her face, her naked shoulders, the scar above her left breast, the wet towel clinging to her skin. "You're right to be afraid of me, darlin'. Right now my thoughts aren't very honorable." His gaze lingered on hers, then he turned and strode toward camp.

She bolted for her clothes, shaking as she dragged them on. The man had no right to make her feel these things. No right at all.

When she returned to camp, she didn't look at either of them. She climbed into her bedroll and turned away. As soon as she got to Laredo and took care of Cecil Boggs, she'd light out on her own. There were far fewer dangers from those murdering Boggses than from Char Daniels.

But, try as she might, she couldn't erase his softly spoken words. Couldn't stop the tingles moving through her woman's body.

Chapter

❋ 5 ❋

Char couldn't sleep, so he got up and sat by the fire, trying to get visions of Jesse out of his head. Over the years, he must have seen a hundred women wearing much less than she had been tonight, but not one of them had affected him the way she had. With moonlight bathing her smooth skin, that damp towel clinging to her sweet curves, and those riotous curls cascading down to her firm rear end, she had resembled a pagan goddess. A bewitching one. No wonder he'd said those things to her. His thoughts *had* been anything but honorable.

But he shouldn't have said the words. Hell, he shouldn't have even thought them. She was a virgin. He could spot one of them in a heartbeat, and it had even been more apparent when she'd watched him undress last night. She hadn't been able to hide her curiosity when she'd explored him with those damned green eyes. She'd been so naive, she hadn't even noticed how her interest had aroused him. Her gaze had shyly skipped that part of him that would have made the fact known.

But he'd known. God, yes. He'd gone to sleep last night dreaming about her, about the soft red mouth that begged to be kissed. About settling himself between her smooth white thighs. Heat stirred in his lower region, and he swore under his breath. This had to stop.

He broke a twig in half and tossed it into the fire, remembering that today was his birthday. He was thirty years old. Single. Without a home. Without direction. Those thoughts were as unsettling as the ones about Jesse.

He wished he could locate his real pa. At least then he might find direction, if nothing else. Wanting to learn what happened to his real folks was like an itch Char couldn't scratch. Maybe it was a need to discover his roots. Or, very possibly, it was his age. But whatever the reason, the drive wouldn't leave him.

He hadn't been lying to Jesse when he said he might find the man he wanted in Laredo. It was possible. Unless he was dead, Otis Daniel *whoever* had to be somewhere, hopefully in Texas.

During his time with the Rangers, Char had searched most of the northern section of Texas, then along the Nueces Strip. But there was a lot of territory to cover yet. Besides, what else did he have to do? Since the Rangers disbanded, he didn't even have a job. No kin, either, since he'd never considered the Websters family.

At the thought of the people who raised him, his stomach turned sour. He refused to think about the barrel-chested farmer or his prune-faced wife. Refused to remember the humiliation he'd suffered that last day, fifteen years ago.

The day he joined the Union Army out of spite.

He smiled, wondering if Deke ever found out Char had sided with those who Deke considered the enemy. He hoped so.

Yawning, he discarded thoughts of the Websters and climbed into his bedroll. Now, if only he could stop thinking about Jesse. . . .

The sky had turned pink by the time he woke, roused the others, and was ready to leave.

Jesse still refused to look at him, which was annoying as hell. But it gave him an excellent opportunity to study her at his leisure. Her big-brimmed hat concealed the blackberry curls he'd watched her stuff inside earlier. Her spine was rigid beneath the man's checkered shirt she wore.

He wondered where she'd gotten it. By the size, he could tell the owner of that garment was a very big man. The jeans encasing her slender legs and hips appeared new and fit well, but the snakeskin boots were worn and too large. Who *had* supplied her "boys" clothes?

The owner of that shirt bothered him. Her family was dead, weren't they? So who was the man in her life? He felt an emotion he couldn't put a name to grind into his middle.

"How much farther?" Buddy complained, wiping his cheek on the shoulder of his shirt. "All this ridin' with no conversation is boring."

"What do you want to talk about?"

The kid's eyes lit with eagerness. "How you learned to be such a fast draw."

What else? Char looped his reins around the pommel and relaxed. "Like I told Jesse the other night, I learned from a hired hand who worked during harvest one year on our farm. I was fifteen—and very impressionable." He paused. "Kinda like you. Anyway, at the time, I didn't know the names of gunfighters, so I wasn't duly impressed with the man's name until later. I was more interested in his expertise."

Buddy leaned closer. "Who was he?"

"Cole Stevens."

The kid's mouth fell open.

Jesse whipped around, her expression startled. *"Cole Stevens* taught you?"

"Impressive, isn't it?"

"Very." She nudged her horse into a faster canter.

Char smiled. Well, at least she was talking to him again.

They crossed the Nueces River in the late afternoon, and Char stopped long enough to snare a rabbit for supper, but he wanted to make a few more miles before they stopped for the night. They'd already wasted enough time with their slow pace and early evenings.

There was no shelter of any kind when they at last settled next to a scrub brush on the open plains. It wasn't a place he would have chosen, but they were exhausted. Yet, as he unsaddled the horses, he became edgy. Their fire could be seen for miles, and it left them vulnerable to troublemakers.

"Let's get supper over and douse the fire," Char instructed as he joined the others.

Jesse continued scooping biscuit dough into a skillet.

Buddy gave the rabbit a turn on the spit. "Are we in Indian country again?"

"No place in Texas *isn't* Indian country. But I'm more concerned about drawing outlaws than a wandering band of Comanche." He lifted the pot of coffee from the side of the flames and poured himself a cup, trying not to notice how the firelight danced over Jesse's beautiful face. "I'm gonna keep watch tonight."

"You'll keep watch *part* of the night," she countered. "You can't ride without sleep any more than the rest of us can. I'll keep guard half the night."

"What about me?" Buddy argued. "I get a turn, too."

Char came to his feet. "This isn't a damned game."

Hill fingered one of his Colts. "Me and Betsy, here, don't play games."

Ah, hell. He threw up his hands. "Fine. I'll wake Jesse when I get tired, then she can wake you." He didn't bother to tell either of them he wouldn't get tired. He wouldn't let himself.

When supper was over, and the fire smothered beneath a mound of sandy dirt, Char unsheathed his rifle and settled his spine against his saddle. In the darkness, he listened to the scuffle of a prairie dog, the caw of a bird, and the sound of Jesse climbing into her bedroll behind a cluster of scrub brush.

The scent of honeysuckle mingled with woodsmoke, causing visions of the way she had looked wrapped in that towel to taunt him again.

He let out a sigh, wondering why he didn't get on his horse and ride out. He didn't want to get tangled up with her. But the thought of leaving her to the mercy of killers didn't set well, either. *Killers who knew she was after them.*

He studied on that, trying to figure out how

54

Davidson Boggs had known she was coming. Who had warned him? Would the others know, too?

The image of Jesse walking into a trap and being gunned down by some back-shooter hardened his resolve to stick with her, at least until he found out who'd warned the outlaws.

A soft thud startled him.

Easing his finger over the trigger of the rifle, his muscles tense, his ears attuned to the slightest rustle, he came to his feet. Someone was very, very close. He could feel them.

A shadow moved.

"Easy, partner," he rasped, raising the Sharps.

"Will you put that thing away," Jesse hissed. "I came to relieve you."

Being alone in the dark with her was not what he needed right now. His senses were too alive. "Go back to bed."

"Not yet," another voice countered. A match flared to reveal three desperados holding rifles. "Drop the Sharps, mister. Slow and easy like," the leader ordered, his weapon pointed at Char.

Another match leapt to life and lit the end of a torch. A harsh yellow glow spread over them.

"Gahl damn, Dutch. This one's a gal!"

Char swung his gaze to Jesse, and nearly groaned out loud. Her hair was down, and now, when she needed it most, there was no sign of that lousy flop-billed hat.

"Ah, *amigo,*" the third man crooned. "She is a beauty, no?"

"She is that," the leader agreed in a husky voice.

The way those no-accounts were staring at her sent stirrings of panic through Char. He had to do something. Quick. "You fellas aren't really thinking of messing with Jesse James's wife, are you?"

The Mexican sucked in a breath. A Springfield rifle wobbled in his grip.

The torch wavered in the hand of a pit-faced younger man.

But the good-looking one called Dutch smiled. "No, I wouldn't mess with Zee James." His flashy grin widened. "We've been friends too long."

Char clamped down on a curse. "What do you want?"

Buddy came lumbering into the light, wearing only his britches and scratching his mop of blond curls. "What's going on . . ." He gaped at the armed men and paled.

The leader shook his head. "Who's this? The Sundance Kid?"

Char ignored the mockery.

Jesse bristled. "Listen, mister—"

"I'll get to you in a minute, beautiful. But for now, drop your gun, then gather the supplies while the kid gets the horses. You, fella," he directed at Char, "put your weapons down and move over to that brush."

Char clenched his teeth. What choice did he have? He set the rifle down, then lowered his gun belt to the ground.

"You can't treat *Char Daniels* like that!" Buddy blurted.

Char swore. He was going to gag that damned kid.

Dutch arched an amused brow. "Zee James, Sundance Kid, and now Char Daniels." He peered into the darkness from where Buddy had emerged. "Who's next? Cole Stevens?"

56

"Probably," Jesse taunted.

Dutch chuckled. "I like your spunk, gal. Now get a move on, before I blow a hole in your friends." He jerked the gun. "You, too, kid." Then he nodded to his men. "Paco, bring our horses in. Matt, you gather their weapons and toss them into that cactus."

After Buddy led the horses to the group and handed over the reins, Jesse plunked down their supply sacks on the ground and gave the outlaws a mutinous glare.

Char was getting nervous. The woman was going to cause a scene. He *knew* it.

"Since it's going to take you at least a day and a half to reach town, you'd better keep one of the canteens for yourself. The rest, you can hand to me, beautiful," the leader ordered.

She didn't budge. "If you want them so bad, then you come and get them." She folded her arms across her chest.

"Jesse, do as the man says," Char commanded in his sternest voice.

"Not a chance."

"If I come over there, honey," Dutch warned, "you're going to pay the price."

Fear tightened Char's gut. *For God's sake, Jesse, give him the sacks.*

She didn't.

Dutch smiled and walked toward her, then in a lightning fast move, he caught Jesse's hands and pinned them behind her back. He dragged her against him and held her, his smile growing wider. "Did you know spirited women excite me?"

Char saw red. He took a step toward the outlaw.

A gun cocked. "No, no, *amigo*. You would not want

to die for a useless reason. The Dutchman, he will not hurt the *señorita*."

The Dutchman. Char stared. He'd heard of the gentleman outlaw who had never killed anyone—yet—and who made it a practice to kiss his female victims. The thought set Char's blood on fire.

"Let me go," Jesse hissed.

The blond leader ignored her as he lowered his head and kissed her, hard and quick.

"You son of a bitch!" Char roared. He went for the outlaw.

Gunfire ripped through the air.

Dust exploded between his feet.

"Amigo. Do not give your life foolishly."

Dutch was still staring at Jesse. He touched her cheek. "Bye, beautiful. I hope to see you again some day." He glanced at Char. "Alone."

Char was trembling with rage by the time the outlaws left.

At least the sidewinders left them the bedrolls, saddlebags, the money they didn't know about in Char's gear, and their weapons, that last giving him pause. Why hadn't they taken their guns? It was almost as if they didn't want to leave them defenseless in hostile country. Was that how the Dutchman had earned the name "gentleman outlaw"? Char should have been thankful whatever the reason, but he wasn't.

"How'd they find us in the dark?" Buddy asked.

"They didn't. They spotted our fire earlier and waited till they thought we were asleep." He glanced at Jesse. "Are you okay?"

"I'm fine." She hefted her saddlebags over her shoulder and glared in the direction the outlaws had taken. "But he won't be the next time he comes within range of my gun."

"What are we gonna do now?" Buddy asked. "How are we going to get to Laredo?"

"We're gonna walk, kid."

It took them the rest of that night and all the next day to cover the remaining distance to Laredo and check into rooms above a saloon overlooking the Rio Grande.

Not that Jessalea noticed. Her skin felt fried to the bone from the grueling heat, and she was so hungry, she could eat a whole steer by herself. But those feelings were nothing compared to the anger she felt toward those despicable outlaws. They had taken Fanny's buckskin, Hannah.

After cooling off at the washbasin, and getting rid of a pound of trail dust, she straightened her dirty clothes and shoved thoughts of the Dutchman's gang out of her mind.

She'd rather think about Char. No, that wasn't such a good idea either. She concentrated on the aroma of sizzling meat wafting up from the kitchens below.

From the room next door, she heard snatches of Char and Buddy's conversation as they, too, cleaned up for supper. Buddy was griping about the blisters on his feet, while Char continued to curse the outlaws—the Dutchman in particular.

Running a brush through her tangled hair, then twisting the curls high on her head, she stuffed it under the hat and reached for her weapons when Char banged on the door. "Come on, Jesse. I'm starved."

She smiled at the irritation in his voice, then strapped on her gun and joined him. "Stop caterwauling then, and let's go."

Buddy raced ahead of them and commandeered a vacant table. A kerosine lamp glowed in the center of the rough wood.

An attractive woman in a yellow satin dress sauntered over. She flicked a glance over Jessalea and Buddy. "Y'all want sarsaparilla, I suppose."

"Milk," Char corrected, flashing her a smile that caused Jessalea's heart to do a funny twist. "Whiskey for me, darlin', and three of the biggest steaks you've got." He winked. "Rare."

Jessalea didn't like his highhandedness, or the way he was treating her like a child, but she was too hungry to waste time arguing.

Buddy's scowl revealed his thoughts were the same.

The waitress hurried off, then returned a moment later. She filled Char's whiskey glass and handed it to him, lingering when his fingers brushed hers. The two full of milk she left for Jessalea and Buddy to get for themselves.

"Milk." Buddy curled his lip as he took a sip. "Who ever heard of a gunfighter drinking *milk.*"

"Cole Stevens does," Char advised, trying to hold onto a smile. "When he was staying at the farm, he had milk with every meal."

Buddy was stunned.

Jessalea arched a disbelieving brow. The man was full of cow manure.

Buddy stared at the glass in front of him with new respect. "After we get some horses, are we goin' after them no-accounts?"

Char, the snake, hadn't taken his eyes off the woman in yellow satin. "No. It'd cost more to search for them than it would to replace what we lost."

"So we're gonna let 'em go?"

"Yes. But don't worry, kid. They'll cross my path again one day."

He sounded so sure that Jesse wondered if he didn't have private plans to take care of the Dutchman's gang. "They'll probably have sold my buckskin by then." *Fanny's buckskin.*

Char covered her hand. "Not if I can help it."

Heat moved along her neck, and she jerked her hand away just as the waitress returned.

The woman set Char's plate in front of him, first, then gave him a warm smile before plunking down the other two. When she spoke, it was only to him. "Y'all in town for the hangin' tomorrow?"

"Nope. Looking for a couple of men. Cecil Boggs and Otis Daniels—or a name close to that. You ever heard of them, darlin'?"

Jessalea ground her teeth at the way the woman glowed when Char spoke to her.

"No." She shook her head of golden curls. "But I'm real bad with names. Why, I don't even recall the name of the man they're stringing up in the morning. Course, I probably won't be awake to watch, anyway." She gave a sly smile. "Since I don't get off till midnight."

Jessalea glared at the steak in front of her. If she wasn't so hungry, she'd shove it in the witch's face. She cut into the meat and poked a piece into her mouth—as much to stop a caustic remark as to appease her hunger.

Char lifted an interested eyebrow. "I might see you later, then—after I see the youngins to bed."

Jessalea choked on her food.

CHAPTER

❦ 6 ❦

Jessalea discarded the wet towel from her bath and flounced down naked onto the bed, reminding herself again and again that she didn't care what that skirt-chasing Char Daniels did. *He could bed every woman in Texas, for all she cared.*

She had other more important things to think about. Like Cecil Boggs. That murdering bastard was somewhere in Laredo, and she would find him.

Dragging on her dusty britches and shirt, she twisted her newly washed hair into a knot at the top of her head and covered it with her hat.

After stomping into her boots, she strapped on her gun belt, checked her Colt, and headed for the door.

A knock startled her. Cautious now, she moved closer. "Who is it?"

"It's me, Jesse. Open the door."

"What do you want?" What was Char doing here?

There was a long, silent pause, then his husky voice penetrated the wood. "I've got something for you."

"What?"

"Clothes."

The man must be nuts. Opening the door, she placed her hands on her hips and stared at him.

Char, looking devastating in his clean black clothes and freshly shaved face, held a paper wrapped parcel in his left hand. His hair, damp from his bath, gleamed like polished onyx beneath the hall's lantern lights. That same light reflected in his eyes, making them glint with blue silver as they explored her.

She felt an annoying flutter in her stomach. "What's this nonsense about clothes?"

He tossed the package on the bed. "Try them on. I'll be back in a few minutes to see how they look."

"I don't want—"

"Do you have to argue about everything?"

"I'm going to find Boggs."

He crossed his arms. "Tonight? How? Do you plan on knocking on every door in town?"

"I'll ask around."

"Then get dressed. There's a dance at the other end of town. There'll be enough folks there to keep you busy for hours."

She was so shocked it took a second to find her voice. "I thought you had other . . . plans."

"Well, you thought wrong." He closed the door.

Not sure she was making the right decision, she opened the package and examined the colorful flowered skirt, off-the-shoulder white blouse, and slippers. She was both pleased and annoyed. She didn't want to go to a dance, but, he was right. A lot of townsfolk would be there—and one of them might know Cecil Boggs.

With the exception of the blouse being too low, everything fit very well. He must have had a lot of experience selecting women's clothes. The thought didn't endear him to her.

After dragging a brush through her hair, she went to the mirror above the washbasin to tie her thick curls back with a white ribbon, wishing the looking glass was big enough for her to see all of herself.

"Jesse? Are you dressed yet?" Char's voice rumbled as he rapped on the door.

She faced the entrance. "Why don't you come in and see for yourself?" She held her breath, suddenly anxious about his opinion—and it bothered her. She'd never cared what anyone thought before.

He walked in, but halted midstride. His gaze ran her length, then up again, stopping at her face. For several seconds, he stared, then he swore. "I knew it was a mistake. I knew damned well I shouldn't have bought that outfit."

"What's wrong with it?"

He cursed again. When he'd bought those clothes at the general store, he never dreamed they'd look like *that* on her. If he'd thought she was beautiful before, it was nothing compared to the vision standing before him now.

Her dark hair glistened against her glowing apricot skin. The white blouse molded to the shape of her unbound breasts, while the flowered skirt clung to her sleek woman's hips and slender legs before stopping above the ankles. He'd misjudged the length. But the slippers fit.

"What do you mean, you shouldn't have bought them?" Jesse placed her hands on her hips and tilted her head, waiting.

"Darlin', believe me, if I stay in this room alone

with you much longer, you're going to find out exactly what I mean."

A flush tinged her cheeks, but she had the good sense to keep her mouth shut.

Not daring to touch her, he opened the door and motioned her through. "Come on. Let's go."

Glowing lanterns hung from ropes draped on either side of the open double doors, more graced the overhead rafters above a plank floor of the timeworn barn. Banjo music mingled with the strum of guitars, while sawdust and sweet scents of toilet water wafted on the warm night air. Laughter and chatter bubbled up like champagne from an uncorked bottle.

"I haven't been to a barn dance since I was a child," Jesse admitted, taking in all the sights at once. Men in their Sunday best and women in smiles and bows whirled and stomped in time to the cheerful music. The multitude of lanterns swung with the beat.

"Who raised you after your family died?"

"My uncle."

"Didn't he ever take you?"

"He was never around much."

Char stared down at her. "Then who took care of you?"

"His mistress, Fanny Dupree."

He didn't care for the idea of an innocent girl being raised by a man's mistress. "Why the hell didn't he send you to boarding school?"

"He wanted me to have a home, and Fanny was wonderful to me."

Disgust filled his tone. "I'll bet—and I can imagine the kinds of lessons you learned."

She stared at him with steady green eyes. "Oh, I

learned plenty, for sure. After all, we did live in a whorehouse."

"You were raised in a *whorehouse?*"

"Impressive, isn't it?"

"Hey, whatcha doing here?" Buddy rushed toward them, hanging onto a glass of lemonade. "I thought you were going to visit that—" He glanced at Jesse and cleared his throat. "I mean, I thought you had *other* plans."

Char wanted to fill the kid's mouth with his fist. "You and Jesse think a lot alike."

She crossed her arms. "Listen, if this is an imposition . . ."

He scowled at her. *A whorehouse, for God's sake.* "If it was an imposition, I'd tell you. Now come on." He gripped her arm and dragged her inside the doors. "Let's dance."

Jessalea was angry enough to stomp her foot. She should never have told him about Fanny. Oh, sure, he was shocked now, but soon the astonishment would wear off, then he'd start looking at her in that funny way, wondering at her virtue. She'd seen it before with Clyde Wilson, a boy who'd courted her a couple years back. They'd met at a church social and had been wonderful friends. She'd come close to falling in love with him . . . until he learned about Fanny and the brothel. After that, the sweet talk stopped and the lewd innuendos began. Then the pawing hands.

"At least *try* to look like you're enjoying yourself," Char grated as he pulled her into his arms for a waltz.

The shock of his body pressed against hers held her speechless. He was so warm. So hard. So very, very male. "L-listen. You don't have to treat me as if I were a child. I'll be fine right here, and I'll have Buddy walk me to my room later. You go on with your plans." She tilted her head to look up at him. "I'm sure it's getting close to midnight."

His hold tightened around her waist. "Now why would I want to meet that waitress when I have you?"

Disappointment and fury shook her. She stepped out of his arms. "Because I was raised in a brothel doesn't mean I'm a whore."

Several ladies on the dance floor gasped and stared.

Furious and humiliated, Jessalea darted through the throng, bumping into several people before she made it outside.

A hand grabbed her arm and spun her around. The fury in Char's eyes was unmistakable. "I never called you a whore, nor did I insinuate you were one. So don't put words in my mouth, woman."

"No. You never said it, but you were *thinking* it."

"The only goddamn thing I was thinking was how I'd like to beat that uncle of yours senseless for allowing you to live like that!"

"Stop shouting at me."

"Then stop blaming me for something I haven't done."

She jammed her hands onto her hips and glared at him.

He glared right back.

Music and laughter drifted around them. The scent of sawdust and leather. The whinny of a horse tethered nearby. The thud of shoes against the barn floor.

Neither of them moved. Neither of them spoke.

Their eyes held in a battle of wills, then something changed. She wasn't sure what, but her senses suddenly came alive and fixed only on him. On the blue-gray of his eyes, the minute crook in his nose, the bronze of his smooth skin, the sensual shape of his mouth.

Her pulse picked up speed. This wasn't supposed to happen. She retreated a step—and came up against the wall of the barn.

He closed in, his eyes never leaving hers, their bodies almost touching. "Want to know what I'm thinking now?" He was so close, she felt the heat of his breath on her lips and smelled the scent of spicy soap.

"N-no."

He gave her a slow smile. "You don't because you *think* you already know, don't you?" He traced the length of her arm with his fingers, leaving tingles in his wake. "You think I've got ideas about touching you, don't you?" He traced the dipping neckline of her blouse. "Or caressing you." He stroked the tip of her breast.

Her breath caught. Fire streaked through her middle.

"Hell, you probably even think I'm going to kiss you."

Jessalea opened her mouth to protest, but his lips were there, warm and demanding. Invading.

He leaned into her, his hands on either side of her shoulders, braced on the wood. The sweet pressure on her mouth increased, then penetrated.

She stiffened in shock. No one had ever kissed her like that. She tried to turn her head. "You must— mmm."

He stole her words and replaced them with the moist softness of his tongue. He teased her, soothed her, then made slow, wicked love to her mouth.

Any resistance she had buckled under the gentle

attack. Heat spread over her flesh. Her breasts grew tight. The place between her legs started to throb. She felt frightened and anxious at the same time. She wanted him to stop yet knew she'd die if he did. The throbbing became a painful ache.

His hands moved to her shoulders, then down to cover her breasts, his palms warm, stimulating. "Do you know what it did to me to see that outlaw kiss you?" he whispered against her lips. "It made me want to take his place." His tongue brushed across her lips, then eased inside.

Hot waves gushed over her. Tingles raced through her veins. His mouth was so gentle. So deliciously arousing. She never wanted the kiss to end. Never wanted the feelings to end.

He leaned into her, his body hard and tight as he molded his length to hers. A tremor ran through him, and he tightened his hold for the barest instant, then released her. "I think we better go inside, darlin'. Before things get out of hand."

She was so stunned by her own shameless behavior, she was speechless. But she knew she didn't want to dance with him again. She didn't want to be anywhere near him. Drawing herself up, she stepped to the side. "You go. I'm going to my room." Not giving him a chance to argue, she left.

She knew he was following her. She could see him a few yards behind, but, at least, he didn't come any closer. When she reached her room, she bolted the door and blew out the lantern.

For several minutes, she sat in the darkness, trying to come to terms with the strange emotions bombarding her. She never knew a man could make a woman feel so . . . so . . . confused. One minute she was appalled at the thought of him touching her, and the next she was aching for him to do so. That was plain stupid. For pity sakes, she had to get her head on straight. She didn't have time for these man-woman games. She was tracking the men who killed her family.

Stripping off her clothes, she crawled into bed, vowing to put Char Daniels out of her mind. Not that it did any good. Those smiling eyes haunted her, teased, and mocked. . . .

By the time she woke up the next morning, she felt as if she hadn't been asleep, and she wasn't in the mood to face the man who'd tormented her the entire night. She was tired and cranky and sticky from the Texas heat that hadn't let up even during the hours before dawn.

After washing and dressing in her britches, she stuffed the rest of her belongings into the saddlebags and slung them over her shoulder. She was going to see what she could find out about Cecil Boggs.

As she stepped out onto the boardwalk, bright sunlight almost blinded her. She took a minute to clear her vision and was surprised to see the town bustling with activity so early in the morning.

Women carrying parasols were escorted by men hurrying toward the east end of town, their voices raised in excitement.

Taking in the chaotic sights, she walked toward a cafe a few blocks down. Before she started her search, she wanted some coffee. Her boots thudded on the boardwalk as she made her way toward the eatery's front door.

She passed a group of men wagering money in front of a barbershop.

"I got a gold eagle that says he'll be kickin' after a full five minutes," one man said.

"I'll take your money, Dicky boy. Way I figure it, with the size of the bastard, his neck'll snap."

Jessalea stared at them from under the brim of her hat. The hanging. They were betting on the outcome of a man's death. Visions of her own father's lynching rose like a demon. Her throat closed, and tears stung her eyes as she rushed past them.

The Boggses had bet on her father's death, too.

Odie Boggs had won.

His name sent bile chasing up the back of her throat. Odie Boggs. Dear God how she hated that man. How she feared him.

Horror-filled memories of that night tightened her spine, and she had to stop and lean against a building to calm herself. She took deep, restoring breaths.

"Here he comes!" someone shouted.

Startled, she swung around.

The sheriff and a deputy rode down the middle of the street. Another man, with his head lowered and his hands tied behind his back, sat on a gelding prancing between them.

Cheers went up from the crowd.

"Let the bastard swing!"

"Hang 'im high, Sheriff!"

"Don't use a blindfold. We wanna see him suffer!"

"Cut his balls off and shove 'em in his mouth the way the Injuns do."

"Show him no mercy, Sheriff. He didn't show Miss Libby none when he carved her up!"

"Murderer!" a woman screamed. "Defiling my daughter wasn't enough for you, was it?"

Carved her up. Jessalea closed her eyes. She could

feel the woman's pain. It was hard to breathe. The ache in her middle became unbearable, and she cradled her stomach. Why would a man do such a thing to a woman? Why? Damn it, *why?*

"Jesse." Char touched her shoulder. "Jesse, it's gonna be all right."

"Do you know what he did?" she hissed. She kept her eyes on the ground, fighting the nausea.

"I heard. I'm just sorry the sheriff got to him before I did."

Her head came up. "You know him?"

Char stared at her tear-streaked face for several seconds, then lowered his hand. "Darlin', the man they're gonna hang is Cecil Boggs."

CHAPTER

❧ 7 ❧

Char watched the expressions flicker over Jesse's face. A second of confusion. Comprehension, anger, then stomach-tightening hatred.

Her frozen green gaze drifted to the man riding between the lawmen. "I want to watch him die."

"Jesse . . ."

She stepped out of his hold. "Don't patronize me, Char. I've got a right to this." Spinning around, she stalked off in the direction of the newly constructed scaffold at the end of Main Street.

He wanted to remind her that a hanging wasn't a pretty sight, but she wouldn't listen. Damned stubborn woman, she'd probably fall apart when it was over. She might try to act tough, but she wasn't near as hard as she thought she was.

Mumbling about the inconsistency of the female mind, he went after her.

He found her talking to the sheriff and pointing at Boggs.

The lawman looked disgruntled as he stared down

at the "boy." Then he nodded in response to something Jesse said.

To Char's utter horror, she walked up onto the platform. The deputy and another man were standing close on either side of Boggs, each holding onto an arm. Even though he was tied, they weren't taking any chances.

Jesse stopped in front of the condemned man. Char couldn't hear her words as she spoke, but he saw the expression on Boggs's face. He looked confused at first, then stunned. He paled. His fat throat started working, his eyes darting as Jesse continued to speak.

She gave him one last gloating smirk, then returned down the steps.

Char met her at the bottom. "What the hell was that about?"

"I wanted to give Boggs a little information to take to his grave."

"What'd you say?"

"Nothing much." She gave a mock smile. "I simply reminded him of his visit to our farm, and how I was going to enjoy watching him die. I went into detail about the horror and agony of choking to death. Maybe too much." She shrugged. "Anyway, then I mentioned how soon the rest of his brothers would join him."

Char felt sick. She was too damned unemotional about the whole thing. It wasn't natural.

A murmur passed through the crowd, and he turned to see a man in a black suit and carrying a Bible step onto the platform. The town preacher.

The clergyman spoke to Boggs, then moved away and nodded to the sheriff.

Jesse was as calm as if she were watching a Sunday sermon. He wanted to shake her. She couldn't be enjoying this.

The sheriff looped the noose around Boggs's neck and tightened it.

Jesse tensed.

Boggs started begging for his life.

The crowd held its breath and watched the sheriff.

The lawman's lip curled into a smirk as he motioned to someone near the steps.

A man wearing a black hood strode up to a long wooden lever that would release the trapdoor beneath Boggs's feet. He gripped the handle with both hands.

Boggs twisted and screamed. A wet stain darkened the front of his pants. "No!" he cried. "No! Oh, God. Don't!"

The trapdoor banged open.

Jesse swayed into Char—and fainted.

The crowd cheered all around him, but he didn't watch Boggs's dancing form. Instead, he lifted Jesse into his arms. It gave him no satisfaction to know that he'd been right about her sensitivity.

As he reached the boardwalk carrying his slight burden, a hush fell over the crowd. He glanced over his shoulder. It was done. Boggs was dead.

A heaviness filled Char. Death did that to him.

In the room, he placed Jesse on the bed, then removed her hat and neckerchief. His brain moved in slow motion as he dampened a cloth in the washbasin, then opened the buttons on her shirt and cooled her throat with the wet fabric. His finger brushed the scar on her breast, and he wondered how she'd gotten it.

He studied her face. This woman had touched him

in so many ways. With her warmth, and spirit, and passion. She'd wanted to see Boggs dead, but she couldn't handle the reality. She was so strong—and so gentle—he ached for her.

He drew the cloth along her jaw, remembering how aroused he'd been last night. How he'd gone to meet with the saloon girl, but lost interest before he even got there and went to his room alone.

Alone. He smiled at that. His body may have been alone, but his mind hadn't been. He'd dreamed of Jesse half the night. The other half he'd spent sitting at the desk, listening to Buddy snore, and trying not to think about her.

Jesse moaned.

He drew the cloth over her forehead.

She opened her eyes. "Boggs?"

"Is dead."

"Good." She lowered her lashes.

So the tough lady was back in place. "It might be good, darlin', but it sure doesn't feel like it."

"I wonder if you'd feel different if it had been your little brother Boggs trampled to death beneath his horse."

"He did *what?*"

"You heard me. That scum dragged my five-year-old brother behind his horse, then stomped him to death while my father and I watched."

"Jesus."

"No. *He* wasn't around to help."

"Jesse, don't . . ."

She massaged her temples. "I don't want to talk about this anymore."

He helped her sit up and brushed a lock of silky hair over her shoulder. "Maybe you should spend some time here at the hotel and give yourself a chance to rest."

"No."

He hadn't thought so. "How do you plan to find the others?"

"I don't know." She drew the front of her shirt together. "What about you? Did you learn anything about the man you're looking for?"

He shook his head. "I asked around last night, but no one's heard of him."

"Jesse! Jesse, you in there?" Buddy's excited voice preceded a pounding at the door.

"Quit hollering and get in here," Char grated.

The kid rushed into the room carrying a box, his blond curls in a wild tangle, his face flushed with exhilaration. "I got 'em!"

"Got what?"

"Boggs's things." He lifted the small crate for emphasis. "But we gotta leave this town fast. I saw that U.S. Marshal talking to the sheriff."

"What marshal?"

"Blake Darcy. The one I heard talking to the sheriff in San Antonio when you were arrested. He thinks you're running with Jesse, and he's been following her since Waco."

So that's why the sheriff in San Antonio didn't follow them. He knew the marshal was on their trail. Char glanced at Jesse. "What happened in Waco?"

She shifted. "I had a showdown with Patrick Boggs there. He was so slow on the draw, his gun didn't clear his holster. Folks started saying I gunned him down."

"Ah, hell," Char swore. "That's all we need."

Jesse's gaze drifted to Buddy. "What's in the box?"

"Boggs's possessions. I told the sheriff I was kin so

he'd give 'em to me. But I didn't figure on no U.S. Marshal. Jehoshaphats, Char. He looks as tough as burnt jerky. We gotta get out of here."

The kid's intelligence amazed Char—and his naivete. He turned to Jesse. "You up to riding?"

"Not until I've seen what's in that box."

Buddy set the crate beside her on the mattress. "Hurry, will you?"

Char joined her and inspected the contents. A six-shooter and holster. A leather vest. A worn felt hat. Some loose silver, a dirty bandanna, and something flat wrapped in oilskin.

Jesse untied the strings holding the oilskin packet together.

Papers slid out.

She sorted through the pages. A bill of sale for horse feed, a receipt for repairs on a Smith and Wesson revolver, an envelope containing a lock of blond hair and a red garter, and the last was a telegram.

Jesse's hands shook as she unfolded the message and read it aloud.

"Marshal wired—Patrick dead Stop
Watch for gunman Stop Warn
Harley in Christi Stop DB"

Davidson Boggs had tried to warn his brothers.

"Christi," she hissed, crushing the paper in her fist. "Harley Boggs is in Corpus Christi."

"How far's that?" Buddy asked.

"Less than a week's ride," Char answered as he knelt in front of her and gathered her cold hands in his. "Are you sure you don't want to rest a few days?"

Empty green eyes met his. "He raped my sister,

Daniels. Harley Boggs held her down and vicious-ly—" her words caught on a choked cry.

His hands shook. God, what those bastards did to her family. What they did to *her*.

Jessalea was hanging onto her emotions by a thread as thin as a cobweb. Visions of Harley Boggs and Susannah stabbed her thoughts again and again. She could still hear her sister's screams. "I'm leaving," she said through a tight throat. "Right now."

Char hesitated for only an instant, then handed some gold eagles to Buddy. "Buy supplies and horses. We'll meet you at the livery."

Jessalea buttoned her shirt, then replaced her hat, while Char gathered Boggs's things and put them in the crate. She stared down at the contents. "Leave that stinking garbage in the hall."

He didn't argue. He set the box outside the door. "How do you feel about using Boggs's horse for a pack animal?"

"It doesn't matter. The gelding's not the same one that killed James. That horse was a paint."

Char led her to the door. "Then we'll have Buddy claim it."

As they rode out, Jessalea tried to keep her thoughts from the Boggses by studying the area. She'd been so tired when they arrived in Laredo, she hadn't even noticed the strange huts that were made of straw and thin tree trunks. "What are those?"

Saddle leather creaked as Char shifted to follow her line of vision. "Jacal huts. They're used as temporary shelters." He gestured to an adobe complex a little farther down. "That's Fort McIntosh. The army es-tablished it right after the Mexican War."

Hill leaned forward, his face alive with excitement. "If I'd been born early enough, I woulda joined the army. I bet I woulda been a general by the time it was over."

"Or a corpse," Char concluded.

Buddy ignored him. "Do you think there's bullets in that adobe wall?"

"Undoubtedly." Char winked at her.

The kid gave a whoop, then dropped the reins to the packhorse and nudged his mount into a trot.

She smiled. "He'll learn . . . eventually."

A chuckle rumbled from Char's wide chest. "He's no different than any other impressionable youngster at that age. Hell, after Cole Stevens left our farm, and I learned the significance of who he was, I was so enthralled, and so shaken up I could hardly do my work. I couldn't believe I learned to draw from Cole Stevens."

"He *is* rather formidable, isn't he?"

"You know him?"

"I see him once in a while."

Char didn't even try to hide his interest. "Is he still as fast on the draw?"

"Faster."

The awed expression on Daniels's face reminded her of Buddy. It was obvious that youngsters weren't the only ones who were easy to impress. Or was she seeing a momentary glimpse of the young boy inside the tough gunman?

Either way, it made her feel warm watching him. "By the way, did you get a chance to talk to the sheriff in Laredo about what happened in San Antonio?"

"No. I didn't know him, and I didn't want to take

the chance on getting arrested. Maybe I'll find some-one in Christi."

Jesse nodded as she watched Buddy guide his horse toward them. Dust rose up from the animal's hooves, and he waved his hat to clear the air. "There wasn't a single piece of lead anywhere that I could see."

Char kept a straight face and inflicted seriousness into his tone. "Scavengers probably took them."

"Yeah." Buddy nodded, gathering the packhorse's reins. "That's what I figured."

Jessalea had to look away to keep from bursting into laughter.

Her gaze fell on the scaffold where Cecil Boggs hung. Oh, God. Why did she have to see that? She started to shake. Memories of her father's lynching rushed through her. In a surge of desperation, she kicked her horse into a gallop, her only thought to get away from the horror. To get away from the ugly reminder of four lonely graves in Missouri.

The thunder of her horse's hooves churned the dry dirt into a choking cloud. Hot wind and sand stung her cheeks. But they were nothing compared to the pain in her chest.

More hooves pounded beside her, then Char's hand shot out and caught her reins, pulling them in.

Her horse skidded to a snorting, prancing halt.

For several seconds, he didn't say anything, then, when he spoke, his words were filled with concern. "Stop thinking about it, Jesse. Recalling the hurt over and over again will make you crazy." He touched her cheek. "I know, darlin', because I've been there. I . . ."

Whatever Char was about to say died on his lips as

Buddy rode up. "Jehoshaphats, Jesse, why'd you take off like that?"

Daniels shot the kid a scowl.

"I'm sorry. I saw Boggs on the scaffold, and it . . . upset me."

"I thought you wanted to see him dead."

"I did. But wanting and seeing are two different things, I guess."

"Yeah, I know what you mean." Buddy looped the packhorse's reins around his pommel. "I felt that way once when I wanted to watch my pa take a bullet out of a man's gut. I never figured there'd be so much blood—or that the man would scream in pain—or that he'd vomit." Buddy shook his head. "It wasn't what I expected at all."

Jessalea met Char's eyes, and a silent message passed between them. They both knew Buddy was in for a sudden awakening when the would-be gunman drew his weapon on a man for the first time . . . and killed him.

"A lot of things aren't what they seem, kid," Char said in a quiet voice. He nudged his horse into a walk, leading hers along, too. "Being a fast gun isn't romantic in the least." He turned his gaze on her. "And revenge is never sweet."

"I don't know, Char." Buddy kept pace with them. "Isn't revenge what you're after when you find that Otis Daniel something-or-other you're searching for?"

Jessalea watched Char's lean features darken. "I don't want revenge, kid. I want to have the satisfaction of smashing the son of a bitch's face."

There was no way she could contain the question. "Who is he?"

A muscle in Char's jaw ticked.

"He's Char's pa," Buddy answered.

Her mouth almost fell open.

"I don't claim him as kin," Daniels ground out. "The selfish bastard got an innocent young girl pregnant, then walked out on her, leaving her stranded and alone."

The anger in him was palpable.

"Is that what your ma told you?"

"My mother died the night I was born. The people who raised me, the Websters, told me about her showing up at their place in Charleston, in the rain, alone, unmarried, and in labor."

"Did she tell them where your pa was?"

"With her dying breath, she told the Websters to take me to Texas, to my father, Otis Daniel—she died before she could finish."

Jessalea frowned. "If he'd run out on her, why would she want to send you to him?"

He looked stunned—really stunned. "I never considered that. I just assumed . . ."

"Maybe you should reserve judgment until you've at least heard his side."

Char stared at her for several seconds, then sent her such a warm smile her belly fluttered. "Darlin', if I was the marrying kind, I'd throw you over my shoulder and haul you to a preacher."

Buddy burst into laughter.

Jessalea blushed to her toes. The mere thought of being married to the rakish gunman did funny things to her insides.

Things she had no business feeling for a man who'd made it clear he'd never settle down.

A man who would die before his time.

CHAPTER

❊ 8 ❊

They made camp that night in the open grassland but didn't risk another fire.

To Jessalea, it was plain eerie, talking to each other in the dark as they ate jerked beef and cold beans from cans. Only a faint glow from the moon silhouetted the men against the lighter background.

"How'd you learn to use a weapon so good, Jesse?" Buddy slurred around a mouthful of beans.

"My uncle taught me a few years back."

"A few years? How old were you?"

"Seven."

"Jehoshaphats. Whatever possessed a man to teach a little girl to shoot guns?"

"He wanted me to be able to protect myself if anyone ever tried to—" She took a breath. "He swore he'd never leave another member of his family defenseless."

She shifted, trying not to think about how she'd suffered during the days after the massacre when she went to live with Fanny at the brothel. "Anyway, I took to the gun easy enough and spent a lot of time practicing."

"Did your uncle go after the men?" Char's question floated out of the darkness.

"He searched for them, but he didn't know who they were, and I never told him."

"Why?"

She set her bean can aside and wiped her hands. "I guess in my seven-year-old mind, I was afraid they'd kill him, too. Besides, I couldn't talk about it. I had nightmares every time I tried. After a while, he avoided the subject, but I know he was hunting them. He would stay away from Fanny's for months at a time."

"And you kept practicing," Char finished.

"Yes."

"When did you decide to go after the men yourself?"

"Last year. My uncle and I had a mock showdown, like the one you and I had. I almost beat him. That's when I knew I could take care of the Boggs brothers myself—and not jeopardize my uncle's life."

"How did you find them?"

"I knew they were from Texas. They told us that during dinner, before everything . . . happened. So, I sent letters to post offices all over the territory asking if anyone named Boggs lived nearby. I received an answer from Waco."

"How old are you now?" Buddy asked.

"Seventeen, last March."

"Wow. That's the same age as me. I never figured that. I thought you were older."

"Hatred has a way of making folks age before their time," Char commented in a quiet voice.

"You're probably right. After that day on the farm, I don't ever remember being a child again."

"I bet your uncle wasn't happy when you left to go after those men."

Jessalea chewed on her lower lip. "He doesn't know. He was gone when I took off."

"When was that?" Char wanted to know.

"Two months ago."

She heard Char shift as if he'd changed positions. "How'd you know this Patrick Boggs was one of the same bunch?"

"He hadn't changed all that much in ten years."

"Was Patrick Boggs the first man you ever killed?"

"Yes." Her stomach drew into knots remembering the horror of the ordeal and how sick she'd been afterward. It hadn't been any different with Davidson Boggs, either. Well, except that her stomach hadn't had anything to give up.

"Why would the law wire Davidson Boggs about you? I mean, how would he even know you'd go after another brother?"

"I'm afraid I was rather vocal when I called Boggs out that day in Waco. I'm sure the whole town heard me vow to kill every Boggs that breathed."

"Was it really a fair fight?"

"I thought it was. Boggs went for his gun first, but I was faster. When folks started accusing me of killing him in cold blood, though, I hightailed it out of there."

"How'd you know where to find the second brother?"

"Before I confronted Patrick, I asked around if he had any kin. Someone mentioned a brother in San

Antonio. I'm sure that's how the marshall knew where to send the wire, too."

"You know," Buddy said with just a tinge of awe, "for a girl, you're really smart."

"Thank you."

Char wasn't so generous. "There's nothing smart about killing people, kid." He paused, then directed another question at her. "Didn't your uncle's friend, Fanny, object to you striking out on your own?"

"I didn't tell her. But I did leave a note so she wouldn't think something bad had happened to me."

Char snorted. "Oh, I'm sure she was relieved to know that you'd only gone traipsing across the country after murderers."

"Ow! *Damn,*" Buddy yelped. "Something bit my leg."

Char was on his feet in an instant. "Jesse, light a lantern."

Fumbling in the dark for the pile of supplies, she located a lantern and box of matches, then lit the wick. She set the glass globe into place before hurrying to Buddy.

Char was kneeling beside him, concerned. "Bring the light closer."

She scooted around so that the lantern was between her and the men.

"God, Char," the boy said through gritted teeth. "My leg feels like it's on fire."

Slipping a knife from his boot, Char sliced open the seam of Buddy's britches from knee to ankle, then parted the material. "Ah, hell."

Jessalea felt the blood leave her face. Buddy had been bitten by a snake. "A rattler?" she whispered, lifting the lantern higher so she could see around the area.

Buddy groaned.

Char shook his head as he examined the wound. "We'd have heard a rattler. It must have been a copperhead. They're quiet bastards."

Jessalea again swept the area for signs of the coppery red-banded reptile. She didn't see it. A small measure of relief moved over her on two counts. The snake was gone, and the bite from a copperhead wasn't usually fatal to bigger folks. Her gaze softened on Buddy's tight features. But it was painful, and he'd be sick for several days.

Char handed her his knife, handle first. "Use the flame in the lantern to sterilize this. Then get me a wet rag to clean the wound after I've sucked out as much poison as I can."

"Is that necessary?"

"I don't know. But I'm not taking any chances." He reached into his saddlebags and drew out a bottle of whiskey, ordering Buddy to drink.

The next few minutes passed swiftly as they worked over the youngster, and to his credit, he didn't cry out. But his low moans were as devastating as a full-bellied scream would have been. He passed out from the whiskey before Char set the hot tip of his knife to seal the open wound caused by the cuts he'd made.

Jessalea tore strips from the hem of her new white blouse and used them for bandages.

When the unconscious Buddy was settled on his pallet, she drew the covers up to his chin and sat beside him, bathing his damp brow with a clean, wet cloth. "We can't travel until he gets better."

Replacing the knife in his boot, Char corked the whiskey bottle and put it away. "I know. But I wish he'd picked a better place. We're too vulnerable here in the open." He stationed his saddle on the other side of Buddy, then drew a rifle from its scabbard and sat down, leaning against the leather. He intended to keep watch again.

"Maybe there's rocks or something nearby where we could hole up."

He stared at her over the light of the lantern. "I hope so, darlin', and come daylight, I'll scout around. But I think it's gonna be a waste of time."

Recalling all the miles of open land, cactus, agave, and sage brush she'd been staring at most of the day, she couldn't help but agree.

He motioned to the lantern beside her. "Douse that, will you? I figure we've announced our location long enough."

When she did, night fell around them like an ebony curtain.

She sat very still, listening to Buddy's heavy breathing, and for the return of the snake. The heat from Buddy's brow radiated up through the cloth she held. She moved it down his cheek then up again.

"You know, Jess," Char's husky voice penetrated the darkness, "I was right proud of the way you handled yourself tonight. You're a tough lady—a strong one, and I like that in a woman. Simpering females grate on a man's nerves." He paused, then added, "I just wanted you to know that."

A glowing warmth filled her, and she smiled into the blackness. Char Daniels knew how to make a woman feel special.

* * *

Sometime during the night, Jessalea dragged her bedroll next to Buddy and fell asleep. She must have, because she woke up beside him the next morning. Shoving the hair from her eyes, she placed her hand against his pale cheek. He was warm, but not too bad, and he smelled of whiskey. Char must have given him more this morning, hoping to keep him unconscious until the worst of the pain passed. She glanced around for Char.

He was gone.

Figuring he was probably scouting for shelter, she yawned and rose, then ambled over to a simmering pot of coffee. The aroma filled the tranquil morning air. "Mmm. Thank you, Mr. Daniels."

She unearthed a pair of skillets, a slab of bacon tied in cheesecloth, and the makings for biscuits.

Char rode in before the bacon was done. "That smells like heaven."

Still basking in the glow of his praise last night, and his thoughtfulness this morning, she gave him a warm smile. "I hope it tastes as good." She stabbed a fork into a piece of bacon and turned it over. "Did you find any rocks or anything?" He checked Buddy, then helped himself to a cup of coffee. "There's a stand of scrub oak a couple miles ahead. Enough to conceal our camp."

Removing the pan of fluffy biscuits from the fire, she set it on the ground. "Should we risk moving him that far—did you give him more whiskey?"

"Yes. No sense in him suffering more than necessary." Char snatched a biscuit and bounced it in his hands to cool it. "And we can move him if we make a litter." He sank his teeth into the hot bread. "Jesus, that's good."

She was pleased by his concern. "Make a litter out of what?"

"The stems of those agave are pretty sturdy. We can tie a few together and cover them with blankets."

She glanced at an agave only a few feet away. It was at least twenty feet high and resembled a thin, leafless tree stuck in the middle of a giant aloe plant. She'd heard they bloomed only once every hundred years and were nicknamed century plants because of it. But she'd also heard they were misnamed because they bloomed every twenty years. "Don't Mexicans make some sort of drink out of the sap?"

Char finished his biscuit and filched a piece of bacon. "Umm-hmm. Pulque and mescal. They also make rope from the stem, and use the thick leaves as fodder."

She barely heard his words, she was so engrossed in watching him munch on the bacon. She couldn't count the times her mother had swatted at her father for stealing bacon from the frying pan. Tears stung the backs of her eyes. Dear God, how she missed them.

"Jess? Is something wrong?"

Moisture dampened her lashes as she stared at his mouth. "You stole the bacon."

"Well, hell. I didn't know you'd take it personal. Stop that. Damn it, don't cry. I won't do it again." He tossed the bacon into the pan. "God Almighty. You can kill a man without batting an eye, then you fall apart over a lousy piece of bacon." He threw up his hands. "I will never understand women." Grabbing an axe, he stalked away.

Jessalea bust into tears.

CHAPTER

❧ 9 ❧

The large stand of spider-armed scrub oak made a decent campsite, Char decided as he laid Buddy on a mat of blankets. There were at least fifty of the rough-barked trees, and they were close enough together that their broad green leaves touched, forming a welcome canopy of shade from the hot Texas sun.

Beneath, there was plenty of room for their gear and the horses. The latter, he'd tied at the edge of the trees where they could graze on the high grass.

His gaze drifted to where Jesse sat sorting through sacks of supplies to find the makings for dinner, and a warmth infused him. He liked being close to her. He liked her scent, her laughter, the feminine shape he recalled under those baggy clothes. He liked her green, green eyes that did funny things to his middle, and he could stare for hours at her beautiful face—well, what he could see of it beneath that stupid flop-billed hat. What he didn't like was the way she made him feel. Aroused and edgy at the same time. Like now.

Distance was what he needed. "Jess. Hold off on dinner a while, and I'll try to round us up some fresh game." Hell, anything was better than sitting here gawking at her like a horny drover.

She nodded, but didn't look at him. She'd been doing that all day—ever since she'd become so upset after he stole the bacon. Never in his born days had he seen a woman act like that—especially over something he'd bought with his own money. It just wasn't natural.

He studied what he could see of her profile. A lock of blackberry hair had slipped from the hat and rested against the smooth line of her jaw. Her cheeks were pale and drawn, her mouth pulled down into a crestfallen bow. It was an expression of deep, deep sadness, and in that moment, he had the strangest feeling that what happened this morning had nothing to do with bacon.

It was on the tip of his tongue to ask her to explain, but he knew it wasn't the right time. Shoving his hat onto his head, he strode toward his horse. A fresh roasted rabbit might put them all in better spirits.

Jessalea wove her way through the darkness toward camp. She was pleased that Buddy had been able to eat some of the rabbit Char killed for dinner and the squirrel for supper. It would help the youngster keep up his strength. She wasn't too sure about the alcohol Char kept giving him, though. Oh, she knew it softened the pain and all, but with Buddy unconscious, she and Char were virtually alone.

Seeing the small glow from their campfire through the trees, she slowed her step. She didn't want to return yet. Didn't want to feel the force of Char's sensual gaze as he stared at her over the fire. His maleness frightened her more than any gunman.

She changed directions and walked to the edge of the trees. For several seconds, she stood there, enjoying the silver glow from the moon as it rippled over the ocean of dry grass. A light scent of woodsmoke from their fire drifted on the air, mingling with the sweet, fragrant aroma of distant, night-blooming yucca. Missouri had never been like this; so vast and intimidating. So exhilarating.

"Spectacular, isn't it?" Char's quiet voice floated out of the night.

Startled, she whirled around to find him right behind her. "I thought you were in camp."

"I was worried about you. You were gone a long time."

She could scarcely see his features in the darkness. "Well, as you can see, I'm fine. Go tend to Buddy. I'll be along in a few minutes."

"Buddy's asleep."

She didn't care if the whole world was asleep, she didn't want to be alone with him. "Char, I came out here to get away from you."

"Why?"

"You *know* why. I've seen the way you stare at me. How you watch my mouth when I talk. Study me when you think I'm not aware of it. I can feel your eyes touch me, and I know what those looks mean. In case you've forgotten, I was raised in a whorehouse. I'm well aware of what thoughts are going through your head."

"What was it like for you there?"

That caught her off guard. She'd expected him to deny her accusations. The man never did what he was supposed to. "In the brothel? It was okay, I guess. Fanny and I had our own rooms on the third floor, and I spent most of my time in them. She taught me reading and ciphering, how to dress and style my hair. A couple times a day, I could play in the yard out back, and on Sundays she'd send me off to church."

"What about your uncle? Wasn't he ever around?"

She smiled with fond memories. "He came as often as he could, then he'd take me shooting, or riding. At night, he and Fanny would disappear, so I'd sneak out of my room and sit on the second-floor steps and watch the girls and gentlemen below. I loved listening to the music and laughter." She didn't mention how she used to pretend she was one of those women— dressed all in fancy satin and feathers.

"Did you watch them . . . ?"

"Never. Fanny made it clear if I was ever caught snooping, she'd send me away."

"Smart woman."

The scent of spice and leather wafted toward her, and she was reminded again of their isolation. She retreated a few steps.

"Did your uncle like bacon?"

"What?" Where did the man come up with these questions? "I don't know. I never paid much attention to what he ate."

"Then why did you cry over the bacon this morning?"

Heat inched up the nape of her neck. "I'm sorry about that."

"Don't be. I just wanted to know what caused you to break down." She felt him move closer.

Folding her arms over her middle, she faced the sea of grass. "My father used to steal bacon when my mother was cooking. When you did it, the memories rushed in, and it made me realize how much I miss them."

His hands cupped her shoulders, and she felt his hard length press along her backside. "I wish I could take your pain away." He nuzzled her ear, his voice feather soft. "Or at least make you forget for a while."

He was doing a good job of that already. The warmth of his breath sent shivers racing through her, sent her thoughts tumbling in directions that frightened her. "I think I'd better return to camp."

"Stop being afraid of me, darlin'. I'm not going to hurt you." He slid his hands down her arms and up again. "I won't do anything you don't want me to."

That wasn't reassuring. His nearness was causing her heart to pound like the hooves of stampeding cattle. "I don't think this is such a good . . ."

He drew his lips along the side of her neck.

". . . idea."

He slid his palms over her breasts.

"Char, no," she half whispered, half moaned.

"Touching you gives us both pleasure, Jesse." He brushed his fingers over her nipples.

They tightened.

He kissed her ear.

The warmth of his breath thrummed through her nerve endings. She leaned into him, let her head fall to his shoulder. She had no power to resist him. He made her feel things that were beyond her control.

"That's it, darlin'. Relax. Let me take you to a special place, where there's no pain . . . only beauty and wonder." He eased a button free on her shirt. Then another. And another.

She wanted to protest, but the words couldn't squeeze past her tight throat.

He parted her shirt, and a slight breeze touched her bare chest. She knew she should stop him, should use the defenses Fanny had taught her, but she didn't have the strength.

With excruciating slowness, he traced the under-swells of her breasts, then the sides and tops. He trailed a finger over her scar.

"How did you get this?"

She didn't want to tell him the truth and remember the pain. "An accident."

He massaged the spot, then kissed her ear, his fingers circling her breasts, following the same path around and around, in ever shrinking circles until he again found her peaks.

Pleasure streaked through her and slammed into her woman's core. A moan rushed up her throat, and she felt him tremble against her spine.

He turned her toward him, one hand holding their lower bodies together, the other burrowing into her hair. His hard length nudged her most sensitive area as he took her mouth in a slow, intoxicating kiss that left her dizzy.

She could feel the soft material of his shirt, the firm muscles beneath, rippling against her bare breasts, the moist heat of his tongue as it brushed hers in lazy caresses. Her bones turned mushy, and she knew if he hadn't held onto her, she'd have sunk into a lump at his feet.

He lowered his mouth to her throat, tasting her skin, nibbling with his teeth. The warmth of his breath sent tremors through her.

Inching his hands inside her shirt, he covered her with his palms. "You have beautiful breasts. Did you know that?" He traced a thumb over her nipple. "So firm and smooth. So perfect." He dipped his head and drew her into his mouth.

Her gasp of surprise turned into a sigh. Her legs began to quiver. Her knees grew weak. Flames licked her middle. She'd never known anything could feel so incredible.

His hands kept moving. They explored the shape of her bottom, her waist, and belly. Then they were inside her britches, cupping her most intimate place.

It was wrong, every moral fiber in her cried, but it felt so right. So good. No one had ever touched her that way, made her feel like she was reeling in circles. She caught the sides of his shirt to steady herself.

His mouth sought hers, and his kiss became urgent, his fingers alive as they massaged her into a state of complete mindlessness.

She pressed closer. Closer.

He penetrated her.

Hot spasms erupted beneath his hand. Wracking convulsions gripped her. Every muscle in her body shook. Her breath became trapped. Her world centered on the hand giving her such savage pleasure.

An eternity passed before she came to her senses and realized he hadn't let go of her. His hand was still nestled between her thighs. Then she felt the heat of his breath on her lips. "I won't apologize for what happened, darlin'. It was too remarkable . . . too beautiful." He released her and righted her clothes.

She couldn't move. She was too numb, too stunned by what had just happened. Was that what the girls in the brothel felt with their customers? Good Lord, and they got *paid* for it?

"Jesse, damn it. Say something."

"Hmm?"

He caught her by the shoulders. "Are you all right?"

"Oh, yes. I'm fine." She smiled to herself. "More than fine."

"You don't sound fine. You're talking funny." He guided her toward the trees. "Come on. Let's get to the light so I can have a look at you."

Did that mean what had happened was going to *show*?

Char wanted to kick himself. Oh, not that he hadn't enjoyed pleasuring Jesse. He most certainly had. But it shouldn't have happened. He only thanked God that he'd had the sense not to take her virginity. But, damn, it had been hard—and now she had him worried. She was much too quiet.

He watched her as he eased her down onto her bedroll. She wasn't acting right. "Jesse. Being upset isn't going to change what we did. What went on between us tonight was natural—and inevitable. You can't put a man and woman together day after day and night after night without *something* happening."

"I never thought it would feel like that. Somehow I got the notion that lovemaking was a chore. I'm not sure where, maybe from the girls in the brothel. But I didn't expect it to be so . . . nice."

Of all the things in the world she could have said, he never once imagined those words. The woman was great for his ego. "Are you telling me you've never been kissed before? Touched?"

"No. There was a boy once who tried, but I broke his nose. He thought I was like Fanny's girls because I lived there." She met his eyes. "I figured you'd start thinking that way, too, and I was right."

So much for being good for his ego. "What went on between us had nothing to do with where you were raised. Hell, you could have come straight from a convent and it would have happened. It has to do with instinct, darlin', not upbringing."

"You mean I could lose control like that with any man?"

"You damn well better not," he ground out, startled by a sudden stab of jealousy. "What I mean is no. I'm sure those feelings only happen with certain people." He knew that was the truth.

"Are you saying only you can make me feel like that?"

She didn't have to make it sound like a death sentence. "Maybe."

"Well, I intend to find out for sure."

"What?"

She rose and began to pace. "I'm not going to spend the rest of my days wondering if my instincts are linked to you. I've got to know if other men can make me feel the same way. My dreams depend on it. I can't marry a man and raise children if our times together are going to be a chore."

"And just how do you plan to do that?"

"Experiment."

"Like hell, you are!"

She turned on him, her eyes bright with anger. "I'll do whatever I please." She poked his chest. "Get this straight, Daniels. It's my life—*and what I do with it is none of your business.*"

He gripped her arms and shook her. "You little fool—"

She gasped in pain.

Horrified, he stared at his fingers digging into her shoulders. "I'm sorry. I didn't mean to—" He jerked his hands down. Never in his life had he touched a woman in anger. He was appalled. Ashamed.

Spinning on his heels, he stalked into the darkness, hoping to regain his sanity before he lost it completely.

He couldn't understand what was happening to him, but he knew one thing for sure. She was getting too close to him.

CHAPTER

❈ 10 ❈

Jessalea figured Char was angry with her since he hadn't spoken more than a dozen words in the last three days—and those had been orders. *Call me when supper's ready. Tend the kid. Don't wander too far.*

"Where's Char?" Buddy asked from where he sat on his bedroll, rubbing his sore leg. Even though his hair resembled a tangled bird's nest, and his eyes were puffy from too much sleep, his color had returned, and he was much better. Of course, the fact that Char stopped pouring whiskey down him yesterday had helped.

"I'm not sure where he went. He left about an hour ago." She didn't mention that he'd done that every day since their argument. Nor did she remark on how Char's features had taken on the appearance of carved granite.

"I was sure surprised when I woke up this morning and saw those branches overhead. How long have we been here?"

"Four days. We brought you here the morning after you were bitten."

He shuddered and eyed the coffeepot. "Is there anything in that?"

She poured him a cup and handed it to him. "How's your leg feel?"

"Sore, but the rest of me's doing fine." He grinned, showing the dimples in his cheeks, then scanned their campsite. "Been any unsavory characters around since I was laid up?"

Not if you don't count Char. "It's been quiet as a Sunday picnic."

"Not for long," Char clipped, stepping from the trees. He glanced at her from beneath his lowered Stetson. His eyes were as hard and dangerous as his appearance. Dressed in black, with twin Colts hugging his lean hips, he appeared satanic. "There are a dozen men riding this way."

A chill moved up her spine. "Outlaws?"

"A posse."

She didn't know which was worse. "Maybe they'll ride on by. We're pretty well hidden."

"Not well enough."

"What are we going to do?"

"You've got to change your appearance, while I hide the horses."

"Change how?"

He motioned to her green checked shirt. "Get rid of that and put on the clothes I bought. Buddy, you go without a shirt." He gestured to her hat lying by her bedroll. "Get rid of that stupid thing and let your hair down. The law's after three men—not a pair of youngsters who ran away from home."

"I'm not a runaway," Buddy defended. "I'm old enough to be on my own."

Char shot him a glare that should have turned him to brick. "I don't care if you're a grandfather. You damn well better make the posse believe you're running if you want to live through this." Spinning around, he stalked into the trees.

Jesse dove for her saddlebags. After using part of her white blouse as a bandage for Buddy, the thing was too short, but it would have to do. "I'll be right back."

By the time she returned, Buddy had removed his shirt, and his curls were hidden beneath his black Stetson, and she was so nervous, her heart felt like it was in her throat.

"I got rid of your hat, but I hope the law don't check my saddlebags and find my irons. They'd know for sure I was partner to Char Daniels—our weapons matching and all."

Jessalea tried very hard not to roll her eyes. There were a hundred young men who wore twin sidearms. "I hope so, too, Buddy." She prayed the posse didn't search the trees and find Char, either.

The thunder of hooves shook the ground.

Buddy tensed.

Jessalea drew in a lungful of air and moved to stand beside him.

He gave an uncertain nod before he turned to watch for the approaching posse.

The sheriff and several men she recognized from Laredo strode into their camp, guns drawn.

"Oh God," Buddy groaned.

Jessalea had to do something quick—before he fell apart. She planted her hands on her hips and faced the lawman. "If our papa sent y'all to bring us home, y'all best git. Teddy and I ain't goin'. Nothin's gonna stop us from joinin' the theater in New York." She gave Buddy a weak smile. "Ain't that right, Ted?"

He nodded, but kept his mouth shut.

She swung toward the sheriff. "Y'all git on outta here and leave us be."

"Whoa. Hold on, gal. Your pa didn't send us." He motioned for his men to lower their guns. "We're after three fellas. Two in black and one in an ugly hat. You seen 'em?"

She scanned the group for a U.S. Marshal but he wasn't with them. "Was one of 'em real tall?"

The sheriff nodded.

"Yeah. I seen 'em a couple days ago, when Teddy was huntin' for our supper. I gave 'em a cup of coffee to wash down the trail dust."

"Which way were they headed?"

She furrowed her brow as if trying to remember. "Up Austin way as I recall."

"Did you see them leave?"

"Sure did. Rode out 'bout half hour 'afore Teddy got back."

"Yeah," Buddy piped in, at last catching onto the game. "I remember her goin' on about the young one in black. Made me right puky, listenin' to her carryin' on about how handsome he was."

Jessalea held onto her smile, and her composure. "He was handsome, you horny toad. Better'n anything I seen in El Paso, that's for sure."

The sheriff gestured for his men to return to their horses. "Listen, if you two see them sidewinders again, you get a wire to the closest law. There should be a U.S. Marshal headin' this way before long, too. If you see him, you tell him what you know, too. Got that?"

"What marshal?" Jessalea asked.

"Fella named Blake Darcy."

She licked her lower lip. "Those outlaws musta done somethin' real bad to have a marshal after them."

"Killed two men. Darcy's been after them since they left Waco. Remember, boy," he warned Buddy, "thems bad *hombres*. If you see 'em, no heroics."

"Yes, sir."

They filed out through the trees, and a moment later the rumble of hooves jolted the ground.

Char stepped from the shadows. "You up to riding, kid?"

"Yep."

"Good. Let's clear camp and get the hell out of here."

Less than an hour later, they mounted up, Jessalea and Buddy still wearing the same clothes in case they came across anyone else.

They rode hard and slept little for the next four days, stopping only when complete exhaustion claimed them. Jessalea's muscles hurt, and her neck ached from using her saddle as a pillow. She was getting irritable, and found herself snapping when one of the men spoke to her.

Char's disposition hadn't eased, either. If anything, he was colder.

Buddy on the other hand had taken a sudden interest in her. He watched her a good deal of the time. Gave her sly looks and secret smiles. He rode at her side every chance he got, and at night, he made it a point to place his bedroll very close to hers.

He was making her edgy as hell. Thank goodness they'd make Corpus Christi today. In fact, she figured they should get there within the hour.

Char reined in and motioned for them to do the same.

"What's wrong?" Buddy drew his horse and pack animal up next to Daniels.

"We've got to split up. We can't be seen riding in together." He gave a curt nod in her direction. "You and Buddy go first. Find a hotel and get two rooms, but leave your horses out front so I'll see them. Hill, make sure the room you get has two beds." He tossed him a gold eagle.

"What about you?" She couldn't stop the question.

"I'll come in later." He spoke again to Buddy. "After you're settled, kid, go to the closest saloon. I'll meet you there."

Jessalea wished they'd keep on riding and leave her alone. But there wasn't much chance of that. Char Daniels had appointed himself as her protector, and, other than shooting him, there wasn't much she could do about it. But she damned sure wasn't going to acknowledge his orders. She nudged her horse toward the town.

Buddy was right behind her.

Sea air, tinged with salt drifted on the cool ocean breeze. The town itself came into view, sitting at the edge of a wide bay where the Nueces River dumped into a channel of water that was separated from the Gulf of Mexico by a long, sandy island.

"Jehoshaphats. This place is something."

"It sure is," Jessalea agreed. Although the town was small in area, it was alive with activity, from the bustling streets, heavy with traffic, to the waterfront, teeming with steamers, swimmers, and boaters.

Guiding her mount along Chaparral Street, she spied the entrance to the Steen Hotel. "There's a place."

They left their horses tied out front at the hitching rail, then ambled into the spacious lobby. Across an expanse of hardwood floor, she saw the hotel desk lining the back wall. She had just taken a step toward it when she noticed another man.

She caught Buddy's arm and jerked him to a stop.

"What?" He stared down at her in confusion.

"That's what." She nodded toward the man who hadn't yet seen them, the man talking to the hotel proprietor. He was tall, well-built, and attractive.

He was the U.S. Marshal.

"What are we going to do?" Buddy asked in a shaky voice.

She pulled him out the door and to the side. "Give me the money, then go find someplace to hide until the marshal leaves. I'll get the rooms."

"What if he recognizes you?" Buddy asked as he handed over the gold eagle.

"Dressed in these clothes? He won't." She checked the street. "Make sure you watch for Char, in case he comes ahead of time."

Drawing in a steady breath, she clamped down on her fear and entered the hotel.

The marshal saw her first. His eyes, the color of warm honey, drifted over her face, then swept her body. He smiled—a beautiful smile, filled with masculine appreciation.

She released a sigh.

"May I help you, miss?" the proprietor asked.

"I need a couple rooms for the night. My brother will be along later, and he needs two beds." When the man gaped at her in question, she added, "One for his . . . dog."

The proprietor, with thick sideburns and a bald head, reached for an open registry and pushed it across the counter. "Sign in, please."

She noticed several *X*s in place of signatures on the page, and she considered doing the same, but changed her mind. She didn't speak or act illiterate, and if she wrote that way, the marshal might become suspicious. She printed her parents' names, Lawrence and Lenore Richardson, before placing Char's gold eagle on the counter.

"Rooms five and six, second floor," the balding man said, handing her the keys and change.

The marshal hadn't taken his eyes off her, but he hadn't said anything, either.

Thank goodness.

Anxious to escape, she shoved the coins into her skirt pocket and hurried toward the stairs. Halfway up, she peeked toward the counter.

The marshal was studying the register.

It was earlier than he'd planned when Char rode into Corpus Christi, but he'd been anxious to get to the general store. After making a stop at Gullet & Company and the Orleans Tonsorial Palace, he went in search of his companions' horses. He spotted the animals tied in front of the Steen Hotel—next to a saloon where boisterous voices and bouncy piano music blared from behind a pair of swinging doors.

Char reined in at the hitching rail and had dismounted when he heard the shatter of glass followed by, "You stupid son of a bitch!"

The music stopped. The voices grew silent.

He closed his eyes and shook his head. He'd bet his ass Buddy was in the middle of whatever had happened. Settling his gun belt lower, he strode across the boardwalk and through the doors.

Patrons scrambled in every direction, knocking over chairs and drinks in their haste to clear a space for the two men glaring at each other in front of the long bar.

One of them was Buddy.

For the barest instant, Char considered letting the kid find out firsthand what gun-fighting was really about, but he didn't want to see the fool get himself killed. Not taking his eyes from the older man with dirty brown hair and a red, bloated face, Char stepped between them. "You got a problem with the boy, mister?"

Buddy bristled. "I can handle—"

"Shut up." He fixed his attention on the eyes of the other man. Brown eyes. Wary eyes, now that he was no longer facing a green kid. "I asked if you had a problem with *my son.*"

Shocked gasps reverberated through the room.

"Yeah, I got a problem, all right. I'm gonna blow the bastard's head off for buttin' in between me and Susie, over there." He gestured to a saloon girl who was holding the torn bodice of her dress together.

Fear shadowed the girl's eyes. Beads of blood seeped from scratch marks on her throat and chest.

"The gal was trying to get away from him," Buddy

defended, his tone filled with hurt because Char had usurped him.

"Mind your own business, you little weasel!" the straggly haired man shouted.

Char handed Buddy the package he'd purchased and turned on the red-faced man. "Doesn't seem to me like the lady appreciated your attention."

"What goes on between me and that whore ain't none of your business."

"That's tellin' him, Pete," someone yelled from the crowd. "We know how them kind like it rough."

The saloon girl paled.

Char's temper went up a notch. He met those puffy brown eyes. "To my way of thinking *all women* should be treated with respect."

Pete's throat worked, and his eyes darted around the room.

A gun cocked.

Char stiffened and turned to see the saloon keeper holding a rifle on him.

"We got a strict rule about ruckus here," the man said in a no-nonsense voice. "We don't allow it."

Just as well, Char thought. There'd be more room to maneuver in the street. He gestured to Pete with a jerk of his head. "Outside."

With no help from the onlookers, the troublemaker swung toward the door.

The man's hog-leg was too cumbersome for a quick draw, and Char had no intention of killing him, but he was going to teach the jackass a lesson in manners.

Buddy mumbled to himself as he followed.

Char ignored the kid. He had to. When facing a man intent on killing you, no matter what kind of weapon he carried, there was no room for anything but concentration. One mistake could land you in a coffin.

The sun didn't quite reach several shaded doors and windows lining the boardwalks and that made him damned uncomfortable. You never knew when a man was going to have a friend nearby to help the odds.

Hoping that wasn't the case this time, Char took a stance at the west end, in front of the Steen Hotel, with the sun above his head.

Pete positioned himself in the shade of a sign, half concealing himself in the shadows. "Any time you're ready, partner."

A calmness settled over Char as he fixed on the man's eyes, waiting for the slightest flicker of change. Sometimes it was a minute narrowing or widening of the lashes, or even a sudden glassiness that preceded the draw.

The man's eyes widened.

Char didn't wait for the movement of his hand. He drew and fired.

The roar of the gun blast deafened him.

Pete flew backward and hit the dirt. His gun discharged into the air. Screaming, he grabbed his bloody leg.

Char rammed his gun into his holster. "Contrary to what your friends may believe, women don't like rough treatment at any time."

Latching onto Buddy's arm, Char marched him toward the hotel. "Tell me the goddamn room number."

"I-I don't know it," the kid whined, barely able to keep up with his furious stride.

"*What?*"

"There was a marshal. Jesse went in alone and said for us to wait until the law leaves."

"Has he left?"

"I-I don't know."

"Shit." He stationed Buddy beside the horses. "Stay here while I check." He peered in the glass above the door of the hotel and saw that the lobby was empty.

Darting inside, he checked the register but didn't see a familiar name. He gave a muttered oath and sprinted outside.

"It's upstairs!" Buddy exclaimed. "Jesse waved from the balcony." He pointed at a railed porch overhead.

"Come on, then." He took the package and stalked upstairs.

Jesse met them in the hall and tossed Char a key. "Room six." Without another word, she marched into room five and closed the door.

Wondering what had her dander up, he handed the key to the kid. "Get in that room and stay there. I'm going to check on Jesse, then order some food brought up. And, tomorrow, I'm putting you on a stage for home."

"But—"

"No buts, kid. I've had enough." He slammed his fist on Jesse's door and opened it. He heard Buddy grumble something about Char being as bossy as his pa before he stepped inside.

Jesse turned from the square-paned glass doors that led to the balcony, her eyes bright with an emotion he couldn't define. "You bastard." With a furious screech, she charged him.

"What the hell? Ow! Stop that." He dropped the package and caught her hands, holding them away from his stinging cheek. He dodged the point of her boot and grabbed her shoulders, giving her a rough shake. "What the hell's wrong with you?"

"Let me go, you—you—*show-off*."

"What? Damn it. Quit kicking me."

"It serves you right for scaring me like that. You could have been killed!" Her knee came up.

He took the blow with his thigh, but he was reeling from the impact of her words. *She'd been scared for him.* Pulling her into his arms, he held her against him so she couldn't do him any more damage. "If you don't calm down, I'm going to tie you to the bed until we get this settled."

"Let me go, you ass." Her heel came down in his instep. Her teeth sank into his shoulder.

"Shit!" He hauled her to the bed, then fell on top of her, holding her hands above her head, her legs locked beneath his, and keeping his upper body a healthy distance from her sharp teeth. "Will you calm down!"

She glared at him, her eyes shooting green sparks, her glorious hair tumbled around her head like a pillow of black silk, her chest heaving with anger. That's when he noticed the hem of the blouse was caught between their stomachs and pulled much too low for his comfort. A tempting amount of white flesh spilled over the neckline, quivering with each breath she took.

He forced his attention to her face. "I don't know what's got you so riled. I was never in any real danger. It would have taken the man a half hour to get that hog-leg out of its holster."

Her eyes widened, as if she'd suddenly realized how much of herself—her concern—she'd revealed. "I—I wasn't worried about you. I was worried about you drawing attention with the marshal in town."

He knew she was lying, but he let it pass. "Did you see where he went?"

"I saw him go into the sheriff's office—*after he checked the register.*"

"What name did you give?"

"My mother's."

"Did he see Buddy?"

"I don't think so, but he seemed real thoughtful when he saw my name."

He stared at the iron rail at the head of the bed, hoping the marshal hadn't associated her with the young outlaw he was tracking. He studied her heart-stopping face. It was scrubbed clean and pink, and her hair glistened from a recent washing. She must have bathed while waiting for him and Buddy. The image of her in the tub caused his stomach to knot. A sweet fragrance rose to tease his senses. She smelled like warm honeysuckle. Jesus, it had been a long time since he'd touched her. "You're a beautiful woman, darlin'. He probably wanted to know your name. I know if I'd seen you sashaying into a hotel alone, I would."

The pulse at the base of her throat started to beat rapidly. "Then what would you have done?"

The feel of her soft body beneath his was playing hell with his control. "Followed you. Talked my way into your room . . . and made love to you."

She arched a brow. "You're pretty sure of yourself, aren't you?"

"Yes."

A tremor ran through her, and she took a shaky breath. "Get off me."

"Not until you've apologized for attacking me."

"Fine. I'm sorry."

He bent his head until their lips almost touched. "The only way I'll believe you is if you say it with a kiss."

"I don't care if you believe me or not."

"Sure you do. Because I'm not going to release you until I'm convinced of your sincerity." He shifted his lower body. "And believe me, darlin', I'd be content to stay like this for a very long time."

"Oh, hell." She lifted her head and pressed her mouth to his, then pulled back. "There."

Char lost interest in the game. The soft warmth of her lips had stirred heated memories of that night on the trail. Their breaths mingled for a heartbeat, then he lowered his mouth to hers.

"Char!" Buddy's excited voice ricocheted through the room. He banged on the door. "The marshal's coming. I saw him from the balcony!"

Leaping off the bed, Char raced to the glass doors. He was in time to see a tall man wearing jeans and a gray shirt step under the covered boardwalk. "Damn."

"Did you hear me?" Buddy yelled again.

"The whole town can hear you," Char hissed.

"Get out of here," Jesse urged from where she now stood by the door. "He knows my room number."

"No. Buddy, make yourself invisible."

She clenched her fists. "You're not my keeper, Char Daniels."

"We'll argue about it later." He stepped onto the

balcony. "If the marshal shows, it's for one of two reasons—to arrest you or to court you. Either way, I'll be on hand if you need me."

"I won't."

Touching the brim of his hat, he smiled, then slipped from sight, praying he wouldn't have to kill a U.S. Marshal over Jesse.

CHAPTER

❈ 11 ❈

Jessalea straightened her clothes and combed her fingers through her hair as she waited for the sound of footsteps in the hall. When none came, the knot in her belly loosened, and she slumped down on the edge of the bed.

A knock rumbled across the room.

She stiffened. He'd been so silent she hadn't even heard his footsteps. Wary, she went to the door, then took a deep breath before she opened it. "Yes?"

The lawman stood with his left hand lowered, a thumb clinging to his belt loop. The position of his arm revealed the badge on his shirt. "Afternoon, miss. I wonder if I might speak to you for a minute?"

"What about, Marshal?" If he mentioned Jesse or the gunfights, she'd die on the spot.

He sent her a very gentle, very male smile. "Supper."

She was so stunned, she could only stare at him.

"I saw you earlier, when you checked in, and, since

I haven't seen a man with a dog show up, I thought you might like to have supper with me."

"That's very flattering, but—"

"Honey, you don't have to worry about your safety with me. It's my job to protect folks . . . not harm them."

She stared at the man standing in front of her, not fooled for a second. There was a wealth of intelligence in those brown eyes. The invitation was an excuse. He wanted information—and he didn't even realize he'd called her "honey." Glancing toward the balcony, she smiled. Of course, Char didn't know that. "Marshal . . . ?"

"Darcy. Blake Darcy."

"Well, Marshal Darcy, I'd be delighted to have supper with you." She might even have enough time to buy a decent dress with the change she had from Char's gold eagle since her satin one was dirty.

Blake Darcy didn't appear surprised by her acquiescence. In fact, those eyes were downright amused. "Is six o'clock too early?"

"Six is fine."

He nodded. "I'll see you then."

As she watched him saunter down the hall, she wondered if she hadn't made a mistake. Although the man was polite and disarmingly casual, the intelligence she'd been aware of made her uneasy.

"That was about the stupidest move I've ever seen," Char groused as he stepped into the room. "What the hell's the matter with you, woman? Are you *trying* to get caught?"

If the marshal made her uneasy, this high-handed male irritated the stuffing out of her. "No. I'm trying to throw the lawman off our trail."

"How? By turning yourself in?"

"Don't be ridiculous. I'm going to enjoy a meal with him and, if I'm lucky, I'll determine how much he knows about the outlaws he's tracking."

"I think that's a super idea," Buddy praised as he came in from the balcony.

Char expelled a harsh breath and headed toward the door. "Neither one of you has a lick of sense."

"Jehoshaphats. What's got his dander up?"

"Male pride. He's used to giving orders and expecting them to be obeyed. I think it rankles him when he isn't in control of a situation."

"He might be right about this, you know," Buddy said with a touch of belated loyalty. "The lawman could be up to something."

"Maybe. But that doesn't mean I'll be snared by his trap, now does it?" She winked.

Buddy rolled his eyes and followed Char.

After he left, she counted the money in her pocket, hoping that eighteen dollars was enough for a new dress. Fanny had always bought her clothes, so she didn't have any idea what they cost. It didn't worry her in the least, though, that the money belonged to Char. She'd repay it when this was over, even if she had to earn money by working for Fanny, scrubbing floors or doing laundry.

She was excited about the engagement this evening because it gave her an opportunity to handle two problems at once—how much the marshal knew— and if Char's kisses were the only ones that could set her on fire.

Char was so furious, he could have ground bullets with his teeth. The woman had no sense. *And the fact that the lawman was good-looking didn't bother him in the least.*

Taking the last swipe down his jaw with the razor, he inspected his face in the mirror. The sooner he got Jesse out of his head, the better off he'd be—and he planned to do that right now.

He rinsed his face, then grabbed the blue shirt he'd taken from the package on Jesse's bed—the one she hadn't even bothered to open before she left the hotel more than an hour ago.

The fact that she'd returned a few minutes ago carrying another package didn't endear him either.

Withdrawing his watch from his pocket, he checked the time. Darcy would arrive within the next fifteen minutes, and as soon as he paraded Jesse downstairs, Char was going to search for his own entertainment.

In the last hours, he'd paced and swore until the walls were peeling—because he'd been so upset over Jesse's dinner engagement. He was letting her get under his skin and it had to stop. He was starting to think about things he shouldn't even be considering . . . like how would it be to wake up next to her every morning.

Hell. Even the thought of marriage scared him. He'd gotten firsthand knowledge of that institution watching the Websters. Wedded bliss wasn't something he wanted to experience.

He remembered the last time he started thinking about marriage—with a gal in Louisiana. He'd gotten away by leaving town and seeking the arms of the nearest whore. Unfortunately, he couldn't leave Jesse and let her get herself killed, but he damn sure could forget her while in the arms of another woman.

A distant knock startled him. It was coming from

across the hall. Reminding himself that he didn't care what she did, he cracked open the door to watch Jesse and the marshal.

Blake Darcy, dressed in a crisp brown shirt and snug jeans, stood with his backside to Char, waiting for Jesse to answer. A Colt, with a carved wood handle was strapped low on his thigh, and his calm stance proclaimed he knew how to use it.

The door swung open, and Jesse stepped into the hall.

Char noticed two things at once—the way the breath caught in his throat, and an expulsion of air hissing through the marshal's teeth.

She was breathtaking. Her hair had been pulled to the crown of her head in a cascade of fat curls beneath a small velvet hat. A cameo hung from a green ribbon at her throat and matched her hat and the low-cut, off-the-shoulder gown that molded to her breasts and middle like wet tissue.

Where had she gotten those clothes? Then he knew. With *his* money, damn her.

"There aren't enough words to describe how beautiful you are," the lawman rasped in a husky voice that set Char's teeth on edge.

She lifted a hand to her bosom, revealing a small purse dangling from her wrist, her white skin a startling contrast to the darker gown. "What a nice thing to say, Marshal."

"Please, call me Blake." He drew her arm through his and closed the door behind her.

She gave him a smile that would have melted a glacier. "Blake. I like that."

Char'd like to see it carved on a headstone.

"Do you care for seafood?"

"Oh, yes."

The marshal smiled as he led her along the hall. "Good. I know of a pleasant eating house by the bay. They use seashells for candle holders and . . ." His words faded as they disappeared down the stairs.

Char was angry and sick at the same time—and the need to seek out a saloon girl increased.

Dragging on his gun belt, he glanced at Buddy's hanging from a peg near the door. When he'd sent the kid for supplies, he'd made him leave his weapons behind, figuring he couldn't get into too much trouble if he was unarmed.

With Buddy occupied, and Jesse gallivanting around town, Char was free to do as he damned well pleased. Shoving his hat on his head, he marched down the stairs.

Smoke, sawdust, whiskey, and wet tobacco clogged the air in the Oceanbreeze Saloon across the street. The small room was packed with customers, some playing poker, some lining the battered bar. A few businessmen were gathered at a corner table, drinking and talking low. On a stage at the end of the room, a woman dressed in black satin and feathers leaned on a piano, her tinny voice raised above the noise in a suggestive song.

Char sighed. He was getting too old for this. Making his way to a vacant spot at the bar, he asked about Harley Boggs, his father, and ordered a bottle of whiskey. He got the liquor but no information about his pa, and only a little about Boggs. He was out of town until the end of the week. Returning to his purpose, Char scanned the room.

Besides the singer, there were two other women meandering around talking to the customers, a chesty redhead with a large black mole under her right eye, and a full-figured woman with mouse brown hair and several missing teeth.

His gaze returned to the blond-haired singer. She was sorta pretty and had a decent figure. Maybe he'd wait for her. Lifting his bottle, he took a slug of whiskey.

Visions of Jesse kept dancing through his head. He tried to remove them with alcohol. Jesse in the saloon, drawing on Davidson Boggs. Jesse wounded. Jesse so passionate in his arms. Jesse the courageous. Jesse the beautiful.

Jesse with another man.

By the time the singer finished, Char had opened his second bottle, and the redhead with the mole had started looking better. She'd approached him several times—as had the other one—but he'd put them off, and now he was glad. The singer was headed his way.

"Howdy, darlin'," he greeted in a cheerful voice, but he had to squint to focus on her face. It was blurry.

"Howdy, yourself, handsome." She drew a finger down his chest. "Buy me a drink?"

He grinned—at least he thought he did. He couldn't be sure, though. His lips were numb. Reaching with an unsteady hand, he latched onto the bottle swaying on the bar. "I got whiskey, darlin', if you got some place private to drink it."

She looped her arm through his and gave him a sultry smile. "I sure do, cowboy."

Centering his attention on his feet, he followed her up a mountainous staircase that kept shifting from side to side, causing him to bang into the rail.

At last, they made it to a small room that had a big, soft-looking bed.

He grinned down at the woman, then caught her by the nape of her neck and planted his mouth on hers.

She giggled and stepped from his hold. "Whoa. Slow down, lover. Let's get your clothes off first."

"Ah, darlin'. A woman after my own heart, at last." Anxious now, he shoved the bottle into her hands and tore open the front of his shirt. Buttons bounced and skittered over the floor. His hat landed on a chair, and he had his gun belt off in the space of a heartbeat. His boots and britches took longer, though. They wouldn't let go of him.

When he was at last naked, he sprawled on the bed, waiting for her to join him.

She just stood there, her eyes fixed on a spot below his waist. "Oh, sugar, you are magnificent."

Magnificent . . . Magnificent . . . Magnificent Jesse . . . The words danced and swirled into a black void.

"I don't think I've ever enjoyed a meal more than I have tonight, Miss Richardson," Blake Darcy remarked, staring at her across the table. The fat candle, seated in an abalone shell cast a soft glow over his attractive features.

"You insisted I call you Blake. Won't you call me Jes— Lenore?"

"Lenore. The name's as lovely as you are." He brushed his fingers across her knuckles. "Almost."

His voice was low and husky, and reminded her of Char, whom she hadn't been able to stop thinking about all evening. "Your flattery is going to my head. Let's talk about something else."

"Like what?"

"Like you. What is a U.S. Marshal doing in Corpus Christi?"

He caught her hand in his, letting them rest on the table. "I'm in hot pursuit of outlaws."

She tried to make her expression appear surprised. "Truly?"

"Mmm-hmm." He studied their linked fingers. "Three of them. They're wanted for murder."

"Oh, my." She hoped he didn't feel the tremor that ran through her. "Isn't that dangerous for you?"

"Only when I catch them."

"Are you sure you will?"

"Yes."

The certainty in that single word sounded like a death knell. "W-who did they murder?"

"Two brothers. One in Waco, and one in San Antonio."

She clung to composure. "My word. You tracked those killers all the way from Waco—to here?" She glanced around, hoping to appear anxious. *"Are* they here?"

"Yes . . . somewhere. But you're in no danger. They don't intend to hurt ladies. They're after another of the brothers."

"One lives here?" She tried to inflict shock into her voice.

"Umm-hmm. One's in Houston, too—and one's in Shreveport, Louisiana."

Jessalea was breathless. He'd told her where to find Odie and Hank Boggs. She forced air into her lungs, knowing this was something she'd keep to herself. "Can't you stop those murderers?"

He squeezed her fingers. "That's why I'm here,

honey. To do just that." He rose, releasing her hand with reluctance. "It's time I got back to my business, too. I'll settle the bill, then walk you to the hotel."

She was reeling from the information she'd learned. Now if she only knew where Harley Boggs lived.

A waitress came by the table carrying a speckled tin coffeepot.

"Miss?" Jessalea summoned. "May I have some of that?" She didn't want any. Her cup was half-full. But she did want information—more than she'd found out when she'd asked around during her shopping excursion. All she'd learned was he lived by the bay.

The woman filled her cup. "Did you enjoy your supper?"

"Very much, thank you. But I was wondering, do you know a man named Harley Boggs?"

"Sure do."

Jessalea's hopes soared. "Do you know where he lives?"

"Near the bay, on Aubrey Street, I believe. He's gone right now, though, and not due to return until the end of the week."

She tried not to show her disappointment. *Three more days.* It seemed like a lifetime. "Will he arrive by stage?"

"Steamer."

"How long has he been gone?" Had he received Cecil's wire?

"Don't know for sure, but I haven't seen him for at least a couple weeks."

He hadn't received it! "Well, perhaps I'll see him before I leave town."

"See who?" Blake Darcy asked as he neared the table.

"An acquaintance." She nodded to the woman, dismissing her, then returned her attention to the marshal. "Ready?"

He smiled and offered his hand.

"You know," Blake said, when he stopped at her door, "I had a good time tonight, and I'd like to see you again if you're going to be in town awhile."

"I'd like that, too," she returned, meaning it. He was a nice man. "But I'm afraid my brother wouldn't approve. As it is, if he's in his room, I'm going to have some fast explaining to do."

"Then I guess this is not only good night, but good-bye."

"I'm afraid so."

He opened the door, then caught her arm. "It's been nice knowing you, Lenore Richardson." Then he kissed her. Slowly. Gently.

She waited for the melting sensation, the streak of fire she experienced with Char.

Although the kiss was nice, it didn't stir anything in her beyond mild warmth.

The marshal gave her a smile. "I'll see you again one day, honey." Then he was gone.

Jessalea stood in the hall for a full minute, fighting disappointment, and making sure he wouldn't return before she hurried across the hall and opened Char's door.

She tried to see into the pitch-black room. "Char? Where are you?"

"Jesse? That you?" Buddy's voice came out of the dark, very close to the door.

"Where's Char?"

"He isn't here."

"Well, where is he?"

"He's, uh, gone."

That told her a lot. "Gone where?"

"Er, out for the evening."

Damn him. She knew exactly where. "When he returns," she managed through clenched teeth, "no matter what time—I want to see him."

"Sure thing."

She marched into her room to wait. For several minutes she paced, fretted, and stared out the glass doors. Then she caught sight of the package on the chair.

Char had left it. Curious, she examined the contents. A beige hat, jeans, tan shirt, and a gold satin pillow.

The clothes were her size, and the pillow . . . She smiled as she fingered the soft material. He'd noticed how uncomfortable she'd been using her saddle. Curse him. Why did he have to be so kind? She didn't want to feel things for him. He was a wanderer and a skirt-chaser—not the kind of man she should get starry-eyed about.

Knowing where he was right now, she felt an ugly emotion slither through her. She paced to the balcony and leaned on the rail, fighting crazy, kaleidoscoping feelings . . . and waiting.

She was still waiting when the sun came up.

CHAPTER

✳ 12 ✳

Char didn't want to open his eyes. He could feel the dull ache sloshing from one side of his head to the other. The light would only make it worse.

He listened to sounds; a muffled snore—not in the same room, but farther away—a barking dog, the whinny of a horse, a child's laughter.

He noticed the scent of cheap toilet water, a woman's body odor, and musky sheets. He knew where he was—or, at least, what *kind* of place he was in—but he didn't remember getting there. His body didn't feel any different, either. That low, gnawing ache was right where it had been last night.

If he hadn't taken care of his needs, what was he doing here? He summoned his courage and cracked one eyelid.

A blast of sunlight slammed into his brain.

"Ah, God." He clamped his eyes shut and grabbed his head.

"So, you're alive," a woman's tinny voice ricocheted through the walls of his skull.

He dug the heels of his hands into his temples, trying to dull the pain. It didn't help. Nausea rolled across his stomach. "Get out of here," he whispered. "Now."

"Whatever you say, cowboy." There was a harsh expulsion of breath, the squeak of floorboards, then a door opened and closed.

Char pried an eye open, spotted the chamber pot and made a dive for it.

After he finished, he stumbled to the washbasin and almost drowned himself in tepid water before he felt human again. Shaky, but human.

Dragging on his clothes and tucking in his buttonless shirt as best he could, he tossed a handful of silver on the bed, then eased his hat onto his throbbing head and crept silently from the room, more for his own benefit than the patrons of the saloon.

When he reached the swinging doors, he took a deep breath before forging into the bright sunlight. A fierce yellow blast blinded him, and he covered his eyes. Ah, Jesus, that hurt.

Using great caution, he cracked his lashes, then opened them very slowly and squinted to see down the street.

The town appeared deserted—probably because it was only seven in the morning. He lifted his gaze to Jesse's hotel window.

He was surprised to see her on the balcony— staring at him with disgust. Then she whirled around and walked inside.

What was she riled about? Deciding to avoid her sharp tongue until his brain settled and he had some coffee, he strode to an eating house a couple blocks down.

It took an hour, and two pots of coffee before he felt hardy enough to face Jesse, but when he got to her room . . . she was gone.

Jessalea couldn't shake the feeling that someone was watching her as she questioned folks on the dock about when Harley Boggs should arrive. Hearing the waitress's statement confirmed, Jessalea glanced again over her shoulder then headed for the beach. Her sleepless night had made her edgy.

No. She wasn't going to think about that—or *Char Daniels*—again. As soon as she confronted Boggs, she was leaving. Alone.

The ache in her middle wouldn't ease, and she didn't understand it, but she knew Char was responsible.

Lowering the bill of the hat he'd bought her, she walked along the beach, listening to the gentle slosh of the waves, the seagulls overhead, and the voices drifting from the docks.

Salt air feathered over her cheek and fluttered the collar of the tan shirt she wore. A misty spray cooled her sun-warmed skin and caused tingles to skip over her flesh, reminding her of the sensation she'd felt when Char touched her breasts, her—.

Stop it! *She would not think of him.*

"Jesse, is something wrong?"

Startled, she whirled around to find Buddy standing a few feet from her, wearing a new brown shirt. "No. Nothing's wrong." She noticed the saddlebags draped over his shoulder. "Where are you going with that?"

"Char doesn't want me around anymore. He said if I didn't get on the noon stage by myself, he'd put me on it." He shrugged. "I came to say good-bye."

A sadness touched her, and she placed a hand over his. "Are you going home?"

He sent her a grin. "Not if you'll tell me where we're heading after Christi."

"Buddy, maybe Char's right. You shouldn't be involved in this."

"If you don't tell me, I'll learn on my own. Char's not right. I think he's forgotten how important it was to him to be a gunman. And if you don't tell me where you're going, Jesse, I'll get off the stage a mile or so down the road and follow you."

"You'll have to follow Char. When I leave Christi, I'll be by myself."

"I figured that—the way you and him have been at loggerheads. But I'll stick with you. You need watching after more than he does."

"I appreciate your concern. But I don't want you following me."

"You don't want me around either, do you?"

"That's not true. I enjoy your company very much. But I think Char's right about you going home to your family. The appeal of gunmen—and the Wild West— is way overexaggerated, and I'd hate for you to learn that the hard way."

"I've never been one to take the easy road. Where are you going next, anyway?"

She shook her head. He was persistent if nothing else. "Go home, Buddy. As soon as this mess is over, I'll write to you." She touched his cheek. "I won't let our friendship end here."

"Can I kiss you good-bye?"

The notion wasn't that appealing. Even though they were near the same age, he seemed so much younger than she. "I guess it would be okay."

As if he were afraid she'd change her mind, he dropped his saddlebags on the sand and caught her shoulders. It was a sweet kiss, one filled with youthful passion, and she was almost sorry when it ended.

"First the Dutchman, then me, the marshal, and now the boy. You do get around, don't you, darlin'?"

Startled, she whirled around. "How did you know about the marsh—*Buddy.*" She glared at the younger man. "You were spying on me!"

Hill scooped up his gear and retreated. "I-I'd better see what time the stage is going to arrive." He ran toward town, his blond curls flapping beneath his hat.

Char didn't take his eyes off her. "You didn't answer me."

"After where you spent the night, I'm surprised you have the nerve to question my actions."

He didn't like that. She could tell by the way his jaw hardened. "I'm a helluva lot older than you."

"You're not *that* old."

"And," he continued, "I'm a man. You on the other hand should be in some fancy girls' school learning how to be a lady, instead of traipsing across the country alone, chasing outlaws—*and allowing men such liberties.*"

"But, Char," she said, her voice laced with mock sweetness. "If it weren't for women like me—what on earth would men like you do?" With a toss of her head, she left him standing there, scowling at her.

In her room, she slammed the door, then grabbed the satin pillow and threw it against the wall. "Arrogant jackass!" It was fine for him to spend the night with a whore, but God forbid if she should kiss a friend good-bye.

She pulled off the shirt *he'd* bought her and tore it to shreds. Stripping off the jeans, she tried to tear them, but couldn't, so she tossed them in the fireplace. The hat, she crushed flat with her boot.

Then she headed for the pillow.

The door opened.

Gasping, she spun around.

Char stood in the doorway.

Heat rushed to her cheeks. She was stark naked—except for her boots. "Get out of here!"

He stepped inside and closed the door, his gaze roaming her length. "Where are your clothes?"

"I tore them up, because I didn't want anything you bought me next to my skin—*and stop staring at me like that.*"

He glanced at the shirt on the floor and the pants in the fireplace, then again at her. "You look better without them."

She bolted for the bed and jerked the quilt around her. "Go, damn you."

"Darlin', you're making it awfully difficult for me to apologize." He came toward her in slow, fluid strides. "I shouldn't have said anything about your morals, when my own leave a lot to be desired—and I wanted to explain about last night."

She recoiled. "I don't want to hear about it."

"Nothing happened." He cupped her shoulders. "I drank myself into a stupor over you and passed out." He stroked the curve of her neck. "I got a good night's rest, but that's *all* I got."

Some of her anger faded. "I couldn't care less."

"Yes, you do." He traced the edge of the quilt across her chest. "We're friends, aren't we?"

Were they? She wasn't sure. "I guess so." She felt like a fool for throwing a tantrum, too. Sitting on the edge of the bed, she fixed her gaze on the floor. "I imagine I should apologize for my remarks, too."

"I deserved it."

"No, you didn't. But to clear the record, I only kissed the marshal to see if he would affect me the same way you do."

He smiled as he knelt in front of her and lifted her chin. "What was the verdict?"

"No."

His eyes lowered to her lips. "Then I won't have to kill him." He leaned closer, until their lips met, then he kissed her with slow, erotic precision. "Let's call a truce, Jesse. I'm tired of fighting."

That sounded good to her. "Shall we shake on it?"

He pressed her back onto the bed. "I'd rather make love."

Her heart almost exploded. She placed her hands on his chest, holding him off. "Don't be silly."

"I didn't know I was."

"Well, you were. Now get off me. I—" She thought quickly. "Want to go down to the bay. Folks say the water's great this time of year."

A chuckle rumbled through his chest, and he stood up. "Coward."

"Lecher."

He smiled as he walked to the door. "Get your jeans, darlin', and put on another shirt. In a half hour, I'm taking you swimming."

Panic held her speechless. *That wasn't what she meant.* For heaven's sake, she couldn't swim a lick. She'd only used that as an excuse.

After he left, it took her a minute to gather enough

strength to sit up. How on earth did she get herself into these situations?

Dragging in a breath, she rose and retrieved the jeans from the fireplace and shook them, then found her shortened white blouse. It was all she had, except for the green checkered one—and she couldn't wear that with the marshal in town.

She had finished dressing and twisting her hair into one long braid when Char strode in.

"Grab a towel, darlin'. The desk clerk told me about a quiet place not far from here."

It wasn't often she saw him in such a good mood, and she didn't want to spoil it by telling him about her inabilities. Besides, he'd probably laugh at her. With a feeling of doom, she did as he said.

As they walked to the door, he tucked the quilt and her satin pillow under his arm.

"What do you need those for?"

He grinned. "In case we get tired."

Tired, my foot, she thought as she followed him downstairs. The man was planning something. Probably something that was going to earn him a black eye.

It wasn't the ocean, she thought as she scanned the small stretch of beach lined by thick grass and surrounded by a forest of trees. In fact, they weren't even on the beach. The "quiet" place was in a bayou. "It's beautiful."

"It's not what I expected," he admitted. "If you'd rather swim in the ocean . . ."

"No. This is fine." At least she wouldn't make a fool of herself in front of a million people when she drowned.

"Okay, here." He handed her the quilt. "Spread this, while I tie the horse."

When she finished, she sat down to wait for him.

He returned carrying the pillow and a bottle of wine.

"What's the wine for?"

"In case we get thirsty." He set the items down on the blanket. "Take your clothes off, woman. Time's wasting."

"What?"

He unbuttoned his shirt and peeled it off. "You weren't planning on swimming in your clothes, were you?"

"Yes."

He arched a brow, then shrugged. "Suit yourself." He removed his boots and britches and tossed them aside, then with a wink, he ran toward the water and dove in, making barely a ripple in the surface.

She closed her gaping mouth. She'd never seen a more magnificent creature—all sleek, bronze masculinity.

"Come on, darlin'. The water's great."

Fear rippled up her spine, and she grabbed the bottle of wine and took several swallows, fighting for breath after each drink. She'd never had spirits before, but she'd seen the girls at Fanny's do it to calm themselves before opening the doors to hoards of customers. Maybe it would help her.

Feeling the soothing warmth of the alcohol slide through her veins, she removed her boots and rolled up her pant legs. Using great caution, she sloshed into the shallow water.

"Dive in."

"I'd rather wade for a while." She dug her toes into the sand, enjoying the gritty coolness. A breeze fluttered the bottom of her blouse against her midriff.

Stuffing her fingers into her back pockets, she ambled along the shore, nudging rocks and pieces of wood out of the way with her toes.

Char erupted from the water beside her.

She let out a startled squeak a second before he swooped her up and tossed her into the lake.

Arms flailing, she hit the water. It surged over her head. Panic consumed her. She twisted frantically, trying to find the surface. She couldn't tell which way was up! Terrified, she clawed at the water. *Help me. Oh, God. Someone help me.* Her throat closed in fear. Her lungs constricted.

Out of nowhere, strong hands gripped her waist and hauled her from the water. "Jesse? Jesse, what's wrong?"

She grabbed him around the neck and clung to him. Violent shudders racked her, and she began to cry.

"What is it?" He held her close. "Did you get hurt?"

Trembling, she shook her head against his chin. "I—I can't s-swim."

"Son of a bitch! Why didn't you tell me? Damn it. I could have drowned you."

She burrowed into his chest and cried harder.

He swung her into his arms and carried her to the blanket, then held her, massaging her back until her cries dwindled into jerky sobs.

"I'm sorry, Jesse. I'm so sorry." He brushed wisps of hair from her cheeks. "I'd have never done anything like that if I'd known."

She sniffed. "I know. But I was afraid you'd make fun of me. Or worse, try to teach me to swim."

"I wouldn't have made fun of you." He eased her away. "Here, drink some of this." He uncorked the bottle of wine and put it to her lips. "It'll calm your nerves. That's it. A little more."

She took greedy gulps of the smooth, sweet liquid. Half the bottle was gone by the time he set it aside.

"Lie down and I'll cover you until you stop shaking." He pressed her head to the satin pillow and drew his shirt over her quivering shoulders, then lay down beside her. "Relax, darlin'. The wine will do its work before you know it."

"You must think I'm such a baby."

"I think you're stubborn, and hardheaded, and irritating. But there's nothing childish about you."

"I bet you say that to every woman you almost drown."

"Only the beautiful ones."

She rolled onto her back. "Do you think I'm beautiful?" Heavens, she felt giddy. How potent was wine, anyway?

His gaze moved over her face, then down her front. He stopped at her breasts—and swallowed. "I think you're exquisite."

She followed his line of vision. The wet, white material of her blouse was almost transparent. It clung to her shape, giving a clear view of her jutting nipples.

It struck her as funny, and she giggled. "Oh, dear. Look at that. You can see through my blouse."

"I know," he said in a strained voice.

She studied her chest. "Do you think my breasts are too big?"

A pulse throbbed at the base of his throat. "They're perfect."

"Hmm." She ran her hand over one. "Doesn't feel

perfect." Taking his hand, she placed it on her chest. "You feel."

He made a choked sound. "Jesse . . ."

She closed her eyes. "I love your hands. They're so gentle. So warm. They make me feel such wonderful things." She moved his hand to her wet jeans, over her secret place. "Like when you touched me here. I thought I would die of pleasure."

A tremor ran through him, and he tightened his fingers the tiniest bit.

"Oh, yes. Like that."

"Jesse, you're too—"

"Did you know you kiss better than anyone? It's true. I know. You have an incredible mouth." Her gaze explored the splendid shape. "Kiss me again."

He removed his hand from between her legs. "Darlin', I'm going to kiss every inch of you one day, but—"

"Oh. I know I'd like that."

"But," he continued, "when I do, I want you aware of what I'm doing . . . and completely sober."

He rose and put on his clothes, and she enjoyed every second of it. "You're beautiful, too."

He hauled her to her feet. "Come on. It's time to go." Lifting her into his arms, he carried her to his horse and put her in the saddle, then mounted behind her. He caught her mare's reins and guided the horses through the trees.

The rocking movement was erotic, and she closed her eyes, leaning against Char's big chest. "You know. I think I'll go to work for Fanny when I get home."

"Over my dead body."

"I like your body the way it is." She trailed a finger

across his thigh and up the inside of his leg. "Hard, and hot, and very alive."

He snatched her hand away. "Stop that. Damn it, I'm not made of stone, and my control has reached its limit. Now sit there, and be quiet—*and don't touch me.*"

CHAPTER

❈ 13 ❈

Char undressed Jesse and pulled her nightgown over her head, trying very hard not to look at her. He was trembling by the time he put her to bed, and the need to make love to her made him ache. The vixen would never know what hell he had gone through to keep from doing just that.

She was getting to him, and he didn't know how to stop her. If only he could leave her. Not worry about her vendetta and the danger she would face when Harley Boggs returned and she confronted him.

But he couldn't.

"Noooo. Oh, please, no."

Startled, he whirled around.

"Leave her alone!" Jesse cried, tossing her head from side to side. "Don't hurt my sister!"

She swung at the air. "He has a knife—Susannah, look out!" Twisting and kicking, she fought imaginary hands. "Let me go! Susannah! *Oh, God, Susannah.*"

Char was beside her in an instant, pulling her into

his arms, holding her. "It's all right, darlin'. Nothing's gonna hurt you."

Tears rolled down her cheeks. "The blood. So much blood . . ."

"Shh. I know. But it's gone now. All gone." He rocked her, talking in soft tones, stroking her spine to calm her.

She wrapped her arms around his waist and cried.

He'd never felt so helpless. "Ah, Jesse. What have those bastards done to you?"

"He k-killed my sister," she said in a shaky voice, her words slurred from the wine, her breath coming in quivering pants against his chest. "Harley Boggs drove his knife into her heart. And Hank—oh, God." She broke into renewed sobs.

He tried to absorb her pain, but he didn't know what to say. How to help her. Yet he understood the depth of her anguish, and he knew what he was going to do about it. Somehow, he would get to Boggs before Jesse.

Soft lantern light filled the room when Jessalea woke later that evening and found Char sitting in a chair by the open balcony doors.

"What time is it?"

He glanced in her direction, then checked his pocket watch. "Almost ten."

"Did Buddy leave?"

"Yes. But I saw him go into the post office beforehand, probably to get information about Boggs—or his kin, so I imagine we'll see him again before long."

There was something different about him, but she couldn't grasp what it was. He *looked* different, though, and his voice was different. Harder somehow.

She sat up. The room spun. Pain shot through her temples. "Ooowww . . ." She grabbed her head.

"Try not to move too much." He dumped a packet of powder into a glass of water. "Drink this. It'll help."

She'd have swallowed trough water if it would have stopped the hurt. When she finished, she handed him the glass and eased her head onto the pillow. "Does wine always make you feel like this?"

A ghost of a smile touched his lips. "If you drink too much of it."

"Do you know that from experience?"

"I've had my share of hangovers, if that's what you mean." He sat down on the edge of the bed. "Are you hungry?"

She rolled her head from side to side. "My stomach feels like someone stomped on it."

"Maybe coffee will help. I'll see if I can find some."

After he closed the door, she lay there for several seconds, but nature's call urged her to locate the chamber pot. By the time she'd finished, the throb in her head had dulled to an annoying ache. The powders really were working.

She wandered over to the balcony and stared at the moonlit night. Then she noticed her damp jeans and white blouse draped over the rail. Char must have done that—*after he undressed her.* Embarrassment burned her face, and she turned away.

Something near the saloon door across the street caught her attention, and she peered into the darkness to see a man leaning against a wall with his arms folded.

The marshal.

Racing inside, she closed the doors.

Char strode in carrying a tray with a china coffee server and two cups. "Feeling better?"

"The marshal's watching my room."

"I know. I saw him."

"What are we going to do?"

Char filled a cup and handed it to her. "Nothing."

She sank down on the bed and took a sip of the steaming liquid. "He makes me nervous."

He extinguished the lantern.

The room plunged into darkness.

"What are you doing?"

"Making him think you went to bed." He peeked through the doors.

Moonlight touched the strong angles of Char's face, bathing them in a silver glow. He was so handsome. Too handsome. She took another drink of coffee. "Did I make a fool of myself today?"

"Don't you remember?"

"Not much. I remember wading, then you tossing me in the water. After that, everything's blurry."

He was quiet for several seconds, then the tiniest bit of humor entered his voice. "You don't remember asking me if I thought your breasts were too big?"

She gasped. "I didn't!"

"Yes, you did. You also told me I had wonderful hands and—I believe you said—an incredible mouth."

Heat burned her neck. She hadn't said that aloud, had she? "I must have been out of my mind."

"No. Only inebriated." He came to the bed and took the cup from her hands and set it aside. The mattress sank with his weight as he sat beside her. "And you were delightful." He brushed his thumb over her lower lip. "By the way, the marshal's gone into the saloon."

That should have pleased her, but she was too intent on trying to see Char in the dark. Now that he wasn't in the moonlight, his features were obscured.

He trailed his thumb over her chin and down the front of her throat. "Do you still think I have wonderful hands?"

Oh, yes. "No."

He chuckled, then lowered his head and swept his lips up one side of her neck. "What about my incredible mouth?"

Shivers chased each other across her flesh. "It's okay." The man was tying her in knots.

"Just okay?" He brushed his lips across hers. "Are you sure?" He deepened the kiss, pressing her down onto the bed, parting her lips with a gentle thrust of his tongue.

Every inch of her body leapt to life. The man had a way of kissing that left her weak. Not one of the others held a candle to him.

The hand at her throat slid down to cover her breast. To knead gently. "You put my hand here this afternoon. Did you know that?" He caressed his way lower until he covered her woman's place. "And here."

She wanted to deny it, but she vividly recalled him touching those exact spots. "I was drunk."

He stroked her through the thin material of the gown. "What about now?"

She couldn't stop a moan. "I must be insane."

"So am I," he whispered, "with wanting you." He lowered his mouth to her breast and traced her nipple through the material.

Pleasure hardened her flesh, and she arched.

Loud voices startled her, then a horrendous crash.

Gunfire roared through the street.

Char lunged from the bed and raced to the balcony, his guns drawn.

"Ah, hell," he swore, holstering his weapons.

"What is it?"

"Someone shot the marshal."

"Who?"

"I can't tell, but he's lying in the street and people are standing around him."

Jessalea got to her feet and started dressing.

"What do you think you're doing?"

"I'm going to see if he's okay."

"No."

She jammed her hands on her hips. "Will you stop telling me what to do. I may not have spent a lot of time with Blake, but he's a decent man, and I'm going to see about him—whether you like it or not."

Char swore and slammed out the door.

Pulling on the rest of her clothes, she hurried to the saloon across the street.

Guilt consumed her as she stared at Blake Darcy lying on a table. She'd wanted to be rid of him. But not this way. "Are you sure he's going to be all right?" she asked the doctor.

"You heard what he said," Char answered. "The bullet only nicked him."

She turned to find him right behind her. "Nicked him in the *head*." She stared at the bloodstained bandage covering the wound.

The elderly physician patted her hand. "He'll be on his feet before you know it. Are you his missus?"

"No!" Char blurted, then regained himself. "I mean, she's—we're both acquaintances."

"I see. Would either of you happen to know where he's staying, then? He needs to be in bed."

"I'll take him to my room," she offered.

"Like hell you will. We'll take him to mine." Char motioned to a couple of patrons in the saloon to help carry the unconscious man. "Room six, across the street."

"How did this happen?" she asked the physician as she watched the men carry the marshal through the swinging doors.

"He tried to stop a brawl, and someone objected." Picking up his bag, he hurried after Char and the others.

In the room, the doc situated Blake in the bed Buddy had used, then checked him over. Satisfied, he told them he'd return tomorrow and left with the others.

Char nodded to her. "You should turn in, too."

"I'm staying here."

"No."

"Yes."

His eyes narrowed. "Fine. Then we'll take up where we left off." He started toward her.

"All right. I'm going." She stormed from the room, vowing to punch that arrogant nose one day.

Char breathed a sigh of relief when the door closed. Thank God. Being in the same room with her was driving him to the brink of insanity, and the thought of her fawning over another man would have pushed him over the edge.

"So, you're Char Daniels."

Char stiffened and turned to find the marshal sitting on the side of the bed holding his head, his eyes wary. Damn. He wasn't prepared for this.

"*The* Char Daniels. I can't believe it." Darcy shook his head. "When the Richardson gal wanted revenge, she hired the best, didn't she?"

"Who?"

"Don't play me for a fool, Daniels. I know exactly who she is—and who you are."

"Then you know a helluva lot more than I do."

"Are you telling me Jessalea Richardson didn't hire you?"

So that was her name. "No, she didn't."

"Then why were you and the kid with her in Waco? And why'd you kill those men in the saloon in San Antonio?"

Char was at a loss. "I was in Waco because I'd handed over a bank robber to the sheriff, but I didn't know she was. The kid was not *with* me. He's been dogging me. As for San Antonio, Jesse was outnumbered so I evened the odds. But I never laid eyes on her before that day."

It was easy to see the marshal didn't believe him. "So why are you tagging along with her?"

"I'm trying to keep her from getting killed. What about you? How did you know about us?"

"I didn't know she was with you when I first saw the names on the register downstairs. I knew Lawrence and Lenore Richardson died ten years ago, so I figured she must be their daughter, Jessalea. Besides, she looks like her ma. But it wasn't until I saw the three of you together on the beach that I realized you were the same ones I'd been tracking." He gave a half smile. "The descriptions witnesses gave were pretty accurate."

Something wasn't right. "So why didn't you arrest us?"

"I'd like to see you succeed."

How Char kept his mouth from dropping open, he'd never know. "You condone what we're—*she's* doing?"

"No. But I understand it. I was there, Daniels. I saw what those butchers did to her family. Hell, I even told her where to find the others."

"Where?"

"Houston and Shreveport."

Char wasn't sure he understood. "You said you saw what happened to her family?"

Darcy massaged his head. "I got there right afterward. I'd been sworn in as a new deputy the night before, and it was my first day on the job. Christ, what an initiation."

"Did you know her folks?"

"I'd seen them a few times. I'd moved to Jefferson City from Saint Louis, to be near my brother and his family the month before." As he spoke, he rose and paced to the mirror to inspect his wound. "I couldn't believe what those butchers did." He met Char's eyes in the glass. "They lynched her pa and stomped her little brother to death beneath a horse. Then they turned on the women." He stared at the floor as if seeing it again. "They raped the older ones and killed them, then one of those murdering son of a bitches cut off her thirteen-year-old sister's breast."

Nausea churned in Char's stomach. "Did they— hurt Jesse?"

"Yes. One of them shot her in the chest. Damn near

killed her, too. The only thing that saved her life was the arrival of her uncle. He stopped the bleeding and got her to a doctor."

Char remembered the scar on Jesse's breast, how close it was to her heart. He closed his eyes, wishing he could get his hands on the man who did that to her.

"Her uncle almost went crazy," Darcy continued. "He tracked them for months that I know of, but never caught them. I tracked them, too, but without any information it was useless. Jessalea wouldn't talk about it, no matter how many times I questioned her—then her uncle took her to Mississippi. Hell, until now, no one knew who did it."

"Jesse knew."

"I know."

"So what now? You just going to let her kill Harley Boggs?"

"As much as I'd like to, I can't. I have to arrest him."

"She'll try to get to him first."

"Yes, she will, and, in the process, she may get herself killed." He gave Char a measured look. "Of course, that could be prevented . . . with help from you."

Char knew in his gut what the man was going to ask of him.

And he knew he would say yes.

CHAPTER

❋ 14 ❋

Char rose early the next day even though he and Blake had talked until well after one in the morning, making plans.

He glanced at the opposite bed. Darcy had already gone to the sheriff's office to let the lawman know about their intentions.

Battling feelings of self-loathing, Char headed for Jesse's room, praying she would fall in with their scheme. If not—well, he didn't want to think about that yet.

"What are you doing awake at this time of day?" she grumbled as she opened the door. She left it ajar and marched to the bed, pulling the covers around her. "The marshall's okay, isn't he?"

Kicking the door shut, Char straddled a chair and studied the beautiful woman sitting across from him. Her delicate features were soft from sleep, her hair tumbled. One long curl fell over her shoulder and brushed the front of her nightgown. "Darcy's fine. In fact, he's returned to his own room."

"Then what are you doing here at this ungodly hour?"

"I want to go fishing."

She yawned and stretched, her breasts pushing against the thin fabric. "So go."

"I want you to go with me."

"Maybe later."

"This is Wednesday, darlin'. Boggs won't be back until Friday. You have plenty of time now."

"I don't like fishing."

"Then you don't have to fish."

Cocking her head, she frowned at him. "What's this about?"

He formed a tale that wasn't really a lie, but one he hoped would play on her sympathy. "The truth is, I want to get away. Half the town knows who I am. If I stay, there's going to be another glory-seeker out to test his speed against the *famous* Char Daniels." He rubbed the nape of his neck, wishing he didn't have to do this. "I'm tired, darlin'. I just want a couple days without having to watch over my shoulder." He knelt in front of her and took her hands. "The hotel clerk told me about a secluded cove on the big island across the bay that only a few folks know about. It sounds perfect—and I saw boats for rent at the dock." He massaged her knuckles with his thumbs. "I'd have you back in plenty of time to meet Boggs's steamer."

"How did you know when—"

"I ask around." He grinned. "I also know his brothers are in Houston and Shreveport, and that he lives on Aubrey Street near the bay."

"But—"

"Darlin', I don't want to talk about Boggs anymore. I want to take you to that island."

She hesitated, her eyes filled with uncertainty, then at last, she shrugged. "Why not. Maybe it'll make the time pass quicker."

He gave her a light kiss, then headed for the door before she could change her mind. "Get dressed. I'll be back before you know it."

Jessalea tossed aside the sheet on her bed and rose to pull on her blouse and skirt. After running a brush through her hair and braiding it, she put on her slippers and sat down to wait.

Fishing, for heaven's sake. She must be out of her mind. The one time her father had taken her, she'd almost gotten sick. Worms made her cringe, and the thought of touching a slimy fish made her queasy. She'd never been in a boat, either. At least Char said she wouldn't *have* to fish.

So what would she do? Stare at him the whole day? The idea did have its appeal, but . . . She gave a light shudder and crossed her arms, hoping she wasn't making a terrible mistake. Her attraction to the man was unsettling.

She was being silly. They'd been together for over a week on the trail and nothing happened. *Almost* nothing.

When he returned a few minutes later, his eyes were alight with boyish excitement. "Everything's ready to go."

Wishing she'd had the good sense to tell him no, she rose and followed him through the door.

The wooden sailing craft was small, with two bench seats and a pair of oars. As Char helped her in, she noticed a large basket sitting on the bottom, right next to a pair of fishing poles and her quilt and pillow.

Gathering the folds of her skirt, she sat down in the rocking boat and watched as he shoved them from the pier and stuck the flat end of the oars in the water.

The swaying motion was frightening and exhilarating at the same time.

He rowed for several minutes without speaking, and she enjoyed the play of muscles working in his shoulders and arms. "Have you been fishing often?"

"I did the first year after I left the farm. I got sick of rabbit and squirrel so I learned how."

"Didn't you learn as a child?" Her father took James from the time he could walk. He tried to take her and Susannah, too, but they were both too squeamish.

"There was never enough time on the farm for play."

"What on earth did you do for fun?"

"I did school lessons, darlin'. No dances, no parties, no fishing. Only work and lessons. Schooling was the easy part, so I considered it fun."

She couldn't believe how the Websters had deprived him of so much, and she couldn't help wondering what else they'd done . . . or not done. "Those people should be horsewhipped."

"I wouldn't waste the energy." The hard set to his jaw revealed how much he meant those words—and how much the conversation bothered him.

She fell silent and watched the water ripple by, listened to the slosh of waves, and the slap of oars. But her thoughts were on the man seated across from her. On what a lonely, unhappy child he must have been.

Hours passed before either of them spoke again.

"Trade places with me. We're almost there." He

pointed to a cove not more than a hundred yards away.

When they'd exchanged seats, he placed her hands on the oars and covered them with his own, showing her the motion. "When we get close, you'll have to keep rowing while I jump out and pull us to shore."

The cove was beautiful with its sandy white beach and grass-covered dunes. But there wasn't another soul in sight.

Determindly recalling their time on the trail, she spread the quilt on the sand while Char got the basket, pillow, fishing poles, and tin of bait.

The food, more than she'd ever dreamed could fit into one basket, was delicious, the pie heavenly, and the lemonade mountain-stream cold.

"Ah, Jesse," he murmured from where he was lying on the quilt. "That was the best meal I've had in a long time."

"It was good," she agreed. Her head was nestled on the pillow, her slippers discarded in the sand. "That apple pie was almost as wonderful as my mama's, too."

"What was she like?"

"Warm and happy. Always smiling, and she was beautiful, with dark cherrywood hair like my sister. They resembled each other a great deal."

"You must favor her, too. At least, the beautiful part."

She smiled. It was the first time she'd thought about her family without pain clouding her memory. "Our eyes were similar. Hers were green like mine, but my hair's mostly black like papa's."

Char fingered a curl that had come loose from the braid. "There's a touch of red in it."

"A blessing of my Irish heritage."

He stared up at the sky. "I've often wondered about my heritage and which one of my parents I resemble."

Her heart ached for him. At least she'd known her family and had memories of their wonderful times together. Char had nothing. She raised herself onto one elbow and explored his handsome features. "With your coloring and the way you like to wander, I think you've got gypsy blood running through your veins."

He chuckled. "You're probably right. In fact"—he lifted her hand—"I think I can read palms."

"Oh, brother."

He inspected the lines across her hand. "Ah, ha. I was right. I can see your future."

"Really."

"Yep. Says you're going to make love to a dark-haired, blue-eyed . . . gypsy."

"Is that a fact?"

"Sure is." He tapped her palm. "Says so right here."

"I see. And does it say when?"

"July 14, 1876."

"That's today."

He stroked her palm with his thumb, and his gaze touched her lips. "I know."

The air had become so still, so thick, she could hardly breathe. "Um, how about some more lemonade?"

He continued to hold her hand for a moment longer, then released her. "Not right now. I need to go for a swim." Kicking off his boots, he rose and discarded his shirt and guns. "I won't be long."

She watched his graceful movements as he strode to

the water's edge, removed his britches, and dove in. He was so beautiful, she almost wished his prophecy would come true.

Almost.

Rising into a sitting position, she marveled at the way he cut across the surface in powerful strokes, then disappeared under water, only to reappear in another spot. He made swimming seem so easy. He made her wish she wasn't such a coward.

She watched for a few more minutes, then started to lie down again when she saw him go under. Smiling and shaking her head, she scanned the water to see where he would surface next.

Several seconds passed, and there was no sign of him.

She stood, a trickle of fear twisting through her middle. Her gaze swept the water again.

No sign of him.

Holding onto her escalating concern, she hurried toward the beach.

Sunlight glinted on the lazy waves.

"Char? Damn it, Char. Come out of there."

Nothing.

"This isn't funny."

The squawk of a gull was the only sound on the deserted shore.

Terror tightened her muscles. Oh, God. *Oh, God.* Blindly, she stumbled into the water. "Char!" She swung from side to side, searching for him. She pressed farther, deeper. Water lapped at her breasts, her chin. *"Char."*

He shot up in front of her, gasping and coughing. "Jesus, woman. I thought I was going to drown before you came in after me."

"What? You mean you scared the daylights out of me on *purpose?*"

He grinned. "I wanted you to go swimming with me."

"You swine!" She swung her fist at his nose.

He ducked and caught her hands, holding them behind her back. "You don't have to get so riled."

She tried to kick him, but between the weight of her skirt and the water it was futile. "Let go of me. You've had your fun, now take me back to town."

"Let me teach you to swim."

"No."

He pressed his naked length against her front and nibbled her ear. "You'll like it."

"No."

He brushed his lips along the side of her neck and over her jaw, then up to the corner of her mouth. "You'll love the sensation of gliding through the water without your clothes."

She swallowed. "No."

"Yes." He lifted her and started walking—away from the shore.

"Char, don't!"

He didn't slow until the water touched his chin and was over her head. "I'm gonna let go of your arms, darlin', and you can either hold onto me or sink." With no further warning, he released her.

She grabbed for his shoulders as her face went under. Sputtering and cursing, she wrapped her arms around his neck. "That wasn't funny, damn you!" She wanted to claw his laughing eyes, but she was too afraid to let go.

"I'm not trying to be funny. I'm trying to teach you something that might one day save your life."

She knew his intentions were good, but the terror was too great. If he didn't take her to shore soon, she was going to become hysterical. "Please. I-I want to go to the b-beach."

Either her words or the shivers racing through her limbs must have convinced him, because he carried her to the sand.

When her feet touched the ground, her legs almost buckled with relief. It took a minute to right herself, then she swung on him, ready to let him have it.

He pulled her to him and kissed her soundly. "Truce, darlin'."

The way he was grinning at her made her go soft, and she couldn't stay mad at him. "Very well. But don't try that again." Whirling around, she stalked to the quilt and plopped down, not caring if she got the thing as wet as she was.

He slipped on his britches and joined her. "Want some wine?"

Remembering what happened the last time she drank spirits, she cringed. "About as much as I do a case of dysentery."

He threw his head back and laughed, a deep, rich sound that glided over her like a warm hand. She willed the erotic thought away. "So, what shall we do to pass the time?"

"I can think of a few things." A devilish gleam sparkled in his eyes. "Like . . . fishing." He sprang to his feet. "Come on, maybe we'll catch one big enough for supper."

"I told you, I don't like fishing."

He stared down at her. "We could make love."

Clenching her teeth against the leap in her pulse, she climbed to her feet. "Fishing is fine."

When he baited the hook and threw the line in the water, he handed her the pole. "You go first. Here, sit. Sometimes it takes a while." He folded his legs and sat down, then patted the sand beside him.

Holding onto the bamboo with both hands, she did as he suggested. She kept her eyes on the water, waiting . . . for what? She didn't know exactly, but several minutes passed and nothing unusual happened.

Suddenly, the pole was almost jerked from her hand. "Oh!" She tightened her fingers around the dancing bamboo. "I've got something!"

He was behind her in an instant, his arms around her, his hands covering hers. "Stand up. That's it. Now walk backward. Not too fast. Easy. Pull him onto the sand."

His closeness was making her heart beat so fast, she could hardly take a step. But she did. One at a time.

The line jerked and twisted.

"Hold on. Don't let him get loose. Look. There it is!"

She gaped at the long, squirming streak of silver flapping on the sand. "Good heavens."

"I'll get him. You hang onto the pole." Char sprinted toward the water. A moment later, he returned carrying the biggest fish she'd ever seen.

"What kind is it?" she asked, unable to keep the awe out of her voice.

"A small black-tip shark."

"Small?" He was enormous.

"Yes, darlin', small. These things grow to be almost as long as you are tall."

"No kidding?" Her blood started pumping, and she

darted a glance over the water. "Do you think there's more out there?"

"Without a doubt. But let me get some bait on your hook."

By the time the sun set, she had caught three more sharks, even one called a leopard shark, a sea bass, and a starfish.

Char let the starfish and all but the bass go. That he cooked for their supper.

"That was wonderful," she praised as she popped the last flaky white piece into her mouth and wiped her fingers on the hem of her skirt.

Lying on his side near the fire, Char braced his head on his hand. "I think I've created a monster."

"Very possibly," she agreed without shame. She'd loved fishing . . . as long as she hadn't had to touch anything slimy. "In fact, I can't wait until tomorrow to try it again."

"Tomorrow?" He gave her a slow, very male smile. "Darlin', that's a long way off." His gaze slid into hers. "A very long way."

CHAPTER

❧ 15 ❧

Their eyes held, and she felt her pulse drum through her temples. Unbidden images of that night on the trail came to her. She remembered the heat of his mouth . . . his hands.

Her belly fluttered.

He rose and extended his palm to her. "Come here, Jesse. I want to show you something."

Every moral she possessed screamed at her to run, but it was no use. Her body had severed ties with her brain. She wanted to go with him. Anywhere. She took his hand and followed him to the edge of the water.

"I want you to go in with me. Not too deep. Just enough to feel the current touch you the way I want to."

Her chest tightened. "I can't."

"Shh." He placed a finger to her lips. "Yes, you can." He lowered his hands to the bottom of her blouse and lifted it over her head.

She trembled when a breeze touched her bare skin.

"Don't be afraid, darlin'. I'm not gonna let anything happen to you." He undid the ties on her skirt, then slid it down her hips and let it fall to her feet.

Moonlight bathed the tense lines of his face as he explored her naked body, but she felt no shame. She burned with a need for something she didn't understand. Something she knew only Char could give her.

His eyes on hers, he undid his britches and pulled them off, then stood proudly before her, giving her time to study him as he had her.

There weren't enough words to describe how splendid he was. She'd seen him naked before, but she hadn't seen him this close, this aroused. He was superb. The need in her expanded.

Without speaking, as if he were afraid to break the tenuous spell between them, he led her into the warm, swirling water.

Foamy bubbles lapped at her ankles, her calves, her knees. She tightened her fingers on his, wavering between fear and excitement.

He took her deeper, and water glided over her thighs, her bottom . . . between her legs.

She tensed.

"Close your eyes. Let the water embrace you. Let it make love to you."

His words were as erotic as the sensations. Lowering her lashes, she bit her lip as the sea snaked its way through her curls, up her belly, around her waist. A warmth spread outward from the pit of her stomach.

"Just a little farther, darlin'." He put his hands on her waist and guided her forward, his thumbs stroking her sides as he backed up, leading her step by step.

The sea swirled around her middle like a soft hand, then rose to caress the undersides of her breasts. Her nipples.

She sucked in a sharp breath.

"Don't fight it," Char's soothing voice whispered around her. "Feel its power, its raw passion." His fingers tightened on her waist. "Let the water love you like I'm going to."

Carnal images danced through her head, and she felt as if she were floating outside herself. She arched her spine, allowing the current to seduce her. Like a greedy lover, it lapped at her breasts . . . slid smoothly between her thighs. Water touched the back of her head, but she didn't care. Nothing mattered but the glorious sensations, the beauty.

Through a daze, she felt Char pull her into his arms, his lips brushing her ear. "It's my turn, darlin'." His hands were as fluid as the ocean as they moved over her bottom and sides, her belly, her middle. Long, liquid fingers flowed down her throat and shoulders and the length of her arms, then rose again to trickle over her spine.

The sea joined his caresses. They were both making love to her.

His fingers grazed the tips of her breasts. "Tell me what you're feeling." He circled the peaks with his thumbs. "Tell me what my touch does to you."

It was hard to find her voice. "You m-make me feel dizzy and w-weak."

He trailed his lips along her neck to her ear. "You make me burn." He sought her mouth and took it, his hands alive as they glided over her bare skin beneath the water.

Their chests touched, their stomachs, their thighs.

His power pulsed against her woman's place, then pressed between her legs, gliding back and forth as the current rocked them. Their flesh met again and again. Waves of need engulfed her.

His tongue penetrated her mouth, filling her, loving her, taking her beyond the edge of reality.

She was distantly aware of him carrying her to the blanket, of his fingers unbraiding her hair and spreading it around her shoulders.

Then he was gone.

She opened her eyes to find him kneeling between her legs, staring at her. He held her gaze as he slid his palms up the front of her thighs, his thumbs brushing the tender inner flesh, brushing her feminine curls.

She had to force herself to breathe. Her lungs were full enough to explode. But he didn't release his hold on her gaze as his hands crept higher, covering her breasts. It was too much, the sensations, the need, the hot desire in his eyes. She lowered her lashes.

"No, Jesse. Look at me. I want to know what my touch does to you."

Helplessly, her gaze clung to his.

He brushed his thumbs over her nipples, then circled the sensitive peaks, rolling them into hard pebbles. Her lungs constricted. Her eyes widened.

His darkened.

He traced her sides with his fingertips, then her belly . . . and lower. He watched her face with feral intensity as he eased his fingers into her curls.

Her spine arched at the stab of pleasure. Her breath stopped. She tried to pull her gaze from his, but he refused to release it. *Oh, God. What was he doing to her?*

With aching slowness, his eyes probing hers, he

parted her folds and massaged the tiny nub they shielded.

A deep, shuddering moan climbed her throat. Her vision blurred. His features wavered, then dimmed.

Through the blessed dark, she felt him slide down beside her, felt him trace her lips with his own. He kissed her, long and deep, intimately exploring her mouth while his hand continued to stroke her.

She absorbed the exquisite craving that rushed through her body, whimpering as his mouth covered her breast, so hot, so moist, so achingly gentle. He caressed her with his tongue, suckled with tenderness, grazed her with his smooth teeth.

Her stomach clenched, and her breath came in short pants.

He kissed his way down her stomach, then the hand between her thighs disappeared and his tongue took its place.

"Oh, *God,*" she cried, bucking at the sharp burst of pleasure.

He covered her completely, tormenting her with tiny jabs, then slow, lazy strokes. He cupped her bottom and lifted her closer, his mouth ravenous as he feasted on her.

Her entire world centered on his movements, on the heat, on pressure building and building. She thrust against his tongue.

He quickened the pace.

She dug her fingers into his hair, her spine drawn into a bow. She was going to die!

He moved lower and plunged into her.

She exploded in a burst of sweet, hot pain so intense, every cell in her body shattered. Convulsions of pleasure shook her. An animal-like cry tore from her throat, then turned into a low, growling moan.

When she was sure she'd drawn her last breath, the spasms began to soften, to release their mindless hold and ease her back to earth.

She became aware of the summer breeze, of the light flutter of leaves, of the gentle slap of waves . . . of Char watching her. "You were magnificent, Jesse. Beautifully, wonderfully magnificent."

Embarrassment burned her cheeks. "I was out of my mind."

He gave her a slow smile. "I know."

She closed her eyes. The man was heartless. But even with her lashes lowered, she couldn't erase the powerful image of his naked body, of the impressive size of his arousal, of the lines of strain in that handsome face. He needed her in the same way she'd needed him.

In that instant, she knew she had fallen in love with him, and she knew she would give him what he needed. She could never give herself to anyone but him. She met his gaze. "I want to feel you inside me."

A tremor ran through him. "Jesus. You take my breath away." He moved over her and kissed her with aching tenderness, his tongue slow and gentle as it stroked hers.

Their stomachs touched, and she felt the weight of his manhood nudge her thigh, then part them. He eased into her the tiniest bit and paused.

Slipping a hand under her hips, he raised her to receive him. His kiss became urgent, almost frantic, his body tight. "I can't wait any longer, Jesse. I can't—" He thrust into her.

A flash of pain caught her by surprise, and she stiffened.

He stilled, his body shaking, but he didn't withdraw. He was giving her time to relax so it wouldn't hurt so bad.

Tenderness welled in her at his thoughtfulness, and she willed her muscles to loosen.

He eased deeper.

The hurt was gone.

He kissed her mouth, her jaw, her ear. "Can you feel me inside you? Can you feel how much I want you?"

Oh, yes. She lifted her hips, pressing closer, answering him without words.

"Don't," he said in a thick voice. "Not yet. Not until we're both there." He remained motionless for several seconds, then released a heavy breath. Slowly, he began to move.

Heat rushed through her veins and centered where their bodies joined. With each long, deep stroke, her senses churned and tightened.

He drew his hand along her thigh. "Wrap your legs around my waist."

She sought his lips and clung to his neck as her legs encircled him. His tongue plunged into her mouth, matching the rhythm of his body. Their breaths became one. Their flesh. Their souls.

He held her head, kissing her fiercely as his body met hers again and again.

She could feel the pressure building again, and she arched higher, reaching for it.

He drove into her. Harder. Faster. Twisting, plunging, taking her up and up.

She exploded into a million tiny shards of pulsating pleasure.

He absorbed her moans with his mouth, shuddering as he found his own soul-shattering pinnacle. Then he slumped and moved to the side, taking her with him, holding her joined to him, so close, she felt as if they were one.

For several seconds, neither of them moved. The sound of their labored breathing filled the warm air, and during those peaceful moments, she knew why Fanny had always smiled after a night with Jessalea's uncle.

Her own smile widened as she snuggled closer to Char. "I don't know which was more erotic, you or the ocean."

He caressed her side and hip as he turned his mouth to her ear. "Maybe we should try it again, and find out."

And they did. Several times.

The next day was the most enchanting, wonderful day in Jessalea's life. They fished, ran from crabs, ate, laughed, and drank wine—very conservatively. They collected seashells, fashioned crowns out of tree branches, chased each other over the dunes, and made love in the soft grass, then again by the light of the fire, and late into the night.

It was a magical day she would carry with her always.

The next morning, she felt the sun warm her cheeks a second before something moist and gentle brushed her lips. She smiled and opened her eyes to see Char bending over her, his eyes soft, his hair tumbled from sleep.

He gave her a lazy grin that melted her heart. "I love waking up next to you."

"You probably say that to every one of your bed partners," she teased, looping her arms around his neck and pulling him down for a kiss.

He chuckled against her lips. "No. Just to the ones who catch sharks."

"How many has that been?"

"Counting all of them?" He nuzzled her ear. "One."

She lost track of the conversation when his lips nibbled their way to her breasts . . . and lower. There wasn't an inch of her body he didn't know intimately by now.

When she opened her eyes again, the sun was high, and Char was dressed, standing at the water's edge, watching something.

Dragging herself into a sitting position, she yawned and brushed the hair from her eyes. Her gaze skimmed the miles of blue, trying to see what he was staring at, but there wasn't anything there.

Relaxing on her elbows, she shook her head. Maybe he was watching for shark—*She didn't see anything.* She jerked upright. The boat was gone!

Scrambling to her feet, ignoring the fact that she was completely naked, she raced to the beach. "Where is it? What happened?"

He didn't face her. He kept his gaze fixed on the ocean. "The boat was gone when I woke up. It must have broken loose during the night."

"You mean we're stranded?"

"For a while."

"But I have to get back. Boggs—"

"Will still be there."

She knew he was right, but somehow it felt wrong. She had veered from her purpose because of Char. Not that she had any regrets on that score. She didn't. But she felt as if she'd betrayed her family.

What was she supposed to have done? she mentally defended. Sat around the hotel for two days, waiting? Watched Char face another gunman? No. She didn't regret coming to the island, but she certainly didn't want to stay there.

As the day progressed, the anger at herself, at her disregard for what mattered most in her life, gnawed at her. Almost as much as the knowledge that Char was avoiding her. He became distant and withdrawn. Uneasy. Several times, he did start to say something, but stopped. She wanted to shake him and demand he tell her what was wrong. Demand he explain his aloofness, when only hours ago they'd been so close.

Determined to do exactly that, she marched over to where he stood and tapped him on the shoulder.

He didn't turn. "What?"

"I think it's time we talk."

"I'm listening."

"No, you're not. You've ignored me since we . . . since you found the boat gone. Now, I want to know why?"

"Why the boat was gone? Or why you think I've been ignoring you."

She clenched her fists. "I'm serious, damn you."

He whirled on her, his eyes bright silver. "What do you want me to say? That I'm feeling guilty as hell because . . . of what happened? Well, you'll be happy to know I am. I'm eaten alive with guilt over this whole miserable trip."

Jessalea felt the blood leave her face. He felt guilty

about making love to her? Anger made her shiver. "I feel guilty, too, Char. I shouldn't have allowed *any* of this to happen." In exasperation, she gathered her skirt and planted herself on a grassy knoll. He continued to stand at the edge of the water with his back to her, his feet spread, and his arms crossed. Sunlight glinted off the pearl handles of the six-shooters draping his hips.

She folded her arms on her upraised knees and rested her chin on her forearms, wishing she'd never taken her mind off her objective. Fanny had always told her; "When you've got something to do, just do it and get it over with. Don't put it off, don't dally, and don't get sidetracked."

"Someone's coming," Char announced.

Startled, she glanced up to find him towering over her, his face drawn and hard. "There's a boat headed this way."

"There is? *There is.*" She sprang to her feet and anxiously scanned the water.

A lone man rowed toward them.

Without another word, Char strode down the hill. She hurried after him.

"Howdy, folks," a smiling man greeted as he climbed out. "Sheriff just told me there was some folks stranded out here, so I come to help."

Jessalea gaped at him in surprise. "The sheriff knew we were missing?"

"Yes, 'um."

"But how did he—"

"Jesse," Char interrupted. "We'll talk about it later. Right now, we need to load our gear."

As much as it galled her, she knew he was right. She hurried to gather their things.

In the boat, the seaman and Char spoke low between themselves as they took turns rowing, leaving no opportunity for her to speak.

Her thoughts turned toward Harley Boggs. Again and again, she saw him rutting over her sister, holding her hands pinned above her head as she screamed in pain and terror. Again and again, she watched him raise his knife and plunge it into Susannah's chest.

By the time they reached the docks, Jessalea was shaking. She swept the area with a critical eye, but saw no sign of Boggs. Figuring they must be early, she was only distantly aware of Char helping her from the boat or their walk to the hotel.

Once inside the room, she changed into her britches, her fingers numb as she buttoned her shirt. Settling her gun belt on her hips, she checked the revolver's chamber to make sure it was full, then shoved her hair under her hat and headed for the docks to wait.

As she stepped into the hall, she almost bumped into Char. He'd been standing by her door. Well, if he thought he was going to stop her . . .

"It's too late," he said in a quiet voice. "Darcy arrested him an hour ago. He knows who you are, and that Boggs was one of the men who killed your family."

"But how—"

"He was at your farm right after it happened."

"But—" It hit her. With blinding clarity, she knew what they'd done. He and the marshal had set her up. Kept her away so Blake could take care of Boggs. "You bastard." She lunged at him, hitting him anywhere she could reach. "You planned this. All of it! You rotten, no-good—"

He didn't try to stop her attack, and when he spoke, his voice was raw with grief. "No, darlin'. I didn't plan to make love to you."

"Liar." Blinded by crushing pain, she whipped her gun from its holster and aimed it straight at his black heart, her hand trembling with anger and betrayal. "I should kill you for what you've done to me."

"Go ahead, Jesse. Maybe it'll make us both stop hurting."

Her hand shook with the urge to pull the trigger. But she couldn't do it. Damn it, she *couldn't*. She fought tears as she stared him straight in the eye. "I hate you, Char Daniels."

"I know," he said in a soft, strained voice.

Fearing she would start crying, she stumbled into her room. Tears blurred her vision as she gathered her things and hastily shoved them into her saddlebags. She was angry and hurt, and she felt betrayed. Still, even through the pain, she knew this wasn't the end of it. Char would try to follow her to Houston.

But this time, she'd outsmart him.

CHAPTER

❋ 16 ❋

Jessalea didn't know when she planned to leave for Houston, but she knew it wouldn't be until she saw Harley Boggs in his grave.

Dropping her saddlebags off at the stables, she headed for the sheriff's office.

Marshal Darcy, a balding man wearing a tin star, and four other men were checking their weapons and loading rifles. "Walt, strap the supplies to the packhorse. Henry, you make sure the canteens are full."

A tall, slim man the sheriff had called Walt, hurried past her. A well-built, older man followed.

"What's going on?" Jessalea directed her question to Blake.

"Sheriff Barker received a wire a few minutes ago. John Wesley Hardin was seen in San Pedro, not far from here, but the sheriff over there doesn't have the manpower to go after him. We're going to try to head him off."

"What about Boggs?"

"He's not going anywhere. He'll stay in the cell

until the circuit judge gets here next week. Deputy Michaels"—he gestured to a young man standing beside the sheriff's desk—"will guard him until then, or until we return."

Jessalea glanced at a door centering the rear wall, the door that led to the cells. "I want to see him."

"I don't think that's such a good—"

She wasn't in the mood to listen. "I'm going to see him, Blake. Right now." Stepping around him, she marched into the rear room.

Darcy was right behind her.

Harley Boggs stood at a small, barred window, watching the street. He had changed in the last ten years, but not so much that she couldn't recognize him. The fat jowls, scarred nose, and small, glassy eyes were the same. He turned as she approached the bars.

"Who the hell are you?"

Jessalea took fierce pleasure in removing her hat and allowing her hair to fall free. "Don't you recognize me, Boggs?"

His mud brown eyes widened in surprise at her gender, then squinted as he licked his thick lips. "You look familiar, sure enough, gal, but I can't place you."

She rested her hand on the butt of her gun. "You don't remember the seven-year-old child you urged Odie to kill?" Her fingers closed around the handle of her gun. "Or the young girl you stabbed to death after you and Hank . . ." She swallowed a rush of nausea. Her hand shook.

Boggs pressed himself to the log wall and darted a wild glance at Darcy. "What's she talking about?"

"The Richardsons' farm."

Boggs's frightened gaze flew to her. His throat worked with fear. He recognized her at last.

Blake stepped closer.

She ignored him and drew her gun. "I'm going to enjoy watching you bleed to death, Harley, the same way you watched my sister." Her finger tightened on the trigger. "Then I'm going after the rest of your brothers."

"It was you," Boggs warbled. "You gunned down my—"

"Yes. I killed Patrick and Davidson," she admitted. "I'm going to kill you, too. Make no mistake about that." She gave him a cold smile and aimed the pistol.

Blake's hand shot out and covered hers, lowering the weapon. "No, honey. Not like this."

"Let go."

He pried the Colt from her stiff fingers and returned it to her holster. "Don't put any more heartache on yourself, Jessalea. Boggs will get his due soon enough, and you'll be right there to watch."

"I want to watch now," she hissed, her gaze raking Boggs with hatred.

Blake captured her hands to keep her from going for her gun again. "Come on. Staying in here is only making it worse." He ushered her into the main room, where the sheriff and his men waited for Darcy.

Blake nodded to the young deputy. "Michaels, I want you to take a good look at this lady and remember that she's not allowed anywhere near Boggs. Is that clear?"

Jessalea jerked her hands free of Darcy's. "Damn you." Slamming out the front door, she headed for the stables to retrieve her saddlebags. She wasn't leaving Corpus Christi until Boggs was dead. But she wasn't about to return to the hotel where Char stayed, either. She'd find another one—at the opposite end of town.

Char felt as if someone had cut his heart into pieces as he walked toward the sheriff's office and found Blake Darcy and several others mounting their horses.

"Boggs is in there," Darcy said, nodding toward the jail. "He'll stay there till he hangs—if you can keep a certain hotheaded female away from him."

"That *certain female* is angry enough to blow a hole in me. Where are you going?"

"John Wesley Hardin was seen not far from here."

"I thought he was supposed to be hiding somewhere in Alabama."

"So did I, but apparently, that isn't the case. Anyway, we should return about the same time the circuit judge arrives."

"When's that?"

"A few days," the sheriff answered. "Got a message from him yesterday."

Char met Darcy's eyes. "If the circuit judge gets here before you, and we miss you, we'll be on our way to Houston." With a nod, he turned to leave.

"Wait," Darcy ordered.

"What?"

"How do you feel about becoming a deputy marshal?"

Jessalea checked into a boarding house on Peoples Street not far from city hall. It wasn't the opposite end of town from Char, like she'd wanted. In fact, only a couple of blocks separated them, but she hoped it would be enough.

Her insides felt hollow as she lay on the bed and stared at the timeworn ceiling. She was torn over her feelings for Char. On one hand, she knew he'd taken her to the island to protect her, to keep her from confronting Harley Boggs and possibly getting herself killed. But, on the other, he'd betrayed her. He'd taken her virginity under the guise of chivalry.

"Damn you," she whispered. "Why did you have to take it that far? Why did you make me fall in love with you?"

A tear slipped from the corners of her eyes, and she angrily brushed it away. She *would not* cry over him.

She went to the washbasin and splashed water on her face, then combed her hair and braided it, determined not to sulk for the rest of the night.

Having missed the evening meal served at the boarding house, she shoved her hair under her flop-billed hat and headed for an eating house she'd seen on the next block. She felt no remorse about using Char's money, either. She'd repay him as soon as she was settled.

After a filling supper of beans and ham hocks, with fried potatoes, corn bread, and mustard greens, she rose to pay the bill.

Late afternoon sunlight burst into the room as the front door flew open, and a winded boy rushed in. "Doc, we need you!"

An older man rose from a table at the rear of the room. "What is it, Luke? What's happened?"

"Jailbreak! Deputy Michaels is hurt. You gotta come quick."

Jessalea's blood went cold. Boggs! Tossing the bill and money on the counter, she ran after the doctor and the boy.

When she reached the sheriff's office, the deputy was sitting up, holding his bleeding head, but he was coherent.

"How'd it happen?" she demanded.

The deputy eyed her warily. "It was my fault. I let a gal come in here carrying a tray for Boggs and didn't go into the rear with her to deliver it. I was so interested in the book I was reading . . ." He shrugged. "Next thing I knew, I was on the floor with a throbbing headache."

"Looks like you were hit from behind," the doctor concluded.

"I'm gonna get his ma," the winded boy blurted, then dashed through the door.

Jessalea was too furious to even speak. Boggs had escaped, and she'd bet money he was headed for Houston or Shreveport.

It took her less than fifteen minutes to gather her things from the boarding house and saddle her horse.

The anger and heaviness in her chest made it hard to breathe. She clenched her hands around the pommel and focused on the dying sunlight and miles of dry grass ahead of her. Everything Char had done had been for nothing.

She rode by the light of the moon for several hours, then guiding her horse around a cluster of cactus, she scanned the area for a place to make camp. She spotted a stand of pecan trees not far ahead.

She started for them, but reined in abruptly, furious at herself for remembering Char's teachings, and headed toward the miles of open range.

In the tall grass, she dragged her saddle off the gelding and hobbled him, then sank down into her bedroll and braced her head against her saddle. The uncomfortable position reminded her of the satin pillow Char had bought for her. The pillow she'd left behind.

She twisted to a different position. It didn't matter. She wouldn't have used it anyway. She didn't want anything he'd given her.

She wished she'd never see him again, but that wasn't going to happen. She knew Char. He was bullheaded enough to come after her. But this time would be the last. She knew what she had to do to keep him from following her. After that, she'd focus only on Boggs.

Closing her eyes, she listened to the rustle of grass in the light wind, the hoot of a distant owl, the soft nicker of her horse. . . .

"Pass me the spuds, little red," Jessalea heard Harley say to Susannah. His squinty eyes were fastened on her bosom. He licked his lips and gave her a jagged-toothed smile, scrunching up his scarred nose. "A man like me packs a powerful hunger."

Susannah was nervous when she handed him the bowl and almost dropped it when his fat fingers closed over hers.

Jessalea saw satisfied smirks pass between the six strangers seated at the table—the men who had identified themselves as the Boggs brothers, "home guards" for the area. Men who were supposed to protect decent folks from outlaws and thieving stragglers left over from the war . . . or so they were told.

"You got room in the barn for us tonight?" the one

called Odie asked. He was the oldest, and the ugliest with his fat jowls and bushy, muttonchop sideburns. He had cold eyes, the coldest she'd ever seen, and his smile was downright scary.

"I'm sure we'll make room," her pa answered. It was easy to see that he was anxious to get them out of the house.

"Then why don't you go along, dear," Mama encouraged Papa. "The girls and I will clear the table."

All the men filed out, with her young brother, James, on their heels.

Mama moved to the sideboard and began pumping water into a pan for heating.

A scream split the afternoon air.

Mama's gaze flew to the window. "Oh, dear God."

"What is it?" Susannah asked as she looked up from wiping the table.

"Run!" Mama yelled, diving for Pa's rifle mounted above the fireplace.

She never made it. One of the strangers burst through the door and tackled her to the floor.

Another plowed into Susannah.

Run! her ma had said. Jessalea bolted for the door. "Pa! Help!" She hit the dirt at a dead run—but came to a skidding halt when she heard her little brother's terrified cry.

In frozen horror, she watched Cecil Boggs ride his horse around in circles, dragging James on the ground behind him. Her brother fought the ropes tied around his wrists, binding him to the horse. He kicked and screamed, clawing at the dirt.

"Come on, Cecil," one of the others yelled. "Stop messin' with that kid and help us."

"Be right there, Odie." Cecil Boggs whirled his horse around and reared it up over James's small body. The powerful hooves came down with killing force.

Her brother's screams fell silent.

"No!" Jessalea cried, running, trying to reach James. Someone grabbed her.

"Lookee here what I got, Odie." The man lifted her into the air like a prize. "A pint-size redhead."

Jessalea kicked and scratched. "Pa! Pa, help me!"

Patrick Boggs tightened his hold on her and gave a harsh chuckle. "He cain't even help hisself, brat, much less you." He snagged the back of her hair and forced her to look toward the old elm outside her bedroom window.

Terror exploded through her body. Odie Boggs was holding her squirming pa up in the air by his legs— and there was a rope around his neck. The other end had been looped over a branch of the tree and was held by Davidson Boggs. "No! Oh, please. Let him go!"

Odie turned his head. "Let him go?" He gave her a cruel smile. "Okay." He jerked his hands away from her father's legs and stepped back.

Horror-struck, she watched her father's body drop. The rope tightened around his neck. Her pa kicked and twisted, his mouth open, his spine bowing as he fought death.

"Pa!" she screamed. She clawed at the hands holding her, trying to get to him, to save him, but Patrick Boggs held on, held her hair in his grip, forcing her to watch until the end.

When it was over, she didn't know how long she stared unseeing, but she was too numb to resist when someone dragged her into the house and shoved her in a corner next to the fireplace. Through a fog, she saw what the men did to her ma and sister, taking turns, over and over again.

Unable to move, she watched Harley Boggs sink his knife into Susannah's heart. She watched Hank Boggs cut off her sister's breast.

In a distance, she heard Harley ask, "What'd you go and do that for?" He stared at Hank, at the bloody flesh he'd cut from Susannah's chest and now held in his hand.

"Gonna tan it like leather and make a tobacco pouch out of it. I seen a trapper once who had a squaw's tit done like that, and I always wanted one. 'Sides, out on the trail, when I get lonely, I'll have me somethin' to play with." Grinning, he flicked the lifeless nipple. "Why don't you get the other one to keep you company?"

Odie Boggs rose from her mother's bloody body and tucked a handful of her beautiful red hair into his vest pocket. "You two quit jawin' and gather some food. Pat, you get the farmer's horse."

Jessalea stared at the man she hated above all the others—the one who had killed her parents—the one who's face she would memorize.

"You gotta kill the kid, too, you know?" Harley said, his glassy eyes on her. "We've cain't afford to leave no witnesses now. Just a couple more raids, and we'll have enough money to start over in Texas."

Jessalea watched Odie Boggs as his gaze drifted to her. She wanted to live long enough to see him die.

Their eyes met and held—and he knew her thoughts as if she'd said them aloud.

With a shake of his head, he drew his pistol, aimed for her heart . . . and fired.

* * *

A sound startled her, and her eyes flew open. Pitch-black surrounded her. But she knew she'd heard a footstep. The nightmare merged into reality. They were coming for her.

Horrified, she huddled against her saddle and drew her knees up to her chin, her body shaking, her chest filled with terror. *Not again. Oh, please, God. Not again.*

CHAPTER

❊ 17 ❊

Carrying a lantern, Char wove his way through the grass looking for Jesse. He'd followed her tracks, and spotted her horse, but he couldn't see her for the shoulder-high blades.

A whimper startled him. It sounded like the cry of a small child.

His worse fears rose like demons. Had Harley Boggs found her? Hurt her? Uneasy, he drew his gun and walked closer, moving the lantern from side to side. When he spotted Jesse, he almost dropped it. She was pressed to her saddle, her eyes glazed, her body shaking. Her cheeks were wet with tears. But she wasn't injured.

"What's wrong?" He held the lantern higher, searching the area.

There was nothing but grass. No footprints. Nothing.

Still, her eyes remained fixed on something only she could see.

He holstered his Colt and knelt in front of her.

"Jesse? Can you hear me?" Concern caused his hand to shake as he touched her cheek.

"No! Oh, please, God. No."

"Jesse." He caught her shoulders and gave her a shake. "Damn it. What's wrong?"

Blinking, she stared straight at him. "Char? Oh, *Char.*" She flung her arms around his neck, pressed as close to him as she could get. "I knew you'd come."

She had him spinning around in circles. "Jesus, woman. You almost scared the pants off me. What happened?"

Burying her face in his neck, she shivered. "I was dreaming . . . about that day on the farm."

He released a breath, thankful that Harley Boggs hadn't caused her scare, and closed his arms around her. "That must have been hell."

As if she realized who held her, she stiffened. "Get your hands off me, Daniels."

He knew he should let her go, but he had to make her listen to him first. "I didn't plan to make love to you. I swear it."

"Of course not."

He grabbed her shoulders, wanting to shake the daylights out of her. "Will you think about it? Why would I use lovemaking to restrain you? For Christ's sake, I'm twice your size. I could have kept you there by force. I didn't have to *seduce* you."

She glared at him. "But it was so much easier, wasn't it?"

He was fast losing his temper. "Think anything about me you like, woman. But never, *ever* think I made love to you for any reason other than because I wanted you. I'm in love with you, Jesse, and what we shared was an extension of that emotion."

She was staring at him. "Do you really expect me to believe that? Well, I've got news for you, Char Daniels, I wasn't raised by wolves. I know exactly what you did and why. You had a mission and you accomplished it. There wasn't anything akin to *love* involved."

"You're right. I'm not capable of loving a woman so much I can't keep my hands off her." He jerked her against him. "But I can damn sure fake it." He took her mouth with barely restrained violence, wanting to hurt her as much as she was hurting him.

She didn't fight him. Nor did she respond.

Frustrated, he shoved away from her and rose, lacing his fingers through his hair. "I'm sorry. That was uncalled for. Sometimes, you make me so crazy, I don't know what to do. But I do know I'll die before I let anyone hurt you."

"You hurt me."

"I wish I knew how to make it right."

She caught his hand and pulled him down to her, placing his palm over her breast. "You could try."

He stared at her in shock. She'd done it again. Change on him. Gone from hellion to seductress. The damned woman was tying him in knots. "Jesse—"

"Shh." She pressed her mouth to his. "Love me, Char."

There was nothing he wanted more. But something wasn't right. He wasn't sure what, but *something*. With caution, he closed his hand around her breast, marveling at the firm fullness filling his palm . . . and waiting for—what? "Are you sure this is what you want?"

"Very."

190

His blood picked up speed as he studied her lovely face in the moonlight. Then, with a groan, he pressed his lips to her throat. "I may end up in a madhouse over this, but, darlin', you're worth it."

She pulled his mouth to hers and thrust her tongue between his teeth.

He lost himself in the sweet kiss. Then it was his turn. He eased her to the ground and buried his mouth in hers. It wasn't enough. He wanted all of her. He trailed his tongue down the smooth column of her throat. "You're skin is so soft it reminds me of fresh churned butter." He dipped his head lower, nibbling her sweet flesh, then nudging aside the shirt to expose her breast. "It tastes as good, too." He drew her nipple into his mouth.

The breath rushed from her lungs.

His own became strained. He circled the stiff peak with his tongue. He suckled it, reveling in the tremors that passed through her.

He kissed his way to her mouth again, then lowered his hips over hers, nestling himself to her woman's mound. Flames of desire spiraled through him, and he deepened the kiss. He thrust his lower body against her, his need so great, he thought he'd burst. Jesus, had it only been this morning they made love?

He rolled onto his back, pulling her on top of him. "Take off your clothes, darlin'. I need to feel your bare skin next to mine."

Her eyes on his, she rose and let the open shirt fall from her shoulders.

Char stopped breathing. He would never get used to her beauty.

She undid the buttons on her pants and slid them

down, then kicked them aside. She stood before him, gloriously naked, her gaze on his britches. "What about yours?"

"You take them off."

With a purely female smile, she knelt between his legs and removed his boots and pants. For several seconds, she studied the evidence of his desire. "Very impressive."

He pulled her over him. "Witch." He plundered her mouth, his hands gliding over her soft curves. He lifted her so he could capture a nipple with his mouth.

She braced her hands on either side of his head on the ground, arching her chest forward to offer him more.

He wasn't sure what game she was playing but it didn't matter. Greedily, he nursed one peak, then the other, while his hands sought the valley between her thighs. She was so warm, so damned tight.

She thrust against his hand.

Blood rushed to his shaft, and he knew if he didn't get inside her soon he was going to disgrace himself. He raised her until she straddled his hips. "Ride me, darlin'."

Her eyes widened, then darkened with understanding. Slowly, tauntingly, she sank over him.

For one awful second, he feared he would spill his seed. He had to take several deep breaths to regain control. When he at last felt the pressure ease, he slid his hands up her stomach and over her breasts. "Move slow, *very* slow. Ah, God. Yes. That's it."

She was so moist, so tight, he didn't think he was going to last much longer. Urgently, he encircled her upper thighs, and found her pleasure point with his thumbs.

She tightened around him, and her head fell back as he brought her to the edge of release. His own body cried out for the same. He thrust upward, grinding into her, increasing the rhythm, bucking and twisting as he sought the ultimate pinnacle. He felt her stiffen, a second before he erupted in a firestorm of white-hot pleasure.

Several breath-stealing moments later, he floated to earth and noticed Jesse had slumped over him, her breathing harsh against his chest.

He couldn't stop a smile of masculine satisfaction as he caressed her sweet backside. "I love you, Jesse." He wasn't sure, but he could have sworn he felt her tense.

But the smile on her face belied the notion. "I'd say the same, but if I don't get off you right this minute and answer nature's call, we're both going to be sorry."

He patted her rear. "Then, by all means, hurry."

She scrambled to her feet and grabbed her clothes, then disappeared into the tall grass.

"You won't be needing those," he declared with a grin. Folding his hands behind his head, he stared at the night sky, enjoying visions of making love to Jesse every night for the rest of his life, of waking next to her every morning. He wasn't sure what caused her to do such a turnabout, but he was thankful for it.

The thunder of hoofbeats jerked him from his reverie. He sprang to his feet. "Jesse?"

Dead silence answered him.

He grabbed one of his guns. "Jesse? Where are you?" He followed a trail of bent grass to where the horses were. *Had been.* They were gone.

Cold realization washed over him. She'd left him

stranded. She'd used her body to lower his guard and run out on him.

Rage consumed him, followed by hurt and anger. He felt betrayed. He felt used.

He felt . . . like Jesse had.

Jessalea drew the horses to a halt in the woods at the edge of the Guadalupe River. She wanted to freshen up from her last two days on the trail before she went into the town of Victoria to leave Char's mount and get supplies.

She knew he'd stop in Victoria, since it was on the way to Houston, and she planned to leave word at the hotels where he could find his horse. She was over two days ahead of him. That was enough time to make Houston, take care of Hank Boggs—and possibly Harley—and leave before Char showed up. *Providing one or both Boggs were there.*

She didn't feel in the least guilty for what she'd done to Char. But she'd rather not have to face his anger.

A soft breeze fluttered the leaves of nearby cypress and oak trees, and she reveled in the coolness of the four hundred acres of woodland bordering the river. After spending so much time under the grueling Texas sun, the shade and water offered an invitation she couldn't resist.

Discarding her clothes, she rinsed them out and hung them over a branch to dry, then waded into a shallow spot in the river. The slow-moving current reminded her of the ocean and the way Char had touched her.

With a sigh, she lathered the soap and began to wash in earnest, hoping that every act she performed from now on wasn't going to somehow remind her of him.

She touched her stomach as another thought occurred. What if there were consequences to their lovemaking? How would she live? For goodness sakes, how could she hope to support a child?

The possibility was too enormous to consider. She could only pray that the few times they'd been together weren't enough.

In the warm breeze, her clothes dried quickly, and she was able to dress again within the hour. After brushing her hair and stuffing it under her hat, she mounted and guided the horses across the shallowest part of the Guadalupe River.

As she rode along the town's main street, *Calle de los Diez Amigos,* Street of the Ten Friends, she marveled at the shops lining the covered boardwalks, wishing she had time to explore a few of them. But she didn't. Nor did she have the money to spare.

Riding past the town square, she studied the old grist mill, watching the hot wind turn the wheel. The entire structure was built of logs that were held in place by wooden pegs, and inside, two grinding wheels, shipped all the way from Germany, crushed grain into feed or meal. She was disappointed by the size, though. In sketches, the "Dutch Windmill" had looked much bigger.

Spotting a livery down the street, she nudged the horses into a trot. She didn't have time for lollygagging. She had to get her supplies and go.

As she dismounted in front of the stables, a sign overhead squeaked as it swung in the breeze. She glanced up, then shook her head at the irony. DANIEL'S BLACKSMITH AND LIVERY.

"Can I help you, boy?"

Knowing she'd never get used to being referred to as a male, she turned to see an older man, with thick arms, wearing a leather apron. "I'd like to leave a horse here for a few days. Three at the most." She gestured to Char's gelding. "A man named Char Daniels will come for him."

The blacksmith's eyes widened, but he didn't comment. "You want him fed hay, or you want grain, too?"

"Both."

"That'll be three dollars."

So much. Sighing, she gave him three pieces of silver. "Where's the general store?"

"Around the corner and down a couple blocks." He caught the horse's reins and started inside, but stopped. "Son?"

"Yes."

"This Char Daniels, he ain't that famous gunman is he?"

"I'm afraid so."

His skin lost some of its color, and he cleared his throat. "I'll take real good care of his horse."

"I'm sure you will."

Jessalea made her way to the general store and had gotten her supplies when she heard the stage roll to a stop at the other end of the street. She watched as a lady carrying a child climbed down and wondered what it would be like to hold Char's baby in her arms. She stiffened. For heaven's sake. She didn't want his child. Gathering her senses about her, she started for one of the hotels to leave word for him. She hadn't gone more than a block when her horse started limping because of a broken shoe.

196

Glad it happened here instead of the middle of nowhere, she led the animal to the livery. But the blacksmith wasn't there. He'd left a note on the open door saying he'd gone for feed.

Stepping into the coolness of the stables, Jessalea looped her mount's reins around a post and sat down on a bale of hay to wait for him, wondering how much replacing a horseshoe was going to cost.

"Well, darlin', we meet again."

She stiffened at the sound of Char's voice, then swore under her breath. Damn it. Wasn't she ever going to be rid of him? Bracing herself, she stood and faced him.

He was leaning on the frame of the rear door, his arms crossed, his manner calm. But she wasn't fooled. The brightness of his eyes gave away his fury. He was on the verge of violence. Well, too bad for him. She lifted her chin. "You made good time."

"Yes, I did, considering . . ." A muscle ticked in his jaw.

"How did you get here so fast?"

He straightened and looped his thumbs over his gun belt. "Does it matter?" He advanced, his movements slow and dangerous.

She retreated. "Char, I had to—"

He caught her shoulders, his fingers digging into her flesh, his hands trembling with restrained rage. "Had to what? Steal my horse? Leave me stranded without food or water? Run away after we—" His grip tightened. "Damn you. *Why?*"

Her insides quivered, but she held her ground. "Let go of me."

"If I do," his voice was soft and low and deadly, "I'll be tempted to teach you a well-deserved lesson."

Her hand inched toward her gun.

His eyes darkened, and a muscle in his neck started to throb. "Think about it, Jesse. Think about it real hard before you reach for that weapon, because this time, one of us will get hurt."

Fear skipped through her. He was dead serious. "What do you want from me? Why can't you leave me alone?"

"No one wants that more than I do. But it isn't gonna happen. I won't watch you get yourself killed." He was so close she could feel his breath feather her lips. "I can't."

She had to get away from him. Her bones were going soft. With a speed she didn't know she possessed, she lunged to the side and ran. She heard her shirt rip, but she didn't care. It only mattered that she escape him.

Tucking her head, she broke into a full run—and slammed smack into a wall of hard flesh.

Clenching his fists, Char stalked after her.

When he glanced down the street to see which way she went, he saw her wrapped in the arms of a tall man dressed in jeans and a blue checkered shirt— *even dressed like a boy.*

Fury hit him so hard, he shook with it. "You've got two seconds to get your hands off her, mister."

The man looked up, then eased Jesse away from him. He eyed her torn blouse, then Char. His eyes glittered with cold rage. "You're a dead man."

Char could only stare. Cole Stevens. *Oh, shit.*

Stevens took his stance.

Wishing he were anywhere but here, Char did the same.

"No!" Jesse cried. She threw herself between them. "Uncle Cole, please, don't."

Uncle Cole?

"It was my fault. I stole his horse and left him stranded—a-and he didn't tear my blouse. I did when I was trying to get away from him."

"Damn it, Jesse. Stop defending me." *Cole Stevens was her uncle?*

Stevens stared at him over the top of her head. "She stole your horse?"

"Among other things." He didn't mention his pride and self-esteem.

"Don't I know you?"

"We met a few years back—in Charleston."

"Charleston?" He swept Char with a curious glance, then smiled. "Char Daniels, of course. Hell, the last time I saw you, you were a skinny kid."

"We all grow up."

"You did, that's for sure—and made quite a name for yourself in the process." Stevens returned his attention to Jesse. "What's this about, pumpkin? Why aren't you home with Fanny?"

Char answered for her. "She's after the men who—"

"Char!" Her eyes begged him not to tell her uncle.

He was tempted to ignore the look. God was he. But Cole Stevens was the only family she had left, and if he was killed trying to track down the Boggs brothers . . . ah, hell. He had to think quick. "She's . . . er . . . after the men who robbed us on the trail. The Dutchman and his gang."

Stevens's eyes narrowed. "What was she doing on the trail with you?"

Jesse got them into this, she could answer that one.

199

He arched a brow at her, then crossed his arms and waited.

She flicked a glance at her uncle, then back to him and sighed. "We eloped."

"What?" Stevens roared.

Char damn near strangled.

CHAPTER

❋ 18 ❋

Jessalea wished Char didn't look so sick. Her uncle was going to get suspicious. Thank goodness the note she'd left for Fanny only said she had something urgent to take care of. She took a breath and faced her mother's brother. "Char and I met at a town dance, and when we fell in love, I knew neither you nor Fanny would approve of me marrying a gunman, so we ran off together."

Char groaned.

Her uncle glared. "Did you *have* to get married?" His gaze lowered to her stomach.

"Now wait a minute," Char hissed.

Jessalea raised her hand to silence him. "No, we didn't. We eloped because we wanted to be together."

Char's eyes blazed, but he thankfully kept his mouth shut.

Her uncle rubbed the nape of his neck.

To give credibility to her outrageous lies, she moved closer to Char and slipped her arm through his. "Once we got settled, we were going to write to you and explain. But we had to find Char's pa first—then we were robbed and, well, Char got angry because I was determined to find the outlaws. We had a fight, and I left and . . . you know the rest."

"My little pumpkin married." He shook his head. "I can't believe it—and to a *gunman*. After you badgered me for years to give up my weapons to stay home with Fanny." He glanced at Char. "I hope you have better luck understanding women than I do."

"I wouldn't understand them if they came with instructions."

"Spoken like a true male." Her uncle laughed. "Well, I suppose we ought to celebrate or something. Have you checked into a hotel yet?"

"No."

"Let's do that first, then I'll buy the biggest steaks in Texas and a bottle of champagne."

Jesse winced, but there wasn't much she could do. She sure couldn't tell him the truth. Wishing she'd learn to keep her mouth shut, she dragged Char along behind her uncle and into the Guadalupe Hotel. She was furious with him, but she couldn't let on.

Uncle Cole ordered two rooms, one for himself—and one for the *newlyweds*.

She stared at the room overlooking the town square. It had the biggest bed she'd ever seen. A bed she was supposed to share with Char.

Avoiding the man seated at the desk, glaring at her, she studied the blue and tan braided rug that took up most of the floor. It matched the quilt on the bed and the blue and tan striped curtains.

"Do you plan to stare at the floor for the rest of the day? Or are we going to talk?"

She'd rather stare at the floor. "About what?"

"For starters, let's discuss that seduction scene the other night."

"I thought you'd have figured that one out by now. By the way, how did you get here so fast?"

"I waved down a passing stage—and quit changing the subject."

"I'm not changing it. I've said all I intend to on the matter. We're even."

"For now," he agreed, but the look in his eyes said it wouldn't be that way for long. He leaned back in the chair. "Why'd you tell your uncle we were married?"

"To save your hide." *Not to mention her own.* She'd seen his temper more times than she cared to. "My uncle's morals may be loose as pudding, but he's a real stickler when it comes to me. If he knew the truth, I wouldn't be able to stop him from demanding a showdown. I'm not saying he could beat you, but one of you would die, and I couldn't bare for that to happen. Not because of me."

"So what are we supposed to do now? Pretend to be married?" He nodded to the bed. "Share that? Not that I'm opposed."

"No, we will not." *Not ever again.* "Besides, we'll only be stuck in here together for a short while. Uncle Cole will go after the Dutchman."

"What makes you think so?"

She shrugged. "My uncle is very protective. Those men robbed me. He won't rest until he finds them. As for our arrangement, we'll simply have to work something out."

"You can't be that naive. You know I can't get within fifty feet of you without wanting to touch you. Much less *share a room with you.*"

"Practice restraint."

"How? By shooting myself? That's about the only way I'll stop these damned feelings."

Her heart took flight. Was he trying to tell her he really was in love with her? It was a heady thought, but a useless one. Even if he was, it wouldn't make any difference. He would never settle down to the life she wanted. "You can make a pallet on the floor."

"I could sleep in the hall and it wouldn't matter. You'd still be too close."

"You didn't have a problem on the trail."

"That was before we made love."

Her stomach tightened. "Pretend it never happened."

"Not a chance."

"Then you'll have to get another room. One my uncle doesn't know about."

"No."

She whirled on him. "What?"

He gave her a wicked smile. "Looks like the score's changed again, darlin'."

"So, Daniels, tell me, how do you plan to support my Jesse?" Cole Stevens asked as he pushed his empty plate to the side and poured himself a cup of coffee.

Char shifted in the straight-backed chair. He wasn't prepared for these kinds of questions. "I haven't decided what I want to do."

"How are you going to live?"

"I have money saved from my days as a Texas Ranger."

"He also has to find his pa before we can settle on a place," Jesse added with an adoring smile.

Char wanted to kiss that grin.

Stevens traced the rim of his cup with his finger.

"Fanny'll be heartbroken if you move too far from Natchez."

The conversation was getting to him, and if he didn't change the subject soon, he was going to set Stevens straight, once and for all. "Jesse says you might go after the men who robbed us?"

"I'm surprised you didn't."

He winced, then formed a whopper of a tale. "I would have, but they were headed north, maybe to Indian Territory, and I wasn't about to leave Jesse or take her there with me." Remembering her lie about their fight, he added, "That's what we argued about. She wanted to go anyway, but I was trying to take her to Fanny's so I could go after them alone."

Jesse kicked him under the table.

He grinned.

"I see." Stevens stared at the red tablecloth that resembled a large handkerchief. "How many were there?"

"Three."

"What'd they get away with?"

"Our supplies. My stallion, Jesse's buckskin, and a black gelding belonging to a kid who was with us at the time. The leader stole a kiss from Jesse, too."

Stevens didn't appear concerned. "I've heard of the Dutchman. Folks say he's after some outlaws that swindled his parents and took their home. Word has it, he only steals what he needs to survive until he finds them. I also hear he kisses every female victim, so I wouldn't get too upset over that."

Char was surprised. He'd expected Cole Stevens to be a real hothead, but the man was downright sensible. "I didn't like the idea of him kissing her." Well, hell, that was the truth.

Stevens chuckled. "I'll be sure to tell him that when I find him."

"You're going after him?" For a minute there, Char figured he wouldn't.

"I have to. The man robbed my niece." Stevens eyes hardened. "No one does that to my family. Not ever again."

This was a side of Cole Stevens that Char had done his best to avoid. "If you'll wait until I get Jesse to Natchez, I'll go with you."

"No," both Jesse and her uncle said in unison, then they laughed.

"No," Stevens repeated. "If you're not around to keep her in line, she might try something stupid, like following us." He took her hand. "I love her to death, but she's the stubbornest female I've ever known."

Char knew that for a fact.

Jesse crossed her arms. "That was a mean thing to say."

"But true." He rose. "Come on. We've got some celebrating to do—and the saloon down the street is a good place to start."

Char didn't argue. He could use a stiff drink.

As they walked into the smokey, lantern-lit saloon with a parquet floor, he remembered the last time he'd been in a saloon. He'd gotten so drunk over Jesse, he'd passed out.

They wove their way through the crowded room and found a table close to the piano, where a man sat at the keyboard, flanked by two others, one with a guitar and one with a banjo.

Saloon girls squeezed through the crowd, dodging groping hands and ignoring lewd remarks.

Char felt uneasy. This was no place for Jesse, even if she was dressed like a boy.

"Come on, Charlie! Play the Virginia reel," one of the customers shouted above the noisy throng.

Within seconds, the band struck up the lively tune.

"Why don't you two dance?" Stevens suggested.

"With her dressed like that? Not a chance." Besides, he didn't want to touch her. He might strangle her.

Stevens grinned, then reached across the table and whipped her hat off. Her glorious blackberry hair tumbled around her shoulders. "Problem solved."

Jesse looked mad enough to spit.

Char swore under his breath. Then, with a sigh, he rose and took her hand.

"You gutless cow pie, why didn't you tell him you didn't want to dance with me?"

"Why didn't you?"

"Because we're supposed to be newlyweds."

"Exactly."

She tried to pull free of his arms.

He tightened his hold. "If you'll settle down, we'll get this over with."

She clamped her mouth shut and glared at his chest.

He swung her around the floor, trying not to reveal how much he was affected by the way her thighs brushed his. In an effort to remain distant, he dragged his gaze from her and glanced around the room. He gave a silent curse. At least half the men in the saloon were staring at her. Before this night was over, there was going to be a fight sure as it snowed in Montana.

Hauling her closer, he swung her in the direction of her uncle.

A burly cowpoke tried to shove him aside so he could wrap his arms around her.

"Let her go, fella," Char ordered. "This one's mine."

"Find another 'un," the man garbled, trying to kiss her neck.

Stevens had started to rise from his seat when Char palmed his gun and shoved the barrel in the cowboy's face.

The music stopped.

A hush fell over the room.

Char kept his eyes on the stranger. "I'm gonna say this once, partner—and only once. The next man that puts his hands on my woman isn't gonna see tomorrow."

A gasp whispered from someone in the rear of the room. "That's *Char Daniels.*"

Shit, Char mentally cursed.

The cowboy paled and edged backward. "I'm sorry, Mr. Daniels. I'm real sorry."

"Yeah, I know." He holstered his iron and gripped Jesse's arm, leading her to the table.

"Show-off," she grumbled.

"He's only protecting you the way I would, pumpkin," Cole Stevens said as he rose.

Char didn't miss the spark of approval Stevens flashed his way.

"Naw. I agree with the lady," a voice said from behind them. "He's showin' off."

Char stiffened. *I knew it.* Clenching his teeth, he faced a cold-eyed youngster wearing a breach-loading Colt. "You got a problem, kid?"

"Yeah. I don't like show-offs. Don't believe you're near as fast as they say you are, neither."

Of course not, Char thought tiredly. "Listen, boy. Make a name for yourself somewhere else. I'm not into killing children." He knew it was the wrong thing to say the instant the words were out.

The kid's eyes narrowed. His nostrils flared. "Them's fightin' words, mister." He jerked his head toward the doors. "Outside."

Char sighed. *Ah, hell. Here we go again.*

CHAPTER

✾ 19 ✾

Jessalea stood on the boardwalk, her fear escalating as she watched Char face his opponent in the moonlit street. The man opposite him was lean and wiry, and probably quick, too. He'd have to be to challenge Char Daniels.

"I don't want to do this, kid." Char tried for the second time to discourage the younger man.

"Scared, are you?"

"No. But I don't cotton to shooting glory-seeking youngsters."

The kid's mouth thinned. "Prepare to meet your maker, *Mr. Daniels.*" He lowered his hands.

Jessalea held her breath, swearing if Daniels got himself killed, she'd never forgive him!

Char positioned himself for the showdown. "Any time you're ready."

"Don't worry, pumpkin. He can take care of himself," her uncle said from close beside her. "Remember, I taught him."

Somehow, that wasn't as reassuring as it should have been.

Silence fell over the onlookers as they watched the two men in the street.

Jessalea bit her lip, nervously watching the other man for signs of the draw.

His eyes narrowed.

Both went for their guns.

Shots exploded.

The younger man fell, grabbing his right leg. "You son of a bitch!"

Char watched him for a few seconds, then shook his head and turned toward her, his features set in disgust. "Damn kid."

"Look out!" Cole shouted.

A gun blast split the air.

Char stiffened. His startled gaze flew to hers, then with aching slowness, his lashes lowered and he folded to the ground.

"No!" She lunged for him.

Her uncle beat her to him, his furious gaze on the young gunman. "Take that back-shooting bastard to jail before I finish him." Without waiting to see if his command was obeyed, he lifted Char. "Someone get the sawbones."

The hours passed like days as the grim-faced doctor worked over Char, shaking his gray head and mumbling about the stupidity of gunfights.

Jessalea paced and cried and vowed to kill the man who did this.

Her uncle's gaze followed her, yet he remained quiet.

"At last!" the doctor crowed. He raised his hand to

reveal a pair of metal tweezers gripping a bloody bullet. "I was afraid I wasn't going to be able to reach it. Confounded thing was lodged between his shoulder blade and rib. The boy was lucky it didn't hit his lung."

Jessalea had to work to keep the hysteria from her voice. "Will he be all right?"

"I think so. Far as I can tell weren't nothing vital damaged."

"How long will he be laid up?" her uncle wanted to know.

"A week or so—providing he stays in bed."

"I'll see that he does," she pledged. *Even if she had to sit on him.*

The doctor bandaged Char's wound and gave her instructions on how to tend him, then said he would return the following day. When she closed the door behind him she saw her uncle standing at the window, staring at the dark street.

"Uncle Cole?"

He didn't turn. "You know, when you first told me you and Daniels were married, I had my doubts, but I don't anymore." He faced her. "He loves you. I can see it in the way he looks at you. You love him, too. With the same fierceness my sister loved your pa. But, pumpkin, you're going to have to get him to settle down before he gets himself killed and breaks your heart."

She wanted to deny her uncle's declaration, but she knew in her heart it was true. "You mean get him to settle down the way I've been trying to get you to do with Fanny for the last ten years?"

"Yeah. Something like that." His lips quirked. "Listen, I'm not going to hang around here for the next week waiting for him to recover. So, I'll put my time to good use. I'm going after the Dutchman."

Jessalea knew her feelings toward the Dutchman were mixed, but his family had been hurt because of no-goods, too. "Don't kill him, Uncle Cole. He didn't harm me. Please, just get the horses and let it go at that."

"I think you've been listening to too much gossip about me. I'm not a cold-blooded murderer. The only time I've ever shot anyone was to keep from getting killed myself."

"I know. But this is the first time anyone's done anything to me since . . . that day, and I don't want you to hurt him because of me."

He chucked her chin. "I won't. I'll only mess him up a little." With a wink, he jammed his hat on his head and sauntered out the door.

She sank down into a chair next to Char, wondering just how much *a little* was.

Her gaze moved to the bed. *And what about him?* She studied Char's pale features, knowing all the love in the world wouldn't change her feelings about gunmen.

Too many times, she'd seen the hell Fanny went through.

But, for now at least, Char would be okay. The doctor had turned him onto his good side, leaving his bandaged shoulder draped by the sheet. His skin appeared darker against the whiteness. His chest rose and fell with his steady breathing, stirring the silky hairs coating that smooth skin.

He was so handsome, even looking at him made her ache with the need to touch him.

Drawing her finger over the tanned hand resting on

the bed and along his firm arm, she marveled at the corded muscles that lay beneath his flesh.

She traced the edge of his bandage and leaned closer, inhaling the fragrance of woodsmoke and spice and leather and a musky scent she couldn't put a name to. But it was his alone—and it reminded her of when they made love.

Heat moved through her, and she snatched her hand away. She wasn't going to start thinking about that again.

She located his bloodstained shirt so she could mend and wash it.

Something heavy bumped her hand.

Curious, she reached in the pocket and withdrew the object.

She stared at the metal star lying in her palm, the one that proclaimed Char as a deputy marshal.

She didn't know if he'd had it before they met, or had somehow gotten it afterward, but it didn't matter. He was a lawman—and a gunman—and always would be.

Battling an empty feeling in the pit of her stomach, she set the badge aside and stitched the hole in his shirt, then rinsed it in the basin.

Seeing his blood tint the water, she felt her chest tighten. He'd come close to dying tonight. So very close. Next time he might not be so lucky.

But she wouldn't be there to see it. She couldn't be, not if she wanted to hang onto her sanity.

After draping the shirt over the window ledge to dry, she found a book about horses in Char's saddlebags and stationed herself at the desk to read.

The book was about as entertaining as watching leaves grow.

"Jesse? Damn it, Jesse, where are you?"

She hurried to the bed. "I'm right here." She took his hand.

His eyes opened in surprise. There was a moment of confusion, then he smiled sleepily. "I dreamed you left me in the desert, bleeding and alone, and without a horse." He tightened his fingers around hers. "I kept calling for you, but you wouldn't come."

Guilt pricked her. "Well, I'm here now, and I'll stay until you're on your feet again."

"Where's your uncle?"

"After the outlaws who robbed us. Want some broth?" she gestured to a tray on the desk.

"No." He rubbed his shoulder. "I hope he gets my horse. Black Duke is a pain in the ass, but he cost me as much as a small ranch. He's supposed to have bloodlines to some English king's fancy thoroughbred."

"Is that why you named him that?"

"I didn't. The fella I bought him from said he got the name from his coloring and temperament, and from his arrogance."

She smiled. "You're fond of him, aren't you?"

"I'd have to be a fool to like a stubborn, mean-tempered, overgrown jackass."

"I know what you mean," she said tongue-in-cheek.

He scowled at her, then began to chuckle. "Shrew."

"Jackass."

"Ow. Damn." He rubbed his shoulder. "What'd that kid hit me with, anyway? A twelve-gage?"

"A .38 center-fire."

"Just as bad."

She picked up the bottle of laudanum the doctor had left. "Maybe some of this will help ease the pain."

He stared at the bottle with revulsion, then shook his head, causing a silky lock to brush his forehead. "It's not that bad."

"Maybe you should try to sleep."

"I'd rather talk."

"About what?"

"You."

"We've already had that discussion. Let's talk about you."

"There's nothing to tell."

"Sure there is. For instance, what did Webster do to make you detest him so?"

He shifted to ease the discomfort in his shoulder, then turned his head to stare at the window, at the sleeve of his shirt fluttering in the summer breeze. "He didn't do any one thing in particular. It was a combination of everything from beatings to vicious barbs to the inhuman workload to downright meanness. *Then* there was the way he kept me tied to that farm. Other than going to church on Sundays, I never left the place until the day I ran away."

Her throat ached for the young boy who'd never known any fun, who'd never known love. No wonder he didn't want any part of family life. To him, family was a dirty word.

"Was Mrs. Webster cruel, too?"

"Sometimes." He stared at the ceiling. "The worst, though, was the day before I left. A family from Tennessee bought a plot of land near the farm, and they came to visit every week or so. They had a daughter that was my age, a pretty blonde with big brown eyes. I hadn't had any experience with girls, but I knew I wanted to kiss her more than anything. One night, they came over for supper and afterward, I asked her to keep me company while I milked the cow. Maybe if I'd kissed her when we first walked into the barn, it might never have happened. But I didn't. I was too shy, too uncertain. By the time I got up the nerve, Ma Webster came looking for us—and found us in each other's arms."

"What did she do?"

"Had Deke strip me naked in front of the girl's parents and beat me with a razor strap. I was used to whippings, but the humiliation was more than I could stand. I ran away the next morning, and I've never been back. But I think that's one of the things that makes me want to chase outlaws. Injustice—in any form—turns my stomach."

She explored his tired features. He was such a complex man, and he'd suffered so much. She knew she could never add to that pain.

Even if she could convince him to join her on her parents' farm, she wouldn't. He'd never be happy. No matter how much she wished it different, she knew beyond a doubt there was no hope for them.

Char closed his eyes so he wouldn't have to face Jesse. Even now, after all these years, the disgrace of being stripped down in front of those people still shamed him.

"With so much work on the farm, how did you find time to practice shooting a gun with Cole?"

He raised his lashes, glad for something to take his mind off that night. "We used to meet in the pasture before dawn and practice until the sun rose and it was time to start the chores. I lost quite a bit of sleep over it, but I was never sorry."

"Do you think you're as fast as he is?"

"I wouldn't want to test him."

"He says I am."

A brow lifted in her direction. "Is that so?"

"Yes." She grinned. "But then, he tends to fabricate sometimes."

"Oh, I don't know. Buddy agrees with him."

"I know. But Buddy also thinks you're a *God.*"

"Touché." He chuckled, then grabbed his shoulder.

She rose, and he enjoyed watching the seductive sway of her hips as she walked to the desk and got a cup from a tray. He remembered how that sweet rear end had felt in his hands and grew warm. But he knew sexual attraction wasn't the only thing that drew him to her. He liked everything about her, from her wit, to her humor, to her courage and determination. Hell, he even liked her stubborn streak.

She held the cup toward him. "How about some broth, now?"

I'd rather have you.

"The doctor said it would help you keep up your strength."

He eyed the mug. Strength, huh? "Sure, I'll have some."

She handed it to him. "He said you should be back to normal in about a week—if you stay in bed."

There's no place he'd rather be—as long as she was with him. He took the cup and was surprised to feel his hand shake. What the hell? He didn't *feel* weak.

He gave an inward curse. Probably another sign of age. As he sipped the chicken-flavored water, he thought about how much he'd wandered over the last fifteen years, and for the first time he felt aimless. As if he came from nowhere and had the same destination ahead of him. Other than capturing an occasional outlaw, his life had no purpose.

It wasn't a settling thought.

"What are you going to do when you find your pa?"

"What?" He rolled his head toward her. What brought that on? "Hell, I don't know."

"Then why do you want to find him? To punch his nose?"

"That was my first intent, but I've decided to give him a chance to explain, *then* punch his nose."

"That's big of you."

"I'm feeling generous."

She shook her head. "Listen, I'm going down to the mercantile. Would you like for me to ask around for you?"

"Might as well."

"Is there anything I can bring you?"

Yourself. "A bottle of whiskey—for the pain."

The concern in her eyes made him wish he'd kept his mouth shut.

"I think you should take the laudanum and try to get some rest while I'm gone."

"The pain isn't that bad." That was the truth. He'd had worse. Much worse.

Not convinced, but acquiescent, she collected some money out of his pockets and stuffed it into hers. "I won't be long."

When the door closed, Char smiled and slipped into daydreams of the nights to come.

After a visit to the mercantile in the east wing of the hotel, Jessalea headed for the telegraph office to send Fanny a wire, hoping the other plan she had formed would help Char.

219

A nice looking man glanced up from a desk behind a half wall. "May I help you, sir?"

She sighed. She really was going to have to do something about her clothes. Perhaps she'd have her cream satin gown pressed. "I'd like to send a telegram to Charleston."

He nodded and fetched a pencil and paper. "To whom?"

"The postmaster."

"How do you want it to read?"

"I want to know if there's a family around there who knew a man by the name of Otis Daniel, or a name close to that, or if anyone had a daughter named Emma who disappeared in 1846. If so, I have some information for them. If there's an answer, have it sent to C. Daniels in . . . Shreveport."

"Louisiana?"

"Yes."

He made some notes on the paper. "Is that it?"

"No. I'd like to send another wire to Natchez." She had to let Fanny know she was okay.

When Jessalea left the telegraph office, she went to a saloon to buy Char a bottle of whiskey.

At least being able to enter a saloon unnoticed was one advantage to her "boys" clothes.

She walked to the counter, but as she waited for the bartender, the hairs on the nape of her neck began to prickle.

"What can I getcha, kid?" the bartender asked, placing a gnarled hand on the battered bar.

"A bottle of whiskey."

As he bent to reach under the counter, someone behind her moved.

She darted a peek over her shoulder to see a man

push through the swinging doors. The panels closed before she could see him clearly.

But the eerie sensation wouldn't leave her.

Telling herself she was being silly, she paid for the whiskey and headed for the hotel.

The sensation grew stronger.

Someone was watching her.

CHAPTER

❈ 20 ❈

Char was at the farm, standing naked in front of the Hendersons, clenching his teeth against the pain of the razor strap tearing into his back.

From nowhere, Jesse appeared, holding a blanket and a six-shooter. She tossed the blanket to Ma Webster and made her cover him, then she aimed her gun at Deke. "If you ever hurt him again, I'll blow a hole in you big enough to drive a buggy through."

Deke laughed and turned the strap on Jesse. The rawhide laid open the flesh on her right cheek.

Enraged, Char dove at him and looped the leather around his neck. He held on, tightening the strap, watching the man's eyes bulge, watching him fight for air. . . .

A soft click startled him awake.

Blinking and glancing around the room in confusion, he relaxed when he saw Jesse set a package on the desk, her cheek unmarred.

She unwrapped the paper and took something from

inside, then came toward the bed. "Are you feeling any better?"

"Fine." He tried to see what she held in her hands, but couldn't. "What's that?"

"Something I saw in the mercantile." She unfurled her fingers and held her hand toward him. "Happy belated birthday. Buddy told me when it was."

There, nestled in her palms was a black hatband with a pair of miniature silver steer horns centering one side. It was several seconds before Char could breathe. "For me?"

"Sure is, and I have another gift, too." She grinned. "I sent a telegram to Charleston, asking about your mother's folks. If the postmaster or anyone knows anything, they'll send word to you in Shreveport."

He was touched—and impressed by her intelligence. He'd never thought to locate his mother's kin because he didn't know their names. "I hope it works. I know I've searched for my father for fifteen years, and haven't yet come across a man named Otis Daniel anything."

"I'm sure it will. There couldn't have been many pregnant women named Emma who disappeared during that time, if she was from Charleston. Besides, it worked before. That's how I found Patrick Boggs. I sent letters to a half-dozen post offices in Texas. Waco was the first answer I received. I may have gotten others, too. I don't know, because I left right after I got that one."

Char tried not to get his hopes up. Her attempt could fail as easy as not.

She placed her present in his hand. "What do you think of it?"

He studied the band, unsure what to say, his chest

heavy with an emotion he didn't understand. "It'll look good on my hat."

"Char, what's wrong?"

"Nothing."

She knelt beside him. "Don't you like it? If not, I can return—"

"No." He held onto it, afraid she might take it. "I like it. Very much. It's just that, no one's ever given me a gift before, and I don't know what to say."

"Not even for your birthday? For *Christmas?*"

"We were too poor, Jesse. We couldn't afford to be frivolous." He didn't tell her he was quoting Ma Webster.

She rose and paced, her arms crossed over her middle. "We were dirt poor, too, Char. But my parents *made* gifts for us. Papa whittled a play rifle out of wood for James and a doll for me. Mama made clothes for my doll from Pa's shirts that were beyond mending. She even fashioned ribbons for my sister's hair out of the same material." She turned on him like an avenging angel. "There was no excuse for what those people did to you. No excuse at all."

He felt such a well of tenderness for this woman, he ached with it. "Come here, darlin'. Let me give you a proper thank you."

"You can do that by shooting the Websters."

"If you don't come over here, I'll come to you." When she hesitated, he started to shove the sheet aside.

"All right!" She plunked down on the edge of the bed and scowled at him.

He smiled and smoothed her hair from her cheek. She was such a treasure. Cupping the back of her head, he pulled her down to him and gave her a slow, lingering kiss. "Thank you."

"You're welcome." She kissed him in return, and he felt the gentleness she tried so hard to hide. With that single kiss, she was trying to absorb his years of loneliness and hurt.

His shoulder ached from the way he held her, but he wouldn't let go. He deepened the kiss, parting her sweet lips, tasting her goodness. He'd never known anyone like her. Anyone so strong and so sensitive at the same time. He buried his fingers in her hair and inhaled the clean scent of her skin.

The hard tips of her breasts nudged his chest, and he released a frustrated moan.

She jerked upright. "Damn. I'm sorry. I didn't mean to hurt you." She rose from the bed. "You're in no condition for this." She opened the bottle of laudanum, and before he could protest, she had poured some into his mouth.

He tried to spit it out but had already swallowed most of it. "I told you I didn't want that."

"Stop being so pigheaded. It won't hurt you."

That's what you think. It made him sick. "Damn it, woman. When are you going to learn to listen?"

He tried to glare but couldn't stay focused. Her beautiful image was swallowed by a thick fog. The room grew dark . . . then faded, only to be replaced by Ma Webster's hated face.

She smiled as she thrust the bottle of medicine into his hands. "Take this, Charlie. Deke did a fair job this time, but if you cain't work tomorra, you know what'll happen."

* * *

The pain in his shoulder disappeared . . . but the nausea began.

Jessalea grabbed the chamber pot just as Char became violently ill. When he finished, she gave him a drink of water and washed his face, but he was only half-conscious when she returned his head to the pillow.

"No more," he slurred. "I don't want any more. I don't care if he does hit me again. I don't care if he kills me."

Her anger rose as she watched him struggle with imaginary hands.

"No . . . Don't . . . *Don't* . . ."

She couldn't stand any more. "Char! Char, wake up." She shook him.

He opened his eyes but they didn't focus. "Why does he hate me? Why doesn't he send me away?"

His voice sounded so childlike. He was scaring her. "Will you wake up."

"Ma, no. Please, no more. It makes me sick. I'll stand the pain tomorrow. I'll work. I swear I will."

Dear, God. What did those people do to him?

Feeling nauseous herself, she walked to the window and stared out over Victoria's lazy streets.

Char's hatred of home life stemmed from much more than overwork and boredom. He associated home with pain and humiliation, and God-only-knows what else. She swallowed against the ache in her throat. No one should suffer like that. No one.

She couldn't help comparing his childhood to the carefree one she'd known—before the Boggs brothers destroyed it. Old pain moved through her, and she gripped the window curtain. At least she could do something about *them*.

Over the next few days, she watched Char grow stronger, but she didn't mention the Websters again. She didn't want to know more about him. Didn't want to feel any more of his pain.

She returned her gaze to the window, where she'd been staring at the dusty street for the last hour—and inhaling the delicious scent of baked apple pie coming from the eatery down the street.

The room was starting to close in on her, and she felt as if she were suffocating. She hadn't left the hotel since the day she went to the saloon.

Well, *that,* at least, she could do something about. Darting another glance at Char, and seeing he was sound asleep, she dressed quickly in her "boys" garb and strapped on her gun belt. She would check their horses, and make sure her mount's shoe was repaired—then see about some of that tempting pie.

Placing her hat over her hair, she quietly left the room.

She hadn't gotten more than a few steps from the hotel door when she saw a man coming toward her. He was thin and unshaven, with a cigar clenched between narrow lips and yellow teeth. His eyes were shadowed by the brim of his hat, but by the way he wore his weapon and carried himself, she knew he was a gunman.

In an attempt to avoid him, she changed directions and started across the street.

"It won't do any good to run," the man called in a gravely voice.

She stopped in the center of the street and turned, her nerves growing taut. "Are you talking to me, mister?"

Dust rose beneath his boots as he took a stance opposite her. There was a confidence about him that was frightening. "I'm not talking to your horse."

"I think you've made a mistake."

He spit out the cigar. "The only mistake I made was waiting around so long for you to come out of that hotel."

"Who are you?"

His thin lips spread into a nasty smile. "Your executioner."

"Listen, fella. I don't know what this is about, but I've got no quarrel with you. I don't even know you." She turned to walk away.

He cocked his gun. "You got two choices, pissant. I can drop you where you stand, or you can test your speed against me. But those are the *only* choices you have."

Char woke in a sweat, his chest heaving, his stomach churning with bile. He'd been dreaming he was at the farm again.

It took a minute to force aside the images and orient his thoughts. When he could think straight, he realized that Jesse wasn't there.

Figuring she'd gone to the kitchen to get their dinner, he rolled out of bed and staggered to the clothes closet. He'd been able to sit for the last couple days, but this was the first time he'd felt well enough to stand, and he wanted to surprise her.

He leaned against the wall by the window and dragged on his pants. The ache in his shoulder made itself known, but the pain wasn't as bad as before.

He turned and caught the window ledge, then

poked his head outside to drag in a lungfull of fresh air.

Jesse was facing a man in the street, her hand hovering above her gun.

"Son of a bitch!" Grabbing his hat and holster, he stumbled down the hall, strapping on his guns as he went. He burst through the front door just as the man reached for his revolver.

Gunfire roared.

The man in the street fell.

Sunlight glinted off of metal, and Char saw another man leaning from a window across the street—with a rifle aimed at Jesse.

"Jesse, look out!" He went for his guns and fired.

A blast exploded from the rifle.

Jesse dove to the side.

The man toppled from the window and crashed through a slatted roof covering the opposite boardwalk.

Char swung his gaze to the street and saw Jesse spring to her feet.

Their eyes met, and he was so relieved that she wasn't hurt, he slumped against a post.

She started toward him.

"What in tarnation is going on around here?" a big man wearing a badge boomed as he stepped from the door of the eatery. He yanked a napkin from the front of his shirt and stalked toward her.

"What happened?" he repeated.

As Char moved to join them, he heard Jesse tell the sheriff the stranger had confronted her in the street and demanded a showdown. The other one, she didn't know anything about.

The sheriff went to examine the bodies as Char approached her. He felt his blood roll to a slow boil. "Why are you always trying to prove yourself? Damn it, couldn't you have walked away?"

"I tried." She searched his face. "You're pale. You need to be in bed."

"Who was he?" Char demanded.

"I can answer that," the sheriff said as he returned. "They're hired guns—Red Daley and Tom Thorpe. I've got wanted posters on 'em." He removed his hat and wiped his brow. "Since both of 'em had a wad of money in their pockets, my guess is someone hired 'em to do a job." He eyed Jesse. "To kill you, by the looks of it."

"Harley Boggs," Jesse hissed.

Char didn't doubt it. He gripped her arm. "Let's go." He marched her to the room.

She pulled free of him the second they were inside. "When I see that pig again, I'm going to blow a hole in him as big as Texas."

"You'll have to get in line behind me, first."

She whirled on him, ready for battle, then her gaze drifted to his bare feet, his naked chest. To his stunned surprise, she burst into peels of laughter.

Fearing she was hysterical, he caught her hands. "Darlin', it's okay."

Her eyes were filled with tears. "I wish you could have seen how you looked, racing to my rescue wearing only your pants and hat. I'm sure the ladies in this town won't forget that sight for some time." Her chest shook with renewed chuckles. "I know I won't."

Damn her. She was making fun of him. "It's not a laughing matter."

"The gunfight, no. But the rest . . ." She wiped a

tear from the corner of her eye. "Oh, Char. You were priceless."

"Priceless," he growled. "I'll give you priceless." He jerked her against him and ground his mouth down on hers.

He felt her in-drawn breath, the way she stiffened, but the taste of her overrode everything else. He pressed his tongue between her lips and sank into her. Jesus, he'd come so close to losing her.

A small feminine moan shimmered over his tongue. She caught his arm, dug her nails into his skin. Her breasts hardened against his chest.

He deepened the kiss, feasting on her mouth, desperate to touch her. He closed his hand over her breast.

Her shivers sent streaks of fire straight to his loins.

"Ah, darlin'. It's been too damn long." His mouth worked its way along the column of her throat, over the swells of soft, white flesh.

He undid the buttons on her shirt and eased the material apart to reveal her beautiful breasts. He stared at the perfection, then lowered his head and drew one stiff peak into his mouth.

"Char, your wound," she reminded breathlessly.

He buried his face in her creamy flesh, teased the taut nub with his tongue, letting her know without words how well he was.

She arched closer.

His hands became impatient, fumbling with the rest of her clothes until they lay at her feet. His pants came next, then he returned to ravage her mouth, to devour her breasts, while his fingers sought the sensitive area between her thighs—the place he needed to be.

They fell on the bed.

She flung his hat to the side and buried her fingers in his hair.

He stroked her moist haven, pleasuring them both until he couldn't take any more. He moved over her and nudged her legs apart, then thrust deep inside.

"Oh, Char . . ."

He loved this Jesse most. The purely female one. He drove into her, retreated, and plunged again. Again.

The astounding swiftness of his climax left him arching and shuddering and calling her name.

The air in the room was heavy, and thick with the sound of their labored breathing as he rolled to the side, pulling her with him. The ache in his shoulder he ignored. Their union had been worth the pain.

"Is it always this incredible?" Her warm breath feathered his neck.

"With us, it will be."

"What's that supposed to mean?"

"It means I want you to marry me."

Surprise held her immobile for several seconds before he saw the look of defeat touch her eyes. "Where would we live?"

"I don't know. After we find my pa, we'll settle in a town somewhere. I'll get a job as a marshal or something."

"A marshal? A town? What about my dreams of returning to my parents' farm?"

"You'll be happy in a town, darlin'. I'll see to it."

"No."

He sat up. "Damn it, Jesse."

She wrapped the sheet around her and rose. "I won't live in town, and I certainly won't sit at home waiting for word that you've been killed trying to bring in some outlaw."

"It's all I know."

"No, it isn't. You know farming."

"I hate farming."

She stared at the handsome man sitting on the bed, his dark hair tousled, his skin flushed from their lovemaking. She loved him, but on this she couldn't—*wouldn't*—compromise. "Char, please try to understand. I lost everything to outlaws. Everything. I can't live a life where I'd be in constant fear of losing you to them, too."

"Jesus, woman. Give me some credit. I know how to take care of myself. I've been doing it for years— against outlaws who make the Boggs brothers look inept."

"So you've been lucky."

"Lucky, hell. I've been damned smart."

She snorted. "Yes. I saw an example of that when you drew on a man and didn't kill him. Because of that, you nearly died. Yes. I guess that's real smart."

A muscle in his jaw ticked. "Cole taught me the same way he did you. *Aim for the heart*. Hell, I can still hear his words. But I don't like to kill people, and I won't unless it's absolutely necessary. That fellow in Laredo and the kid here in Victoria had one thing in common. They'd both had too much to drink, and had let their egos override their common sense. I can't see killing a man for something he'd regret when he sobered up."

"Regret," she hissed. "What makes you so sure that fellow in jail isn't going to come after you when the sheriff releases him?"

"If he does, *then* I'll kill him."

"If he doesn't kill you first."

He grinned. "Yes. There is that."

"This isn't funny!"

"No, it isn't—and neither was my not-so-conventional rescue—but I know we could work things out between us, if you'll give it a chance." He held her gaze. "Say you'll marry me, darlin'."

Yes, her heart cried. She wanted to be his wife. But for how long? Until someone shot him?

"I can't." Trying to hold herself together, she pulled on her clothes and left the room. She made it halfway down the hall before she fell apart.

Curled into a ball against the wall, she cried until there was only cold, frozen pain left. But she knew she'd done the right thing. She and Char would never be happy together. No matter how much they both wanted it.

It was time they stopped torturing each other. His wound was almost healed. She had to leave.

When Jesse hadn't returned in half an hour, Char knew she was gone again. Because he knew *her.* She was hurting, and the way she dealt with hurt was by running.

Wincing as he dragged on his clothes, he thought about their problem. He knew she loved him. That was something she couldn't hide. But he also knew she'd never give up her dream of raising a passel of kids and living the rest of her days on that Missouri farm. Nor did he want her to. She had a right to it.

That only left one solution. They would have to find a compromise. One they could both live with. Now if he could only figure out what.

Fingering the tiny steer horns on his hatband, he

smiled. He would think of something. Settling his black Stetson on his head, he walked out the door, wondering if he could catch her before she reached Houston, and wondering if Buddy would be waiting for them. He knew the kid had talked to the postmaster in Christi, and he'd bet his new hatband, Buddy had learned the whereabouts of Harley Boggs's kin.

He shook his head as he walked down the hall. Yeah, the kid would be there all right—*if* he hadn't already gotten himself killed.

CHAPTER

❋ 21 ❋

Jessalea guided her mount through a shaded grove of pecan trees, listening to the thud of her horse's hooves strike the soft dirt.

She heard a rider coming behind her. A streak of fear shot through her. Was it Char? Or someone else? Reining sharply into the woods, she waited. Moisture dampened her palms. A pulse at the side of her throat pounded. Her hand closed over the butt of her Colt.

Then she saw him.

Char drew his mount to a halt in front of her, his gaze fixed on the ground—on her horse's tracks. He sat motionless for several seconds, then said in a quiet voice, "I'm tired, Jesse. Don't make me come in there after you."

Loosing a resigned sigh, she nudged her horse into the open. What else could she do? She'd never get away from him. He knew where she was going. "You should be in bed."

He glared at her from beneath the brim of his hat. "I would be if you hadn't run out on me."

"All right. I'm sorry. But you're going to have to stop making love to me. Damn it, Char. You're only making things harder between us. We don't belong together."

"That's your opinion. Besides, you could have said no."

"I will from now on."

He didn't argue, but his eyes said she was dead wrong.

Shaking her head, she nudged her horse into a trot. As expected, Char followed.

For the next three days, she kept her word. Every time he got close to her, she moved. Every time he gave her that look that curled her toes, she turned away. At night, she bedded down several yards from him, and determinedly kept her eyes averted while he shaved in the mornings. She would make him understand. She had to.

Thank goodness they only had one more day—and night—before they reached Houston.

"Jesse, wait."

She twisted in the saddle. "What?"

"Riders coming."

She glanced behind them and saw two men hauling three riderless horses. "It's Uncle Cole, and he has my buckskin!"

"Darcy's with him."

"*What?* But how do they know each oth—" Fear choked off her words. Had Blake told her uncle about the Boggses?

Her uncle reined in and drew the two mounts he was leading to a stop. "We missed you in Victoria and have been riding day and night to catch you."

Uncertain, her gaze darted from one to the other. "How—"

"We met a few years ago," Uncle Cole explained. "Then again on the trail. Since Darcy was heading for Houston, we teamed up."

Her insides sagged with relief. He didn't know about Boggs. She couldn't contain a smile as she moved her horse closer to Fanny's buckskin. "Hello, Hannah." She scratched behind her ears. "I sure have missed you."

The buckskin nickered and nuzzled her arm.

"Well, I haven't missed this ornery varmint," Char denied as he stroked Black Duke along the jaw.

She could have sworn the horse sniffed.

"You want to switch mounts now or wait until we make camp," her uncle asked.

"We've only got a couple hours of daylight left, might as well keep going," Char answered. He flicked a glance at the marshal. "You find Hardin?"

"No." Blake Darcy's jaw ticked. "It wasn't him." He glanced at her. "I'm sorry about Boggs, honey."

Jessalea stiffened.

"Who's Boggs?" her uncle asked.

Panic gripped her.

Darcy turned to him. "I thought you knew."

"Knew what?"

"Darcy!" Char snapped.

"He has a right to know, Char."

"Know what?" Cole Stevens demanded.

"Not now," Char insisted.

"Be quiet, Daniels," her uncle ordered. "Now, Blake, what are you talking about?"

The marshal shifted in his saddle. "Harley Boggs, the man we're talking about, is one of the men who killed your sister's family. I arrested him, but he broke out of jail in Corpus Christi."

An icy calmness settled over her uncle. His eyes glittered in a way that scared her.

"Who are the others?" His voice was laced with barely contained fury.

"They're all Boggses. Six brothers. Three are dead."

"The rest?"

Jessalea swallowed. Uncle Cole's voice was much too calm.

"One's in Houston, and one's in Shreveport. Harley is probably headed in that direction, too."

Not a muscle moved in her uncle's body. He sat very still. Very quiet. Then he turned those glacial eyes on her. "You knew all along who they were, didn't you?"

Instinctively, she moved closer to Char. "I couldn't tell you. I was afraid they'd kill you, too."

"Who got the other three?"

"Jesse shot two of them," Char answered. "The other hung for a similar crime."

"How do you fit into this?"

"I've been doing my damnedest to keep her from getting that beautiful head blown off."

"I see." Her uncle swung out of the saddle. "Daniels, take care of the horses. Blake, you start a fire." He turned on her. "You, young lady, follow me. We're going to have a talk."

Her heart in her throat, and feeling a lot like a naughty child, she eased her leg over the saddle horn and swung down. But, as she did so, she heard Char's quiet voice. "Don't be too hard on her, Stevens."

The "talk" wasn't as bad as she'd expected. Her uncle, even with his quick-tempered fury, was a sensible man. He understood her fears. Of course, she hadn't told him about the hired guns in Victoria—or that she and Char weren't married. One problem at a time.

After a quiet night, with sparse conversation, they mounted up the next morning.

"We should reach Houston by this evening," Cole said to the marshal as they lagged behind on their horses.

"Won't be soon enough for me," Darcy returned.

Char sent Jesse a smile from where he rode right beside her, as he'd been doing since they'd left Victoria. It was as if he were afraid to let her get too far away from him.

Last night, though, had been the worst. Since they still had to maintain the ruse in front of her uncle that they were married, she'd had to sleep with her bedroll next to Char's, and the need to touch him had almost been more than she could stand. Her confession to her uncle, and the temptation last night, combined with the warm, knowing smiles Char kept giving her, had shredded her nerves.

She was jumpy and irritable, and frustrated.

"I hope that anger isn't directed at me," Char said as he drew his stallion closer.

The warmth in his voice was a soothing balm, but she couldn't allow herself to respond to the sensation. As soon as the Boggses were taken care of, she'd never see him again. "It isn't. I have no feelings about you one way or the other." The lie sounded convincing to her, but when his eyes darkened with hurt, she wanted to recall the words.

He nudged his horse into a gallop, leaving her behind.

"Trouble on the home front?" her uncle asked as he joined her.

He was so astute, he made her nervous. She tried avoiding the subject. "No. By the way, what'd you do to the Dutchman when you found him?"

"Gave him a firm warning . . . and a new shape to his nose. Now what about you and Daniels? What's the trouble?"

She never had been able to distract him. "Nothing much."

"Can I help?"

"Not unless you know a way to make him content to settle down on a farm."

"What does he want to do?"

"Chase outlaws, while I sit at home and worry."

He removed his hat and scratched his thick mat of dark hair before wiping his brow. "There might be a solution to that, but let me think on it before I offer an opinion."

"I've thought of nothing else. There isn't one."

He quirked his mouth. "Oh, I don't know. I could break both of his legs so he'd be forced to stay home with you."

"He might object."

"True. But what could he do?"

"Shoot you."

He laughed. "You're probably right. I'd better think of something else."

"Think of something else about what?" Blake asked as he guided his mount alongside theirs.

"A way to keep Char home with Jesse instead of roaming around chasing desperados."

For goodness sakes, did he have to tell the whole world?

Blake gave her a questioning look. He knew she wasn't married to Char. Fortunately, he was smart enough not to mention the fact. "I see."

She was sure he did.

"Isn't there some saying about honey attracting more bees than salt? In this instance, that might be the approach she should take with Daniels."

"I don't understand." She really didn't.

"I'm saying, give Daniels a reason to *want* to stay home with you."

Jesse stared, completely baffled, then jumped at the sound of thudding hooves. She swung her head around to see Char riding toward them.

He drew his horse to a stop, his smile jubilant. "Eagle Lake is less than a mile ahead. I don't know about you, but I could sure use a break from this heat in those cool waters."

"You don't have to convince me," Blake voiced.

"Me neither," her uncle seconded, urging his horse forward.

Anxious for a long soothing bath, herself, she didn't hesitate to follow the men. But as she rode, Darcy's words kept swirling through her thoughts. *Give him a reason.* But what reason, for heaven's sake?

As Char watched Jesse saunter toward the lake carrying a towel, he ached to follow her, to make slow, sweet love to her in the water. The image was almost more than he could take.

"Why don't you go with her?" Cole asked from where he stood with his foot braced on a log, cleaning his boots.

"What?" Char couldn't have heard him right.

"She is your wife, Daniels, and I know you two haven't had much of a chance to be alone."

The lie was starting to grate on him, and he had to struggle for a reply. "I . . . don't want to embarrass her."

"You won't. Jesse's so much in love with you she aches with it."

He tried to control the leap in his pulse. "But—"

"No buts." He gave Char a light shove. "Go. I'll keep Darcy entertained for a while."

Anxious and hesitant all at the same time, Char moved toward the lake shielded from camp by thick hedges and high grass, remembering Jesse's vow to say no.

He wedged his way through a break in one of the hedges and froze at the sight of her—*completely naked*—lying against a rock with her eyes closed.

Every male instinct in his body leapt to life. He devoured her satin flesh, her full rose-tipped breasts, her slender waist and long, long legs. His gaze fixed on the dark triangle between her thighs.

Blood pulsed through his shaft, and he reached for the buttons on his britches, not once taking his eyes from her.

When his clothes lay in a pile next to hers, he slipped into the water without a sound. He glided toward her, then when he came within a few feet, he ducked under the surface.

With his eyes open, he could see her outline. He grabbed her legs and pulled her under.

She fought like a tiger, clawing until he released her.

They shot up out of the water.

Fear glazed her eyes until she recognized him.

"*Char.* Don't you *ever* do that again." She hit his chest. "I thought someone was trying to drown me."

He caught her by the waist and pulled her to him until their naked bodies touched. "Maybe I was."

"Stop that! My uncle—"

"Insisted I join you. He thinks we need to be alone for a while."

"He *what?*"

He nuzzled her ear. "Remember? He thinks we're married."

"But we know we're not. Stop that!"

He traced her ear with his tongue. "But we're gonna be."

She shivered and clutched his shoulders. "No, we're not."

He slid his lips over hers.

Jessalea thought she'd drown in his kiss. His mouth was so hot. Her breasts grew hard, achy.

"I'm gonna marry you," he said against her mouth, "and I might even consider living on that boring little farm with you. Anything's better than being without you."

Her heart soared—but only for an instant. Char was willing to settle down with her, but for how long? Would he ever be happy? Or would her way of life eventually tear them apart? Besides, he hadn't said he would—only that he might *consider* it.

"It won't work. No matter how good your intentions are, you'd hate that life." She cupped his face. "I won't do that to you."

"I'm not going to let you get away, darlin'."

The conviction in his voice made her shiver, but she knew she was right.

"I think we'd better go." She tried to leave his arms.

"Not yet. We need to bathe first."

"Oh, no, you don't." She shoved him away and scrambled to the shore. If he made love to her right now, she knew she'd give into his foolish plans.

Dragging on her clothes, she went to join the others—with Char right behind her.

As she reached the hedges that separated the lake from camp, she heard a familiar voice.

Her gaze flew to Char's.

"I knew it," he growled. "I damn well knew that little shit would show up."

Char shoved his way through the hedge and glared at Buddy who was gazing at Cole Stevens with reverence. "Damn it, Hill. What are you doing here?"

The kid pulled his eyes from Stevens. "I just came from Houston and was coming to warn you—but saw my horse with these fellas." He gestured to Cole and Blake. "I recognized the marshal, but when I saw . . ." His gaze returned to Jesse's uncle. "Are you really Cole Stevens?"

"Warn us about what?" Char demanded.

"Huh? Oh, about Hank Boggs."

Jessalea stiffened. "What about him?"

"We're not going to be able to reach him. He owns a big ranch north of Houston." The kid's attention was still fixed on Stevens. "Did you really teach Char to draw?"

"Buddy!" Jesse hissed. *"Why* can't we reach him?"

Sighing, he faced her. "He's hired some fast guns to protect him."

"What gunmen?" Stevens demanded.

"Charlie Walker and Bill Ellis."

Blake Darcy whistled.

Char was shocked, then angered by Boggs's cowardice. "That yellow-bellied, son of a bitch."

Jesse didn't appear upset by the news—and that made him uneasy. "Jess?"

"That won't stop me," she said in a tone so quiet it sent chills up his spine.

Char glanced helplessly at her uncle.

His mouth was set in a hard line. "You're going home."

Thank God. Someone with sense at last.

"It won't matter if you send me to Fanny's. I'll come back, and I'll keep coming until I meet Hank Boggs face-to-face." Her eyes grew bright with unshed tears. "Uncle Cole, he's the one who . . . *cut* Susannah."

Stevens paled, then his eyes took on such a deadly glaze that Char winced, making him glad he wasn't on the receiving end of that fury. "Daniels, I'm going in after him. You keep my niece here until it's over."

"No."

"What did you say?"

"You're not going after Boggs without me. If anything happened to you, Jesse would never forgive me. Besides, after what that bastard did to her, how she's suffered, I'm going to be there to see he gets his due."

Darcy cleared his throat. "Char's right. We might have a better chance if we all went together."

"I'm ready," Buddy chimed.

"I'm going," Jesse announced with a stubborn set to her jaw.

Cole looked like he wanted to murder every one of them.

Chapter

❊ 22 ❊

When they reached Houston, Stevens checked them into the Harris County Hotel near the new rail line that joined Houston and Galveston. They made plans to meet later to talk about plans to penetrate Boggs's stronghold. As usual, Jesse and Char were expected to share a room—a problem she could have done without.

The ceilings were low, and the rooms were musky from the humid heat, but they were clean, even to the brown linen curtains and bedspread. It was a masculine room, though, with heavy furniture and a bearskin rug lying in front of a stone fireplace. She could almost imagine that fireplace dancing with yellow flames, illuminating her and Char as they made love on the bearskin.

It was a heady vision.

"Want to share your thoughts with me?" he asked as he dropped their saddlebags by the door and tossed his hat into an overstuffed chair.

She didn't know what possessed her to tell him the truth. Maybe it was because she knew one of them could die tomorrow. "I was wondering what it would be like for us to make love on that rug."

The hand at his side gave an involuntary twitch, then he let out a slow breath. "Woman, you're going to be the death of me."

"I was only being honest. I think about making love to you all the time." What was the matter with her? She was *asking* for it. Self-conscious, she walked to the window, damning herself for the stupid feeling that kept her unbalanced.

He slipped an arm around her waist and settled his hard length against her backside. "I think about it, too, darlin'. A lot." He caressed her belly. "But I think about other things, too, like how it would feel to see you carrying my child."

Why did he have to say that? Why did he have to make her believe there was a chance for them? Tears stung her eyes, and she leaned her head against his shoulder and lowered her lashes. *Tomorrow, one of them might die.* But, tonight . . . "Make love to me."

His hand trembled, then with a soft sigh, he nuzzled her ear. "Woman, I'm gonna love you until we both collapse from exhaustion." He traced her earlobe with his tongue. "And I'm gonna do it very, very slowly." He turned her in his arms and kissed her until she was limp . . . then lowered her to the bearskin rug.

By the time he carried her to the bed and stretched out beside her, she *was* exhausted. Completely. Visions of them swinging their child under the old elm by her bedroom window made her smile as she closed her eyes. . . .

* * *

Char's body still pulsed with remnants of the most incredible climax he'd ever experienced. *Climaxes.* He smiled and turned his face into her hair, inhaling her provocative scent, and knowing that from this day forward, he'd never rush lovemaking with Jesse again. The slow sweet torture had been worth every agonizing second.

He trailed his hand along her side and over her breast, shaping her with his palm. She stirred and nuzzled his neck.

The response of his body shocked him. He couldn't believe he was ready again. The woman really *was* going to be the death of him.

He eased away from her the tiniest bit, then relaxed when she didn't try to close the distance. For a time, he listened to the even sound of her breathing.

She was such a marvel. All defiance and determination one minute, then passion and fire the next. She kept him spinning in circles with her whispered words of love, then her stubborn refusal to marry him. He wished he knew what to do with her.

One thing was sure. He wasn't going to let her anywhere near Boggs. He'd rather take a bullet himself than place her life in danger. But she wasn't about to let him leave her behind.

Somehow he had to stop her.

Jessalea stretched long and hard, feeling more alive than she ever had before. Char's lovemaking did wonders for her—in more ways than one. Smiling, she reached for him.

He wasn't there.

Prying open her eyes, she scanned the room, then

closed them when the morning sun almost blinded her. Morning? Good heavens, she must have slept straight through. She wondered where Char could be, then hoped he'd gone to fetch them some breakfast. She was starved, and he was probably as hungry as she was after last night.

She smiled and snuggled deeper into the feather tick. But something nagged at her. Something wasn't right. What, for heaven's sake?

The curtains were gone.

Her eyes snapped open. The curtains? She reached to shove the blankets aside. They were gone, too.

In utter confusion, she stared at the bare feather tick where she sat, at the unadorned windows, at the place where her and Char's clothes had been piled next to the rug, at the spot where the saddlebags had been.

Everything was gone.

She brushed the hair out of her eyes, trying to make sense of what was happening. Why would Char take the curtains? The bedding? Her clothes?

Attempting to clear her sleep-fogged brain, she went to the door to peek down the hall.

Locked?

She stared at the latch, then the bed and window. Her eyes widened. *"That son of a bitch."*

She kicked the overstuffed chair, then winced when pain shot through her toes. "Damn you, Char Daniels!"

Hobbling to the bed, she sat down and massaged her sore foot. Tears stung her eyes. Damn it, he couldn't do this to her. She wouldn't let him. Somehow, someway, she'd get out of here.

A knock at the door surprised her.

"Mrs. Daniels?" a woman's voice came from the other side. "I've brung your breakfast."

Embarrassed by her nakedness, she darted behind the overstuffed chair as the woman opened the door with a key. An elderly lady in a calico dress entered, her eyes averted as she set a tray on the floor, then turned to leave.

"Wait! Where's Ch—my husband?"

"I don't know."

"Could you bring me some clothes?"

A gray curl slipped from a bun at the nape of her neck as she stared at the floor. "No. I was told to bring you food, a small towel to dry with after you wash and to lock the door. I was warned not to bring you nothing else. Especially not clothing." She hesitated. "Well, not for two days, anyway. After that, it's okay."

"Who told you that?" Jessalea demanded.

"Your husband . . . and your uncle."

They were both in on it. Her stomach gave an uncomfortable twist. "Why two days?"

"Didn't say. They just told me if they didn't return in that time to give you your clothes."

A feeling of doom spread over her. They'd made provisions in case they didn't return. "You can't keep me prisoner," she insisted in as stern a voice as she could manage while squatting naked behind a chair.

"That U.S. Marshal said it was for your own protection."

Blake Darcy. That rotten— "Where's the young blond man that was with the others?" Maybe Buddy would help her.

"Rode out with the others at first light. I'm sorry, lady, but I can't talk anymore. I got work to do." With a dip of her head, she closed the door and locked it.

Jesse rose from behind the chair, her legs and arms trembling with rage. They damn well better not get themselves killed. And they were not going to stop her. *They weren't.*

She shoved her fingers into her hair and paced. There had to be a way out of the room. Her gaze darted to the window that overlooked the street. She could climb onto the roof, then swing down. But without any clothes? Not likely.

For an instant, she considered waiting for the woman to return with her dinner, then overpower her. But the truth was, she didn't want to hurt her, nor did she want to wait that long. Every minute counted.

She scanned the room again, praying for anything she could use to conceal her nakedness. There wasn't a single thing. Char had been extremely thorough.

Her jaw clenched with another surge of fury, but it dissipated when her gaze landed on the bearskin rug.

Maybe he hadn't been quite so thorough.

She had to think this through. All right, so she escaped wearing the bearskin, providing she could lift it, then what would she do for clothes? A horse? Char had taken her buckskin, hadn't he?

Even if he had, she decided, her own garments—or someone else's—had to be in this hotel. She simply had to slip in the rear door and find them. The horse might be a problem, but perhaps she could borrow one.

She approached the rug and inspected it. The fur was heavy, but not as bad as she had thought it would be. It would be better, though, if she could get rid of the head with its open, snarling mouth.

She glanced at the tray, at the fork and knife lying

next to the plate, and her spirits soared. At least *all* the fates weren't against her.

It took her nearly an hour to saw through the tough hide, but the result was worth the effort. The rug was much, much lighter and big enough to cover her entirely. But she had to make ties to hold the thing in place.

She felt no remorse when she took the knife to the feather tick.

Once she was wrapped and confident that nothing vital showed, she headed for the window. It was nearing noon, and the air was humid and hot, so not many folks were about. A couple of men stood down the block, talking in front of a saloon, and there was a drunk slumped against the wall of the crockery across the street. She couldn't see under the porch's roof, though, but she didn't hear any sound, so she hoped no one was there. *Did she ever.*

This was the best opportunity she'd have, and she'd better make it quick, before the woman returned with her dinner.

Taking a breath, she swung her leg over the windowsill and climbed onto the slanted roof. She couldn't stop a smile when she remembered how Char had been in a similar position the first time she'd seen him.

The drunk stirred.

Afraid he would awaken, she hurried to the edge of the overhang and, using great care, wiggled around until her belly rested on her hands on the edge and her feet dangled in midair. Now, if she could only lower herself down until she hung by her fingers and her feet almost touched the ground, it would be a short, painless drop from there.

She pushed back.

The brunt of her weight slipped over the edge. The tie around her waist caught on a protruding nail.

She tried to wriggle free, but it was no use. The bearskin and tie were thoroughly snagged. She couldn't go up or down. She was hanging on the edge of a roof in full view of the town—and the damned fur was halfway up her thighs.

Cursing, she twisted from side to side.

"You're going to fall if you keep that up," an unfamiliar voice predicted from the porch below.

She couldn't see who it was, but she could hear the amusement in his tone. Embarrassment turned her skin so hot she thought she'd faint.

"If you'll allow me to hold your legs, you'll be free to use both hands to unhook yourself."

"What choice do I have," she hissed, certain that she'd die of humiliation the minute he set her down.

She thought she heard a chuckle before a man's arms encircled her legs and his chest pressed against the front of her thighs. He lifted her the slightest bit. "Okay, little one, I've got you. See if you can free yourself."

Since she now had use of her hands, it only took a second to lift the tie from the nail. "You can put me down."

He did so by sliding her along the length of his body until her feet touched the ground, and she was looking into his laughing eyes. She blushed to her toes. "Th-thank you."

Those arresting eyes sparkled as he nodded. "My pleasure—and I don't mean to pry, but where are your clothes?"

"They were stolen."

"You don't say? Do you know who took them?"

She took perverse satisfaction in telling him. "Cole Stevens and Char Daniels."

He gave a low whistle. "That's pretty dangerous company for a small gal like yourself to keep."

"So I discovered," she said, not wanting to prolong their conversation any longer by explaining.

"Perhaps I can be of service again." He pulled off his hat and turned it in his hands. "If you'd like to wait in my room for a few minutes"—he pointed to a hotel down the street—"I'll see if the general store doesn't have some ready-made things that might fit you."

The idea of being in a stranger's room didn't set well at all. "No, thank you. But I'd appreciate it if you'd check the stables and see if there's a buckskin in there."

His mouth quirked. "Are you going to stand here in the open while I do?"

"Well, I—"

He took her arm. "Come on, little one. You can wait in my room—and before you object, here, take this." He withdrew a small pearl-handled derringer from his waist and handed it to her.

The tenseness in her relaxed as she followed him to his room.

It didn't take him more than a few minutes to return, carrying her saddlebags.

She stared at the leather pouches, knowing Char had left them behind in case he didn't make it back. Damn him.

The man retreated down the hall to wait while she dressed.

Grabbing the only item of clothing in the bags, she

spread out her cream gown on the bed, then dampened a rag to smooth out the wrinkles the best she
could.

Brushing her hair with her fingers, she sighed and
opened the door, wondering how she was going to ride
in a tight dress.

She approached the man waiting at the end of the
corridor. "Thank you, er, Mr. . . . ?"

"Wilkins. Pete Wilkins."

"Thank you, Mr. Wilkins. I'm forever in your
debt."

He eyed her with appreciation. "That's an interesting thought. May I be of service in any other way?"

She caught the gleam in his eye, but ignored it. "No.
I have everything I need, thank you." She even had
Char's money that she'd put in her saddlebags when
she'd bathed in the river yesterday.

Hiding his disappointment, he extended his arm.
"At least let me walk you to the stables."

Now that she wasn't so flustered, she noticed he
carried a cane and walked with a slight limp. His
clothes were those of a gentleman, or a banker . . . or
a gambler. Yes, she thought as she studied his profile.
He did resemble the gamblers she'd seen on the
Mississippi paddle-wheelers.

When they reached the livery, he turned her around
to face him. "I don't know what this is about, sweets,
but I'd advise you to use caution. I don't know
Stevens or Daniels except by reputation, but from
what I've heard, they're not mean-spirited toward
women. They must have had a reason to want to keep
you here."

She wasn't surprised at his perception. His eyes

were filled with intelligence—much more than was expected on such a young face. "I'll be careful."

He touched his hat and nodded, then walked away. As he disappeared from sight, two things struck her at once. She still had Mr. Wilkins's derringer, and she wouldn't get far if she rode boldly onto Hank Boggs's ranch demanding a showdown. She needed a plan.

One that was foolproof.

CHAPTER

❊ 23 ❊

Char left Cole sitting by his saddle cleaning his rifle
and wandered to a break in the pecan grove that
overlooked the fence bordering Hank Boggs's ranch.
For more than two hours, Darcy and Hill had timed
the guards' rounds. One of six men rode by every five
minutes. There was a half mile of open expanse
between the trees where Char stood and the grove
inside the fence.

There was no way to cross that distance in five
minutes without being seen, at least not in broad
daylight, and he was sure the riders guarding the gate
weren't the only source of Boggs's protection. The
gunmen he'd hired must be at the house, surrounding
their benefactor in a nice, safe cocoon.

Removing his hat, he traced the steer horn band
with his finger, fighting his guilt over having left Jesse.
He had no doubt she was chomping at the bit by now,
and planning his funeral. But no matter how much it
pained him, he knew he'd done what was best for her.

He'd vowed to himself to protect her, and he would—even from herself.

But, God willing, he would take everyone of the Boggses to her in a coffin.

"Worrying about Jessalea?" Cole asked, as he joined him.

"Yes."

"There's no sense in it. She'll be okay once she realizes she can't escape. Hell, she might even have settled down to the point where she won't throw anything by the time we return."

Char doubted that. He glanced to where Darcy and Hill sat playing a hand of gin. "Has she always been so headstrong?"

"No." Stevens braced his arm on the trunk of a tree and crossed one ankle over the other. "She was a touch on the stubborn side when she was small, but after the massacre, she changed. She drew into herself and became solemn, private. I never saw a child so quiet and withdrawn. She was plagued by nightmares for the first year after it happened. There wasn't a night that went by that she didn't wake up screaming and crying. It damned near killed me and Fanny to watch her. I spent months searching for anything that would lead me to the men responsible for the murders and her nightmares, but it was no use."

He stared at the trees on the other side of the fence. "I had a hunch she knew their identity, but every time I tried to question her, she'd go to pieces. After a couple years, I stopped questioning her. But I never stopped searching."

"She was afraid of losing you, too."

"I know. In her eyes, I was the only family she had

left. Of course, little girls don't think about the time when they'll grow up and let someone else into their lives. One who will mean much more than an aging uncle."

Char had to smile at that. Stevens was a good man, a sensible one, and the guilt of leaving Jesse coupled with the guilt of deceiving her uncle was more than he could handle. "There's something I'd like to tell you, if you'll give me your word you won't pull a gun on me until you hear me out."

"I'm listening."

Uncomfortably, Char noticed he hadn't given his word. "Jesse and I aren't married."

A dangerous silence thickened the air.

"How long do I have to wait to draw?" Stevens asked without a trace of humor.

Char felt the hairs on his arms prickle. "I love her, Cole. I know she loves me, too. But she refuses to marry me. I've asked her twice."

"Did she say why?"

"She wants me to stop being a lawman and live on a farm." He took a big chance by turning his back on Cole. "I told her I'd consider it, but she still refused."

"Why?"

"She was afraid I'd be unhappy."

"She could be right."

Char tried to control the hardening in his jaw. "I couldn't be any more unhappy than I am now."

"Have the two of you . . . ?"

Char faced him and nodded.

"I see." A muscle throbbed in Stevens's temple. "Did you tell me this so I'd force her to marry you?"

He would have if he'd thought it would do any

good. "No. I told you because you had a right to know, and because there could be a child to consider."

"I was afraid of that, and the way I see it, there's only one solution to this mess."

"There is?" That was news to Char. He hadn't been able to find one.

"Yes. The two of you are going to have to find a compromise. She doesn't want you to chase outlaws, and you don't want to live on a farm. There's got to be something in between that'll make you both happy."

"What?"

"How the hell should I know? I just know that's the solution."

Jessalea snapped the buggy reins, hurrying the horse toward Boggs's ranch of which she knew the exact location, thanks to the proprietor at the general store. He'd also given her the name of Boggs's neighbors, Roy and Eula Scott, which fit right in with her plan.

Now all she had to do was hope.

By the time she reached a fork in the road that was only a mile from Boggs's, she was flushed and damp with perspiration from the hot Texas wind. It was nearing evening, and the Scotts' place—her supposed destination—was another ten miles down the left fork.

Everything was perfect.

She reined in and drew the buggy to a halt. Picking up the parasol, she raised her arm and struck the umbrella hard on the door of the vehicle. The wooden post inside the filmy material snapped. She tossed it onto the floorboards and reached for her bodice. She hated to destroy her favorite gown, but she had no choice. Clutching the middle of the neckline, she yanked to the side, tearing the front until the swells of both her breasts were exposed. The pearls she always wore with it, she put in her pocket.

She bent over and mussed her hair, then withdrew Mr. Wilkins's derringer from her other pocket. She stared at it for several seconds, then replaced it and reached for her own six-shooter beneath the seat.

Her pulse picked up speed. She was ready. Flicking the reins, she forced the horse into a trot, then a full gallop. She was wrenched from side to side as the wheels bounced over the rough road, but she held on with one hand while she aimed the gun through the window with the other and fired three times.

Tossing the weapon on the floorboards, she kicked it under the seat and grabbed the reins with both hands.

"Okay, Boggs. Here I come."

Three men were riding toward the gate when her carriage roared through.

She hauled in on the leather, bringing the conveyance to a grinding, shuddering halt, then buried her face in her hands and began to wail.

One of the guards approached, and she fell into his arms, hiding her revulsion as she hugged his hairy neck. "Oh, thank God. I thought they were going to kill me."

The man tried to pry her arms loose, but she hung on. "Who? What are you talkin' about?"

"S-some men. I was o-on the way to my aunt and uncle's, the S-Scotts, when those awful men stopped me. One of them tried to . . . to . . . hurt me, but I fought him. I h-hit him with my parasol and got away, but they chased m-me. *They shot at me."*

The man finally freed himself from her clinging hold. "What men?" His gaze fastened on the open front of her bodice.

The other two riders fixed on the same place.

"Outlaws," she whined. "They were outlaws. They had bandanna's over their faces and gun belts criss-crossed over their chests." She threw her arms around his neck again. "You saved me."

She felt his head move as he glanced up at his companions. "What do we do, Tom?"

"Hellfire, Jack. Why are you askin' me? I don't know. We cain't take her to town. It's too late—and it's too far to take her to the Scotts'. Maybe we should send Willie to tell the boss."

"Why do I have to go?" the one called Willie complained.

"'Cause me and Tom say so," Jack said, his thick chest rumbling against her ear. He caught her wrists and pulled them from his neck. "Now, girlie. Why don't you sit in the buggy and wait until Willie gets back with the boss's orders."

"I'm afraid," she whimpered.

His gaze remained fixed on her breasts as he patted her shoulder. "Don't you worry none. Me and Tom's gonna stay right here. We won't let no one bother you."

She gave him a watery smile, then glanced at the other man. His thick lips were wet with saliva, his eyes roaming her bosom.

She suppressed a shudder and smiled at him, too.

His eyes turned hot.

A jolt of fear shot through her, and she climbed into

the buggy to wait. It felt safer, and when Willie returned, she'd know if her plan had worked or not.

"I'm going to strangle her," Char hissed through clenched teeth. *"Then I'm going to beat her."* When he'd heard the shots and seen her racing toward the gate in the buggy, his heart had nearly stopped. Then he realized it had been a plan. A damned dangerous one that would probably be the death of her. He swallowed down a surge of panic.

"How did she get out of the room?" Stevens grumbled, his attention, like Char's, on Jesse and the two men standing next to her.

"I have no idea. But next time, I'm gonna tie her to the damned bed." *Please, God. Let there be a next time.*

"I don't like it any more than you, Daniels, but you have to admit, she got inside the gate and may very well get next to Boggs, which is something you and I were still trying to do."

"She might get herself killed, too." Char took a breath to ease the fear clawing through his chest.

"No, she won't. It's almost dark. We'll go in before Boggs—*or anyone else*—can do damage." Settling his hat firmly on his head, he checked his weapons, then strode to where the others were seated. "Stow the cards. It's time to go."

Making sure his own guns were loaded, Char followed, then stopped next to Stevens. "If I don't make it out of this, tell Jesse there's a note to her and our child—if there is one—in my saddlebags." He knew it was foolish, but he never wanted any babe of his to have to wonder about his pa. He'd spent hours that afternoon telling his child everything there was to know about Charleston Daniels. Everything there was to know about his love for Jesse.

Stevens gave him a sour look. "You can tell her yourself *when* we get back."

There were five men standing around her buggy by the time Willie returned. Jessalea held her breath and waited for him to dismount. Had she succeeded or failed?

Willie motioned Jack over to where he stood by his horse. They spoke for a few seconds, then turned to her.

Her heart was beating so fast, she was afraid they'd hear it.

Jack headed in her direction. "Mr. Boggs told Willie to bring you to the main house."

Her shoulders sagged with relief. She'd done it. "Are you sure his wife won't mind?"

A lewd smile twisted Jack's mouth. "He ain't got no missus." He nodded to the boy. "Follow Willie. He'll lead you in." His gaze sweeping her bosom one last time, he touched his hat, then motioned to Willie.

Revulsion climbed up her throat and made it difficult to swallow, but she managed to force a sincere-sounding "thank you" before she snapped the reins.

As the buggy moved down the rutted road behind Willie's horse, she looped the reins around the brake and reloaded the missing shells in her revolver, then put it in her pocket. The derringer, she stuck in the opposite one. She knew she would need all the firepower she could get to kill both Boggses—*if Harley was there*—and hold off the guards until Char and the others arrived. Although she hadn't seen them, she knew they were hidden close by, and she knew they'd hear the shots and come after her.

She was betting her life on it.

The spanish-style stucco house sat in the shape of a U in the center of a huge pecan grove. Beyond the acres of trees lay miles of open grassland. In the dying evening light, the house stood like a shadowy tomb encircled by tall, yawning demons.

She clenched her hands into fists around the reins. Had Hank used blood money from the raids to buy this? She'd bet her horse, he had.

A man she didn't recognize stood on the covered porch, his hand resting on his hip, very close to the six-shooter at his side. His bottomless stare, the grim set of his mouth, and the calm, yet alert stance told her he was one of the gunmen Boggs had hired.

Willie dismounted and helped her down. "Is the boss inside, Ellis?"

The gunman's eyes didn't leave her. "Yeah. He's waitin' for his"—his gaze lowered to her open bodice—"supper."

She gave an involuntary shiver. She'd heard of Bill Ellis, but she never thought she'd see him in person. His size wasn't that intimidating, but the lack of emotion in his eyes, together with the scrubby growth of hair on his chin and upper lip, gave him an aura of danger like she'd never seen before.

Willie's spurs clanked as he crossed the veranda and opened the door for her. "Right in here, miss."

The aroma of chili and corn bread wafted from inside. If she'd been anywhere else, she might have welcomed the homey scents.

Squaring her shoulders, she walked into the main living area of Hank Boggs's house, a garishly furnished room that was designed to leave an impression rather than for comfort. The entire rear wall was lined with glass doors that led to a courtyard. On either side of the doors, halls extended back to additional rooms.

"This the girl?" a man asked from where he lounged near the left hallway.

"Well, she damned sure ain't no hired hand, Walker."

Charlie Walker, Jessalea thought with a tremor. She'd seen a wanted poster of him once. She'd never been able to forget his glassy-eyed stare or thickly bearded face, or the deep grooves spreading out from both sides of his nose. Her nervousness increased. Unless she could get him out of the room, she had no chance of confronting Boggs.

The outlaw studied her, his gaze lazily exploring every visible inch of her body. "No. Couldn't mistake this beauty for no hired hand." He curled his fist and slammed it on the wall beside him to alert someone down the hall. "Hank! Your guest has arrived."

A door opened, then footsteps drew near.

Jessalea shook off nervous tremors . . . and waited.

Hank Boggs's bloated form stepped into view. His eyes met hers, and he gave a start, then his thick lips spread into a smile. "Welcome, my dear."

Her hand inched toward her pocket, and she had to clutch her skirt to stop herself from going for her gun. Hatred engulfed her. Visions of the man's knife cutting into her sister's flesh caused her stomach to roll, and it was hard to speak. "Thank you."

His pig-eyes swept over her, then shifted to Willie. "Close the door on your way out—and tell Ellis to keep a sharp watch." He nodded to Walker. "You guard the rear. Shoot anything that moves."

Walker arched a brow, then shrugged and sauntered out.

Relief that he'd left eased her tension, but she feigned concern as she faced Boggs. "Is something wrong?"

"Not anymore." Keeping his eyes on her, he returned to the corridor he'd just left and motioned to someone.

Two men emerged.

Fear struck swift and hard. She reeled from the impact. *Oh, dear God.*

Harley Boggs's fat lips curled into a smile as he moved to join Hank.

But it was the other man who held her attention. Stricken with terror, she stared into the lifeless eyes of Odie Boggs.

CHAPTER

❈ 24 ❈

C har gave the rope around the guard's wrist a final yank, then rolled the unconscious man into the trees. He searched for Cole and found him finishing with his man. "Where's Darcy?"

"I'm right here," Blake said, strolling from the trees with Buddy on his heels. "Hill and I took care of ours. That only leaves two more—and they should show up any minute."

"You should have seen me, Char." Buddy beamed. "I hid in the grass and jumped him. Knocked him out cold."

"Good work. But right now, there's two more, and God only knows how many at the house. You and Darcy stay here, finish with the fence riders, while Stevens and I check the house."

Cole pulled his gun. "I'll take the front."

Nodding, Char drew his Colts and sprinted into the trees. But with every step he took, his fear for Jesse mounted. His stomach churned. His hands shook.

He stopped and wiped his sleeve over his face.

Damn. He had to get hold of himself. Her life could depend on his quick reactions. His steadiness.

It was the jolt he needed. His nerves settled into a lethal calm as he silently crept through the trees and circled the house.

Candlelight glowed from inside, spilling over a courtyard flanked on three sides by the building. Through a line of glass doors, he could see the shadowy figures of several people. He knew Jesse was one of them.

Controlling his fear for her, he crept closer, his gaze searching for the men he knew would be guarding the house. Something moved on the right.

A match flared, illuminating the face of the man lighting a cigarette. Charlie Walker.

Straightening, Char stepped into the open.

Walker stiffened and went for his gun.

"Do it, Charlie, and you're a dead man."

His hand froze. "Daniels? Is that you?"

"Yeah, and I'd hate to have to kill the man who once saved my life."

"I don't cotton to back-shooters, Daniels. You know that."

"You still saved my life, and now, I'm returning the favor. Get out of here, Charlie—and take Ellis with you. Boggs has my woman, and I'll kill any man who stands in my way."

"Alone?"

"No."

Walker drew on his cigarette, causing the red tip to glow. "How many?"

"Four."

"Anyone I know?"

"Cole Stevens."

"Shit."

Char smiled.

"Listen. I already got paid, and I ain't got no business in the middle of whatever this is. I'm gonna get Bill and hightail it outta here. Give me five minutes." Walker started to turn, but stopped. "For old times sake, there's two by the barn to take down first, then three in the house."

Char felt something cold crawl up his spine. "Who's inside?"

"Three Boggs brothers."

Unable to move, Jessalea stared at Odie Boggs. Her hands trembled. Nausea rolled through her stomach and pushed its way upward. Beads of perspiration dampened her flesh. He was going to finish what he hadn't accomplished ten years ago. He was going to kill her.

Odie Boggs fingered a muttonchop sideburn, his cold eyes locked on hers. "I always wondered what you'd have looked like grown. Course, I figured I'd never know since I thought you were dead. Imagine my surprise when Harley told me about your visit to the jail." He leaned against the wall, resting his hand on his sidearm, his manner relaxed and insolent. "What do you think, boys? She resemble her ma?"

"Sure does," Hank agreed. "Damned near pissed my britches when she walked in, she shocked me so much. Thought I was seein' a ghost."

Jessalea lowered her hand to her pocket.

Harley drew his revolver. "Get your hands away from your skirt, girl. Hank, see what she's got."

"Sure thing." Hank ran his hands over her breasts and hips, then down her thigh, smiling as he squeezed her flesh. His hand hit the pistol. "Well, I'll be . . ." He pulled the Colt from her pocket and stuffed it into his waistband. He checked the other pocket and found the derringer.

"Don't try anything else, gal," Harley warned. "Killin' you would give me great pleasure. 'Specially after the way you talked to me in Christi. Tellin' me how you was going to kill my brothers." His eyes narrowed. "How three were already dead."

"Settle down, Harley," Odie commanded. "Holster your gun. You'll get a turn at her in a minute." His gaze sliced into hers, and hatred flared from the murky brown depths. "We all will."

Panic hit her so hard, she reeled from the force. In that instant, she knew her fate would be the same as her mother's and Susannah's. *Oh, God, Char. Help me.*

Hank inched toward her. "Been a long time since I had me somethin' this purdy." His fat lips spread into a smile. "'Bout ten years, I figure." He fixed on her chest. "Been needin' a new tobacco pouch, too. The other one's worn to a nubbin from so much handlin'."

She swallowed down a rush of bile. Prickles of terror skittered over her flesh.

"Take off your clothes," Odie ordered. "Let's see what you got under them rags."

Shaking with revulsion and fear, Jessalea edged toward the door.

Hank and Harley circled to either side of her, blocking her only escape.

Odie came straight for her. "If you're thinking about fighting like your ma did, go ahead. Makes it more exciting." He stopped in front of her. "She was a real wild cat. Gave me the best screw I ever had."

"You *bastard!*" She lunged at him, raking her nails down his face.

He slapped her so hard, her head slammed into the door behind her. Pain blinded her. Blackness wavered in and out.

Odie stood in front of her, fingering a line of blood down his cheek. "Hold her for me, boys. She's got claws."

Her arms were wrenched out to the sides and pinned to the wall on either side of the door. Mindless with hysteria, she twisted and kicked. "Let me go! Get away from me, you pig!"

He ripped the front of her dress to the waist, then gripped the edges and tore outward, exposing her entire chest. His eyes came alive with lust as they roamed her heaving breasts. "Hey, Harley. One of those beauties is going to make a fine pouch. A lot bigger than the last one. Hell, I might even take one, too."

Hank grabbed a breast, squeezing brutally. "Goll damn, thems nice. Too bad she ain't got another one for me."

Fear closed her throat. Her heart pounded so hard she thought it would beat her lungs to death.

Harley latched onto her other breast. "Yep, they sure are fine. Soft, too. But you'll get one, Hank. I'll give you my old one."

"Quit jawin' and lay the bitch on the floor," Odie instructed. "I'm as stiff as a bull's horn."

Horror-struck, she fought and screamed and kicked as they dragged her to the floor in the center of the room and shoved her skirt to her waist.

"Hold her down," Odie commanded, reaching for the buttons on his pants.

Hank kept a grip on her wrist, while his other han caught her ankle. Harley did the same. Grinning a each other, they spread her legs wide.

"Nooooo!" she cried, struggling to get away wit every ounce of strength she possessed.

"Hurry, Odie. She's harder than hell to hold, Hank urged. "And I'm 'bout to go off just watchin her wiggle."

Odie knelt between her legs. "Close your yaps boys. I got other things to concentrate on." He opene the front of his pants, his eyes wild with lust, his large stained teeth bared between thick lips.

An explosion of glass shook the room.

Gunfire erupted.

Hank clutched his stomach and toppled backwar over a chair.

Odie grabbed her and pivoted until she covere him, protecting him from flying bullets.

The front door burst open. More shots blasted.

Harley screamed.

Odie leapt to his feet and yanked her in front o him, shielding himself. He grabbed her around th neck, turning her so that her spine was against hi flabby stomach. The barrel of a gun pressed into he temple. "Drop 'em, or the girl dies."

In frozen horror, she watched Char rise from be hind a chair, shards of glass dropping from his clothe as he tossed his Colts onto the floor, his eyes on her his fear for her palpable.

The anger and concern in her uncle thickened th air as he straightened from the front door and did th same.

Marshal Darcy rose from his crouched position by

an open glass door. His revolver hit the oriental rug covering the stone floor.

Sick with fear, she made a quick survey of the room, searching for Buddy, but didn't see him.

"Odie, help me," Hank cried. He was curled on the floor, holding his stomach, blood running from the corner of his mouth. "I've been gut-shot."

"All of you, get over there." Odie waved his gun toward the fireplace.

Char hesitated, then moved with Blake and Cole as instructed.

Odie glanced at his brother. "Hank, can you stand?"

"I cain't. I'm dyin'," he whined. Blood gushed from between his fat lips. "Kill 'em, Odie. Kill that bastard in black." He made a gargling sound. "Show 'em the wrath of Otis Daniel Boggs."

Jessalea went numb. Otis Daniel? Odie? No, not *Odie*. O.D. Her gaze flew to Char. Oh, God. O.D. couldn't be his father.

Char's skin went pale, and she knew he was thinking the same.

Hank gasped for air and gagged, then slumped, lifeless.

She felt a tremor of fury quake through O.D. as he cocked his gun and aimed it at Char. "This is for you, Hank."

"No!" She grabbed his arm.

Gunfire exploded.

Char hit the floor.

Jessalea went wild. Kicking and scratching, she tried to tear Boggs apart with her bare hands.

The barrel of his gun struck her jaw.

Through a foggy haze, she saw her uncle and Blake lunge for him at the same time.

O.D. fired again.

Both men dropped to the floor, scrambling for their weapons.

O.D. didn't waste any more shots. He knotted his fist in her hair and dragged her through the door and into the black depths of the pecan orchard.

She was too dazed and too numb to struggle. Was Char dead? Hatred tumbled over her like an avalanche, and without thought, she threw herself at O.D., knocking them both to the dirt. She kicked and clawed and bit, trying to hurt him anywhere she could reach. This bastard had taken everything from her. *Everything*.

Grabbing her hands, he jerked her to her feet and shoved the barrel of his gun to the underside of her chin.

"Let her go," Char said in a cold, dangerous voice.

O.D. tensed.

Jessalea nearly fainted with relief. Char was alive.

"Toss the gun over here right now," Char ordered. "Or I'll blow a hole in your fat head."

"I'll take the girl with me," O.D. threatened.

"She'd be better off dead than living with the memory of your hands on her."

O.D. cocked the gun beneath her chin, his eyes on Char as he slowly backed deeper into the trees, dragging her with him.

Jessalea fixed on Char. There was a danger emanating from him that made her shiver. Anger brightened his eyes. "Take another step, and you're dead, Boggs."

"You'll have to shoot her to get to me." O.D. positioned her dead center in front of him. "Like I said, I'm taking her with me. After I kill you." He turned the gun on Char.

Gunfire roared through the trees.

Boggs stiffened. A chocked sound bubbled from his throat. He twitched and gasped, then his arms fell away, and he crashed facedown in the dirt. Blood gushed from a crater in his back.

In stunned surprise, Jessalea saw Buddy standing beside a tree . . . holding a smoking gun.

CHAPTER

❋ 25 ❋

Char tossed down another whiskey and slammed the glass onto the counter. Where was Jesse? He and Cole and Buddy had searched the whole countryside and hadn't found a trace of her for the last two days.

Pouring another shot, he cursed O.D. Boggs, and prayed the bastard wasn't the man Char had been searching for. The mere thought that O.D. could be his father made him sick. He twisted the glass in his hand, fighting the ache closing in on his throat. It was as bad as the one in his heart. Jesse would never be his. Even if they could have overcome their other difficulties, *this* one was insurmountable. He'd lost her.

He tossed down another whiskey, hoping to dull the pain, and wishing he'd listened to his instincts and left before she ingrained herself so deeply in his heart. Loving her hurt too much.

The swinging doors behind him banged open.

He glanced over his shoulder out of habit.

Jesse, dressed in her britches, checkered shirt, and flop-billed hat, stood at the front doors.

Their eyes met and held for a heartbeat, then she turned and left.

Char was torn between relief that she was all right and wanting to shake her. "Damn it, Jesse, wait a minute." His whole life was walking out the door.

By the time he reached the street, she was standing beside her buckskin, tightening the cinch. "I came to say good-bye," she said in a quiet voice, her gaze fixed on the horse.

Char felt his life slipping away. "Where have you been?"

"On the range. I needed to be alone to think. To make a decision."

"Jesse, O.D. Boggs's name is probably a coincidence."

"It could be," she admitted. "But you said yourself, you'd been searching for fifteen years and never came across the name before." She lifted a hand to the pommel. "Not that it matters to me whether he was your pa or not. It doesn't. You have nothing to do with the past. But nothing has changed between us, either."

"Darlin', give us a chance."

She leaned her forehead against the saddle and rolled her head from side to side. "I can't." She mounted, refusing to look at him, her spine stiff. "Good-bye, Char." As she turned her horse, he saw the tears glistening on her cheeks.

He closed his eyes and arched his head back, his throat so tight he could barely breathe. "Damn it, Jesse, you're tearing me apart."

For several seconds, he fought to control the stinging behind his eyes, the crushing weight rolling across his chest. He took deep, restoring breaths, then at last, when he felt composed again, he turned for the saloon. He needed to ease the pain.

A movement startled him, and he swung around, coming face-to-face with Cole. His thumbs were curled over his gun belt, his eyes concerned and filled with sympathy. "She's confused, Daniels. For years she's focused solely on the men who killed her family, and now that they're dead, she doesn't know where to go from here. Give her some time."

"A century wouldn't be time enough to change how she feels about gunmen."

"She's—"

"It's over, Stevens. We *all* know it." Fearing he would shatter if he didn't leave right that second, he sidestepped Cole and strode into the saloon.

Blake was standing at the bar, but, to his credit, he had the good sense not to mention Jesse. "So, where do you go from here?"

Char reached into his pocket and handed Darcy the badge he'd given him. "I don't know. But I won't be needing this."

"Going to continue searching for your father?"

"I think I may have found him."

Darcy downed a shot glass full of whiskey. "O.D. Boggs wasn't your father."

"How would you know?"

"While you and the others were trying to find Jesse, I checked. From 1844 to 1846, Boggs was in prison for selling rifles to Indians."

"Are you sure?"

"Yes."

Relief washed over Char, and for a fleeting second,

he thought about going after Jesse. But he couldn't. His parentage wasn't their problem. "Thanks, Darcy." He rose and offered his hand. "I appreciate everything you've done."

"I did it for both of you."

"I know." With a last nod, Char returned to the hotel and packed. He wasn't sure where he was going, but he figured he'd start at the post office in Shreveport, to see if there was a response to the wire Jesse sent to Charleston about his mother's folks.

When he went to shove a shirt into his saddlebags, his hand touched paper. It was the letters he'd written to Jesse and the child he thought she may have conceived.

Staring at the parchment, he crumbled it into his fist and tossed it on the floor. He'd laid open his heart—for what? Nothing, *that's* what. Jesse's stubbornness had killed any chance they had.

He thought about the possibility that she carried his child, and he knew that before he left Houston, he would see Cole. If there was a child, Char wanted to know.

After finding Cole in his room and promising to check with him often, Char looped his saddlebags over his shoulder and headed for the stables.

Buddy Hill was sitting on a bale of straw near Black Duke's stall. The image reminded him of the time in Victoria when he found Jess—No! He wasn't going to keep torturing himself. She was no longer a part of his life. "If you've got ideas about following me again, Hill, forget it."

Buddy's blue eyes, that used to be so full of life and excitement, were now shadowed with maturity. "I don't. I knew you'd be leaving, and I wanted to say good-bye. I'll be leaving myself on the next stage for Boston."

Char felt regret for the kid's lost innocence. "Going home?"

"Yes. I decided I like healing folks a lot better than . . . than not."

Fighting the urge to embrace him, Char set about saddling Duke. "You'll do real good, Buddy. You've got a smart head on your shoulders. Hell, by the time you're my age, you'll probably be in charge of some fancy hospital."

He smiled and rose, extending his hand. "Be seeing you, Charleston Daniels."

Char shook it. "Yeah, kid. One of these days."

Hill made it to the entrance before he turned around. "You know she loves you, don't you?"

His whole body clenched against the pain. *"Good-bye,* Hill."

Jessalea stood at the back door of the farm, staring out at the newly raked yard, at the stump from the old elm tree outside her window that Uncle Cole had cut down. He'd accomplished a lot in two months.

The barn had a new coat of paint, the fields were fertilized and tilled, ready for planting next spring. She glanced toward the house where her uncle and Fanny were inside discussing the best way to fix the veal for dinner. She was so glad they'd come to stay with her. Everything was perfect. Like she'd always imagined.

But it wasn't. No matter how hard she wished it otherwise, it wasn't.

Sniffing, she glanced down at the letter she'd received from Buddy today. He was happy, at least.

He'd gone home to become a doctor like his pa. If he'd left the letter at that, she would have been okay. But he hadn't. Her gaze drifted over the second page as she reread his words.

The day Char left Houston, I went by his room before I found him in the stables. He had wadded up these letters and thrown them on the floor. I thought you might like to have them.

She stared at the enclosed wrinkled pages, at Char's bold writing.

One was a letter to their child that told about Char's lonely life on the farm, his fear of being a father. It told about his reasons for becoming a lawman when he left the army, about being afraid of marriage, and his absolute terror of returning to a life like the one he'd escaped.

Then he told their child about his love for her. She knew he'd written the letters because he didn't think he'd survive the confrontation with the Boggs brothers.

She stared at the other page. In the one to her, Char reaffirmed the words he'd written to their child. *I'll always love you, Jesse, whether in this world or the next.*

Lowering the parchment, she wiped the tears from her cheeks.

"Dinner's ready, pumpkin," Fanny called out from the kitchen.

"I'll be right there." She folded the pages and put them in her skirt pocket, knowing she'd never be able to do the same with her thoughts of Char. She missed him so much. Everywhere she looked, she saw his laughing blue eyes, his mischievous grin . . . his tortured features when she left him in Houston.

The pain was unbearable.

When she walked into the kitchen, she caught her uncle and Fanny exchanging a tender kiss. Uncle Cole had changed a lot since they left Houston. He had put away his guns and encouraged Fanny to sell the brothel and become his wife. He was even building them a home at the edge of the north field. Their wedding was planned for November.

"It's about time you showed up, gal. I'm near starved to death." Her uncle winked. "If Fanny hadn't distracted me, I'd have been gnawing on the table legs by now."

Fanny rolled her expressive brown eyes, then smiled in a way that always made Jessalea feel special. "You hungry, pumpkin?"

No, she wasn't. She hadn't had much of an appetite since—. She clamped down on her thoughts. "I could eat a bite or two."

As they sat down to enjoy the veal and gravy Fanny had fixed, Uncle Cole grinned at her. "Did Fanny tell you we found that special wallpaper she wanted for the parlor?"

Jessalea's fork stopped halfway to her mouth. Was that really her uncle talking? It was so different hearing him discuss such mundane things. Not that she didn't like him this way, she did. But it was . . . odd. "I don't think Fanny mentioned it, no."

He nodded. "Old Jake down at the mercantile got some in from Charleston yesterday."

Charleston. Oh, God. Where was he? Was he still the fast draw? Or had someone finally beaten him? The words in his letter hummed through her head. *I'll always love you, whether in this world or the next.* Her stomach rolled, and she rose abruptly. "Excuse me." She made it to the yard before she got sick.

"Are you all right, honey?" Fanny asked, placing an arm around her shoulders.

She buried her face in her hands and began to cry. "No. I don't think I'll ever be all right again. Nothing's like I thought it would be. I can't remember the good times here anymore. I try so hard, but it's just not the same. There's no laughter here. No joy. Only loneliness." She caught Fanny's hand. "Why am I so unhappy? Damn it. I have everything I've dreamed of."

"Not everything." Fanny knelt beside her and lifted her chin. "You don't have the most important thing. A home isn't a place, honey. It's something you share with someone you love, whether it's a grand castle overlooking the ocean . . . or a bedroll under a tree." She wiped a tear from Jessalea's cheek. "Go after him, pumpkin. It's time for both of you to stop hurting."

"I can't. He's a gunman and always will be. Even if I could convince him to come to the farm, it would destroy him."

"Go with him, then."

"Sure. Then I can live like you did—worrying constantly, crying at night, and fearing every day that I'll get word he's been killed."

"I did those things because I wasn't *with* Cole. It would have been different if I could have been beside him." Compassion filled her eyes. "Besides, I think your problem goes deeper. I think you're afraid of being hurt again. Afraid to lose another loved one. Aren't you?"

"Yes."

"Dying doesn't necessarily have to happen in a gunfight, you know."

"What?"

"I'm saying, death can happen anywhere. I could fall from a stool in the kitchen and bust my head. Or Cole could trip and land on a pitchfork. Pumpkin, there's no guarantees on how long a body is going to live. When Char's time is over, the Lord will take him . . . and not a second before, whether it's in a gunfight or behind a plow."

"But at least I won't be there to see it."

"No, you won't—and you'll never have to grieve over his death. Instead, you'll grieve for the rest of your life for what could have been."

Jessalea let the tears fall freely. "I don't know what to do."

Fanny smiled in that gentle, special way. "Do whatever your heart tells you."

Hanging her head, Jessalea tried to reach into her heart for the answer. When it came to her, she smiled through her tears. She knew exactly what she wanted to do.

"Is that a decision I see lighting your face?" Fanny teased.

"Yes."

"For heaven's sake, don't keep me in suspense. Tell me what you're going to do?"

"Send a telegram."

"To Char?"

"No." Without further explanation, she rose and gave Fanny a hug, then headed for the barn.

She sent the telegram from Jefferson City that afternoon, then returned home to wait. She figured it would be a month or more before she received an answer.

But she was wrong. Two weeks later, when Fanny and Cole were at the new house putting on a cedar roof, Blake Darcy rode into the yard.

She stared at him over her dining-room table, hardly able to believe he'd made it so fast.

Bracing his elbows on the white linen tablecloth, Blake folded his hands and rested his chin on them. He studied her for a long time. "Are you sure this is what you want?"

"Yes." *It was the only way.* "And hurry, before my uncle and Fanny get here. It's going to be hard enough to tell them I'm leaving, but I don't think they'd understand about this."

"That makes three of us."

She didn't have time for him to be difficult. "What do you want me to do?"

"Get married, raise a passel of kids, and forget this nonsense."

"Blake."

He sighed. "I don't even know if I *can* do this, and I know I'm going to regret it, but here goes." He rose. "All right, imp. Let's get it over with."

She sprang to her feet and waited anxiously.

"You ready?"

"Yes."

"Then raise your right hand . . ."

CHAPTER

❋ 26 ❋

Is this where you were raised?"

"Yes." Char surveyed the crumbling house and overgrown pastures . . . and the grave markers of the Websters. They'd been dead for years now. Deke during the war, and Ma Webster a couple years later of consumption. He knew he was supposed to grieve for their loss, but he couldn't.

He glanced at the man standing beside him and again experienced an eerie sensation at their resemblance. His father, Otis Daniel Duvall, Dan to his family and friends, looked like an older version of Char, himself. But his eyes were green, and his black hair was tinted with gray at the temples.

Char would forever be grateful to Jesse for helping him find Dan. When Char had arrived in Shreveport, there'd been a telegram waiting for C. Daniels. A telegram from Char's maternal grandmother, Lillian Martin.

"I can't believe you were this close, and I never found you," Dan said in a disgusted voice. "After I

eturned to Charleston and found that your mother
ad disappeared, I searched everywhere for her—and
ou, since I figured you were born by then. Damn it, I
now I came to this house, too."

"You probably did, but Deke's wife was barren, and
e wasn't about to hand over the only free laborer he
vould ever have. That's probably why he wouldn't let
ne go anywhere but to that small church in
Vashburn's glen, either. He was afraid someone in
own might question my parentage or notice a family
esemblance to you or the Martins."

"I wish that son of a bitch was still alive."

Char didn't. "What happened is in the past. Let's
eave it there."

"How did you become so wise?"

"I must have inherited it."

Dan laughed, a full, rich sound that made Char feel
ood all over. His father. He couldn't believe it. He
vanted to touch him to make sure he was real.

Dan's chuckles died, and he became serious. "You
:now, I wish I could be as generous as you and leave
hings in the past, but I can't. I'll never forgive your
:randfather, Herbert Martin, for what he did to us. To
ou. He was so afraid Emma would fall for a fortune
unter who was after the Martin money, he smoth-
:red her with protection—and it finally killed her."

"How?"

"He discovered we were going to elope and had me
irrested on a false charge, then he used the Martin
nfluence and money to have me taken to a jail in
\ustin, Texas. It was his fault she ran away that day.
Iis fault she wasn't at home where she should have
)een—with a doctor close by."

Dan braced a foot on the bottom rung of the rail

fence and gazed at the distant hills. A soft breeze ruffled the collar of his tan shirt. "I hated Herbert. He didn't care how much Emma and I loved each other. All he cared about was his money, and he was so sure I was after it, he didn't even bother to check my background. If he had, he'd have known I was heir to a publishing fortune. But he didn't. He assumed I was a drifter, and because of that, my Emma died." He gripped the railing until his knuckles turned white. "God. If I'd only known money was the reason . . ."

Char could understand his grief. "I'm sure he regretted what he did."

"Lillian says so, but Herbert never said a word to me before he died. He had damn near as much pride as he did money." Dan gave him a derisive smile. "Some family, huh?"

"A very unique one."

Dan chuckled. "So, are you planning to move to Charleston and be near your *unique* kin?"

"No. I'm going to Missouri and see if I can't buy a small farm. Other than chasing outlaws, it's what I know best."

"I thought you said you hated farming."

"I was wrong. I just hate this place." He nodded to the shuttered house. He knew he was right, too. His grandmother owned one of the biggest plantations in South Carolina, and he'd enjoyed the two months he'd spent with her and his father, getting acquainted. When you were with people who cared about you, nothing was bad. Hell, he'd even plowed the north field, and for the first time, he'd *liked* what he did.

"When are you leaving?"

"Why?" Char winked. "Are you in a hurry for me to go?"

"I won't dignify that remark with an answer."

Feeling another rush of warmth, he placed his hand on his father's shoulder. "I have to go soon. There's a woman . . ."

"Jesse?"

Char lowered his arm. "How did you know about her?"

A smile touched the corner of Dan's mouth. "You and I have something besides our looks in common— we both talk in our sleep."

Ah, hell. What had he said?

As if his father had read his thoughts, he smiled. "You said you wanted her to marry you." He cleared his throat. "And you promised you'd never rush lovemaking with her again."

Jesus. Why didn't the ground open up and suck him in?

"I believe," Dan continued, "you also said something about a child." He gave Char a steady look. "Does this mean I'm going to be a grandfather?"

He shifted, feeling very uncomfortable. "It's possible."

"Are you going to let her raise the babe without you?"

"No! I mean, not if I can help it. That's why I'm leaving. I've got to find her."

His father thought on that for a minute. "What if there is no child? Then what?"

"It won't make any difference. I'm going to marry her either way—even if I have to hold her at gunpoint to do it."

"You sound a lot like I did thirty years ago." Sadness touched Dan's strong features. "I only hope you have better luck than I did." His gaze drifted over Webster's farm. "Is your mother . . . buried here?"

Char's heart went out to him. He knew exactly how he'd feel if Jesse disappeared without a trace. "Yes. In the peach grove out back. When I was ten, I put a large stone where the wooden cross had been and chiseled her name on it."

"Do you care if I go alone?"

Unable to speak for the welling emotions, he shook his head.

He sat on the fence rail and waited until his father returned.

The ride to the Martins' ranch was somber, each reflecting on the woman they loved.

With a promise to visit often and write at least twice a month, Char left the next morning and headed for Missouri. But as the days passed, insecurities set in. If Jesse didn't want to marry him, there wasn't anything he could do. He was being a fool. She'd made it clear as glass she wouldn't marry him for any reason, so why was he laying himself open for more hurt?

By the time he reached St. Louis, he was certain he was making a mistake. Jesse wasn't going to change. She had more pluck and determination than any *man* he'd ever known.

But he wanted to see her one more time. He had to make sure there wasn't a child. What if there was? he thought. Then what? He didn't have an answer, but he knew he'd never force Jesse to marry him.

Deciding to let Cole know he was coming, Char sent a wire before leaving St. Louis.

Uncertainty gnawing at him, he rode most of the next two days and nights before reining in near a creek at dusk. Even though it was fall, the weather was still hot.

But the weather wasn't near as bad as the heaviness in his chest. With no appetite, he stretched out on his bedroll and clasped his hands behind his head to watch the pink sky fade to black—like his hopes had.

He closed his eyes against the ache in his chest.

The hammer of a gun cocked.

He went for his Colts before his eyes even opened.

"You're not as fast as you used to be," a voice floated out of the trees. "I could have shot you three times before your gun cleared the holster."

He rose and holstered his revolvers. "What are you doing here?" He didn't want to think about how much the answer meant to him.

"Waiting for you." Jesse stepped out of the trees, and the moon bathed her in silver. She was wearing her usual boys attire—with one exception. A vest.

He drank in the sight of her, but his muscles were so tense he thought they would snap. "Why?"

"I think you know."

His hopes clawed up from the ground and grew wings, but he wasn't taking any chances. "There's been a lot of misunderstanding between us, darlin'. This time, I don't want any mistakes. Tell me plain out what you want."

"You."

His heart jumped into his throat, and he had to swallow to keep from strangling. But he remained leery. "You didn't want me three months ago. What's changed?"

"I have."

"What about me being a gunman?" Damn it. Why was he trying to give her an out?

She crossed her arms and stared up at the sky. "It doesn't matter. None of it does. No matter what kind of work you do, I can't stop loving you." She gave him a halfhearted smile. "Believe me, I've tried."

It was becoming hard to breathe. "It doesn't matter if I chase outlaws?" His voice sounded like a dying frog's.

"It matters. But I'll be right there to see that you stay safe." She shoved aside her vest to reveal a deputy marshal's badge pinned above her left breast.

Shock held him immobile, then he felt his eyes burn at the significance of what she'd done. She had given up her dream for him. She had given up everything. He had trouble finding his voice. "What if I want to become a farmer?"

"No. You be yourself. That's the man I fell in love with—the charming, smooth-talking gunman with beautiful blue eyes."

He wanted to touch her, but he was afraid he'd fall apart. "Yeah? Well, I fell in love with a smart-mouthed, sassy imp, with a stubborn streak as long as the Mississippi." He approached her slowly, but stopped short of touching her. "And she's going to become a farmer's wife whether she likes it or not."

"Why?"

He explained about spending two months on a plantation, but he didn't tell her who it belonged to. "It wasn't farming I didn't like. It was the Websters."

"Don't do this for me," she said softly.

"I'm not. I'm doing it for both of us." He moved closer. "How did you find me?"

"I was on my way to search for you when I stopped in Jefferson City for supplies. Nelson, the man who runs the telegraph office, saw me and waved me down.

He gave me a wire for Uncle Cole. Since it wasn't sealed, I read it." She gave him a sheepish grin. "I knew you'd be somewhere between Jefferson City and Saint Louis."

"I think there's something you need to know."

"What?"

"My father's name is Otis Daniel . . . Duvall."

"I told you that doesn't matter. It never did."

"It did to me—and, you're the one who helped me find him."

"I did?"

"Yes. I remembered the wire you sent to Charleston, so I went to Shreveport, hoping to find out if my mother had any relatives. My grandmother had answered the wire. I have a whole slew of aunts, uncles, and cousins." He finally allowed himself to touch her. He traced the column of her throat. "The plantation I stayed at was my grandmother's."

She was breathless. "Was your father there?"

"He was by the time I arrived. Damned near killed his horse riding up from Augusta, Georgia."

"I thought he was in Texas."

"He was the night I was born." He explained about his grandfather's treachery, and the fact that Herbert Martin hadn't known his daughter was pregnant until after Dan had been sent away. "Anyway, Dan sat in jail for six months, but he wrote to my mother every day. The letters were intercepted by my grandfather. Except one. The day I was born, he was in Savannah buying a new plow team, and someone else went for the mail. When my mother realized what her father had done, she was so angry, she ran away to join Dan in Texas."

"They loved each other, darlin', and if I hadn't

chosen that night to come along, they might have still been together."

Tears sparkled in her eyes. "At least you have your pa, now."

"I have a lot more than that." He pulled her into his arms. "I have you."

Smiling, she placed his palm on her slightly rounded stomach. "That's not all you have."

His hand shook and tears stung his eyes. "Ah, God, Jesse. I love you."

She brushed her lips over his. "I love you, too, and I always will—*whether in this world or the next.*"